DARK CONSEQUENCES

K. BOOZER

DARK CONSEQUENCES

K. BOOZER

AUTHORS NOTE

Your mental health matters to me.

This story explores dark themes and may contain content that some readers find distressing. If you prefer to dive into this book blind, please do so with the understanding that it is a dark romance. For those who would rather know what they're stepping into, a detailed list of potential triggers is provided below.

If you have any questions or concerns about the content, feel free to reach out to me at **authorkboozer@gmail.com**. If you are in need of support, please know that mental health resources and crisis lines are available, and I encourage you to seek help if needed—your safety and well-being comes first.

Trigger Warnings include but are not limited to: Graphic depictions of violence (including torture, murder, and death), graphic depictions of sexual content, threat of sexual assault, thoughts of abortion, thoughts of suicide, sex trafficking, kidnapping, parental loss (happens off page), mental and Physical abuse (not between main characters), swearing, drugs and alcohol.

This is a work of fiction. I do not condone or support the actions or situations depicted between characters. That said... I hope you **enjoy the ride**.

Interested in listening to the songs that inspired this story?
Check out this playlist.

This is for those who believe themselves to be too broken, too damaged, and too tainted to ever be loved again.

You can and you will.

Now, Raphael DiAngelo says to be his 'good fucking girl' and wait for him in the pantry.

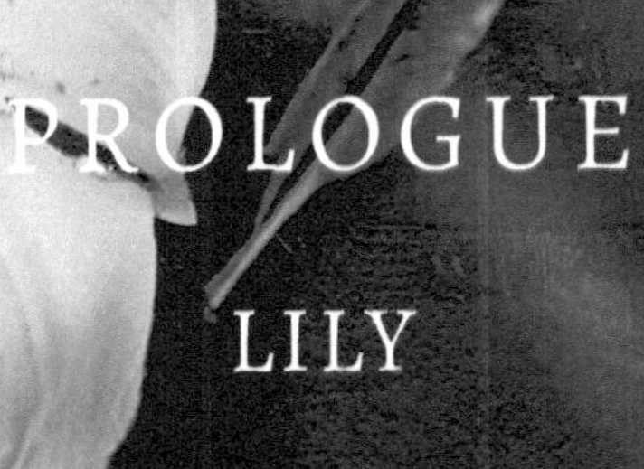

PROLOGUE

LILY

COLUMBIA

Another monstrous mosquito lands on my arm. One so large, I can actually count the stripes on the blood-sucking dinosaur as I watch it stick its needle into my flesh.

Bastard.

I would smack the damn thing and send it back to the hell it came from, if I wasn't busy helping keep a man's intestines inside his body.

As painful as the sting the bug leaves behind on my body after it drinks its fill and flies off to find its next victim, it's nothing compared to how our tent of war-torn patients feels. I gaze at the overflowing cots and makeshift gurneys with an inward sigh. Another attack on a helpless village has left dozens of innocent men, women, and children dead or injured. So many families have been torn apart as a result of a war they never wanted. So many lives destroyed...

I was an emergency doctor in Chicago for a couple of years and saw it all. At least, I thought I had. Bullet holes and stab wounds are elementary when faced with full-body chemical burns and partial disembowelment. I once saved a man who came in with a knife sticking out of the side of his neck, but here…I'm losing patients left and right because there's just not enough help, medicine, or technology.

Accepting and understanding the harsh reality around me is enough to make me ache for home, and I take nothing for granted anymore.

My current team and I have been in Columbia for a few weeks now doing relief work. This is my third rotation over the last year. It's not always like this—no, that's a lie. It is. I like to think my presence here is helping, however small or large that is, and for the most part, that's why I keep coming back. But to be completely honest, the pay for three months' work here is almost the same as an entire year's salary back home, and I have a mountain of student debt to pay off with big plans for the future. I want to buy a condo, get a new car since my old beetle is on its last leg, and take a really long vacation where I spend more time in a bikini than scrubs.

"He's crashing! Get the paddles!" the lead doctor shouts. A moment later, she's yelling, "Clear!" We all step back with our hands in the air.

My eyes lock on the black computer screen, willing the green line to correct itself, but it remains flat.

"Again! Clear!"

I glance at the patient, and my heart sinks at the sight. His face is pale, and his lips are turning blue. He's gone. It's clear as day, and the lead doctor knows it too because after one final attempt, she calls time of death.

"Dr. Song!"

I raise my head and turn in the direction of the person who called my name. It's Dr. Cole, and he's waving me over frantically. I snap my gloves off and tug my protective apron off, tossing both in the trash bin, and hurry over. When I step up, a nurse hands me a set of new gloves and an apron.

"What do we have?"

"Six-year-old girl with an open compound fracture to her left arm. I need to set it, but she only speaks Spanish and won't calm down."

I lean forward and give the terrified girl a kind smile before asking her in Spanish. "What is your name?"

She whimpers in loads of pain but latches on to the familiar language. "Louisa."

"Hi, Louisa. My name is Dr. Song, but you can call me Lily. All of my favorite patients do." I wink at her and earn a small smile and giggle in return. I glance over at my co-worker, and he nods. Turning back to Louisa, I try to assure her as best I can. "Now, I understand your arm hurts, right?" She nods meekly. "Well, my friend here will help you feel all better, okay? But first, tell me what's your favorite color?"

"Pink," she admits right away.

"Really? I like pink too. Okay, so once Dr. Cole has fixed your arm, we'll wrap it in a really pretty pink cast. How does that sound?"

Louisa nods before the brave little girl steels herself. I glance at the nurse beside me and ask in English. "Where are her parents?"

The nurse shakes her head solemnly. "She came in alone."

I sigh. It's unfair and cruel to leave an innocent young girl like this all alone in the world. An orphan in the blink of an eye. So many children have the same story, the same uncertain future, and I hate knowing the pain and fear they'll face in the coming days.

Of course there are programs to offer assistance for

orphaned children of war and extended families who may be willing to take them in, but that's not always the case.

I tried to keep up with the children during my first rotation, but there were so many that it became impossible. For my sanity, I lied to myself and imagined each one had a happy ending. Even though, realistically, I know differently. It's just easier sometimes to believe in the fictional.

By the end of my shift, it feels like I ran a 5k...in the rain and wind, through the mud and then up a hill...wearing a weighted vest and hung over. All I want is to soak in a tub and sleep for a week, but out here in the forests of Columbia, that's not an option. There is no Hilton nearby. We live in shared tents that make my camping trips as a kid look like a resort stay. Our showers are outdoors and no matter what time of the day, you're sweating even while you shower, making the entire effort pointless.

"Hey, there you are."

I look up and see Dr. Rodriguez approaching. The man gives me the creeps. And that's putting it mildly. It's my first rotation serving with him and hopefully my last. Something in the way he looks at me sets every warning bell off in my head. And I'm not alone. Several of the nurses and other female staff share the same opinion.

His eyes roam over my covered body, and I tighten my cardigan anyway, as if the thin fabric will somehow shield me from his lecherous gaze.

"How can I help you, Dr. Rodriguez? Did I forget to fill out a chart or something?"

He holds up a bottle of what I can only assume is alcohol of some kind. Alcohol isn't exactly forbidden since it's a favorite way for many team members to deal with the stress of the job, but I've never been a fan of the hard stuff. I'm a wine and spirits kind of gal.

"A little nightcap?"

"Not tonight, but thank you for the offer." I hate having to be polite, but he's technically my boss, and, like I said, I need the job.

He sighs like my rejection hurt him, and I can't find the energy to really care if I did. I'm exhausted, and if I can't soak in a tub, then I just want to take my sweaty shower and go to bed beneath my mosquito net.

"I heard about the guy and the kid whose parents were killed," he says. "Sounds like a tough day. Are you sure you don't want one little shot? It'll take the edge off and help you sleep."

I lean forward and rest my elbows on the wood railing, swallowing my groan of annoyance. Glancing around, I search for anyone who might help get me out of this awkward situation, but dinner is still being served, so this side of the base is empty.

"Come on. Just one shot?" Dr. Rodriguez pushes again.

"I'm really tired and just want to get ready for bed. Next time, swear."

"Please?" He pouts. "I promise to leave you alone afterward. Look. It's just, I had a bad day too and could use the company."

I take a deep breath and blow it out hard. Fine. A shot would help take the edge of the day off, and if it will at least make the man shut up and go away, I'll do the damn shot.

"Okay, just one, and then you really need to go find Dr. Cole or someone else to drink with. Deal?" I tell him and then turn away as he grabs two plastic cups to pour the alcohol into.

He holds one out to me, and the powerful smell of whiskey invades my nose. He clinks his cup against mine, like there's anything cheerful to celebrate in this war-torn country. In a hurry to get this over with, I toss back my glass and wince as the bitter taste slides down my throat. It's almost nauseating, but I manage.

"Thank you, Dr. Rodri—"

"Call me Joe."

I blink hard, my eyes suddenly tired from the day. I've always been a bit of a lightweight, but one shot is a little odd. When was the last time I had a drink, anyway? Back in Chicago? Or at Sarah's birthday party? That was months ago. No. It was the week before I came to Columbia. Right?

"Dr. Rodriguez, I think I'm going to call it a night."

"Joe, please."

I try to tell him it's not professional, but my face feels heavy. I take a step back and stumble.

"Whoa, my dear! Careful now." He rushes forward and wraps his arm around my waist, pulling me forward flush to his chest. I try to push back against him, but my arms won't work.

"Wha-what's-what's going on?"

Dr. Rodriguez brushes my light hair from my face, and there are two of him in my vision now. "You've been teasing me ever since you arrived."

No, I haven't. I've barely said more than six words to the man outside of a case.

"And well, I'm done waiting for you to make the first move."

He leans forward. Black rushes from the corner of my eyes. I try to resist its overwhelming force, but it's relentless, weighing me down, and I've never felt so helpless.

I'm trained to save lives...but who will save me?

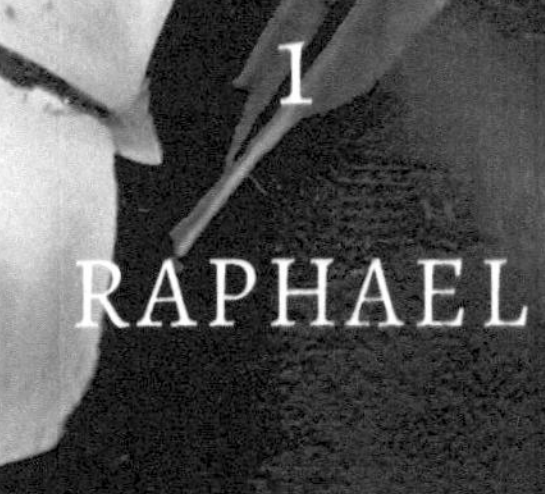

1

RAPHAEL

"The rat's in the henhouse. I repeat, the rat is in the henhouse."

My cousin Dominic's voice fills my ears, and I respond by rolling my eyes at his childish antics. Not that he can see me, but it at least makes me feel better.

"It's fox in the henhouse, not rat," Enzo corrects him through the headset. He's watching what Dominic and I see through our cameras on a laptop while he waits in the car. Although he's back on his feet, his injuries haven't fully healed, which prevents him from joining the front lines. As a result, he has absolutely no tolerance for anything. "Dumbass."

I adjust my rifle, aiming it toward the house, and peer through the scope to get a clear view of the man I've been waiting for.

"I see him," I tell them both, relief drowning away the anxiety and worry I had coming in to tonight's mission.

It's taken weeks to gather the intel necessary to confirm the location of the Triad leader's home. We finally had our big breakthrough with the help of Evelyn, my future sister-in-law Rose O'Leary's best friend and Enzo's...actually, I'm not sure what the two of them are, but whatever it is, she has the gruff,

Viking look-alike wrapped around her prim little English finger.

If there were ever a more opposite-looking couple, it would be those two. Evelyn is a real-world lady hailing from Britain with hacker skills and professionalism enough to warrant jail time, but the woman is impeccable at covering her tracks. Besides, if she were ever caught, her family name and fortune would be enough to buy her a suite at the finest jail. If it even got that far.

I'm still not clear on how Evelyn did it, but she located an image of our friendly neighborhood Triad rat leader, Xiao. The man thought he could hide his face from technology, but nothing stays hidden forever.

This leads us to now, with me perched high on a branch in the tallest oak tree outside Xiao's residence, staring at the bastard through a rifle scope with a trigger finger itching to fire. He's smoking some kind of cigar, a Cuban by the looks of it, and wearing a silk robe, open to his bare chest...correction, make that open to his naked body.

"Please, God, tell me he's not naked," Enzo begs, seeing what I do.

"As the day he was born."

Dominic groans. "Because the last thing I want is to see his pencil-thin dick."

"Bigger than—" Enzo starts.

"If you're about to say my dick, I'm going to come over there and kick your ass."

"Oh no," Enzo taunts. "Big words for a small dick."

Keeping the two of them on a mission is like herding cats. In the dark. During a hurricane.

"Can we focus, please?" I ask, interrupting what is about to become an annoying and unnecessary conversation if I don't.

"Sorry, boss," Dominic mocks with a chuckle.

I'm glad I'm not the boss anymore. With Michael's fertility proven with the birth of his son, Liam, and his pending marriage to Rose O'Leary, he has officially been renamed heir to the DiAngelo family, leaving me in the clear.

Kind of.

Before the truth of Rose's identity came to light, Dad entered into a marriage contract between me and the youngest daughter of the Sicilian Cosa Nostra leader, Emilia.

Strategically, I understood why he did it. I was the heir at the time, and he felt pressured to have me married. But my fiancée is younger than my baby sister, Gabriella. At eighteen years old, the girl is fifteen years younger than me.

Now, listen. I've enjoyed the company of women her age before, but I've never wanted to marry any of them. Holding a conversation with one is like talking to a foreigner, and I'd much rather they use their mouths for something far more productive than struggling to hold an intelligent conversation with me.

When the dust settled following Michael's drama, Dad canceled the marriage contract. However, Emilia's father asked if our family would still host his daughter over the holidays since she's never been Stateside. Even a blind man can see what her old man is trying to do. He's hoping there's a possibility that after we meet, I'll like her. No chance.

The girl is due to arrive next week, and I'm hoping that while she's here, I'll be too preoccupied with our sleazy rat friend here to even give her the time of day. Maybe if I ignore her long enough, she'll get annoyed or bored and just return home. Either way, it'll be a win-win for me.

"We're on the clock here, remember?" I remind the pair.

"You're right," Dominic replies, all silliness gone from his tone.

"Alright. Killing the power in thirty seconds," Enzo tells us. "You have ten minutes, at most, before they get control back."

The plan's pretty straightforward but also extremely risky. Once the power's out, Dominic and I will infiltrate the house, taking advantage of the chaos caused by the blackout, and get Xiao out, preferably alive, but dead is fine too.

"Three, two," Enzo counts down. "One." The house goes dark. "Now."

I snap on a pair of night-vision goggles, sling my rifle over my shoulder, and rappel down the tree, meeting Dominic by our entry point at the back door. The home is well guarded, but with no moon in the sky and with us wearing all black, we're practically invisible to the naked eye.

A second later, the door swings open, just as we expected, and a pair of Triad guards rush out. We each grab one and simultaneously snap their necks.

I check my watch. That took less than thirty seconds. Not bad.

We step inside and work as a team, moving through the bottom floor, searching each room for our prey, and taking out every Triad member we find. If tonight ends up a bust, at least we got to exterminate some fucking rats in the process.

"Five minutes left," Enzo announces in our ears.

Where the fuck is Xiao?

Despite Evelyn's best efforts, she couldn't find a blueprint or floor plan of any kind for the house, so we're in the dark here as well, primarily relying on intuition and basic house building. "Are you sure he hasn't left, Enzo?"

"Positive. Unless he somehow actually turned into a rat

and slipped out, he's still in the house. Somewhere. May I suggest you two divide and conquer?"

I don't like it, but with the clock winding down, we have no choice. My eyes flick toward the second floor. "I'll take the upstairs, finish—"

"We're not splitting up," my cousin interrupts because he knows what I'm about to order.

"Really? We don't have time to argue about this."

"I'm not arguing."

"Then what do you call this?"

"Sorry to interrupt what I'm sure is about to be a very fun back-and-forth on should you stay or should you go, but you have four minutes left," Enzo says.

Dominic clenches his jaw, hating how we both backed him into a corner before he nods. "Fine. I'll finish clearing the downstairs, but if you get yourself killed, don't come crying to me."

I can't help myself, and as I slip by him, I say, "If I do, your ass is the first I'll haunt."

"Fuck off."

Chuckling under my breath, I rush up the stairs, relieved the carpet absorbs the sound of my hurried steps. I round a corner and come face-to-face with a Triad guard. Burying my knife in his neck, he's dead before he even hits the ground.

Fewer rooms are up here, so I systematically clear each one until only the one behind the double doors at the end of the hall remains. The knob is locked, but since it's a standard model, I swiftly pick the lock without much effort. As soon as it's open, I glide through the dark room like death's shadow, ready to claim another soul.

In the center of the room sits a massive canopy bed. As I

draw closer, I notice a distinct lump beneath the sheets. Someone is lying there. I raise my gun, finger on the trigger, as I reach out, pull the sheet down...

... and lock eyes with the most enchanting sapphire-blue eyes I've ever seen.

2

LILY

Once upon a time, in a land far, far away, was a girl who believed in fairy tales. She dreamed of handsome heroes riding in on gallant white horses to fight the evil dragon and save the day. She believed in true love and soulmates and happily ever after.

That girl was also stupid and naive and far too innocent for the real world.

Once upon a time, that girl was me.

"Mommy?"

I glance down at the small body tucked into my side and then kiss the dark crown of her head. She giggles before squirming closer to me and continues sounding out the words from her pop-up book.

For a four-year-old child, Mei is significantly gifted for her age. Arguably, I'd like to take all the credit for her smarts, but I only contributed half her genetic makeup. Mei's father is brilliant as well, as much as I hate to admit it.

I thought I saw the worst of humanity working as a doctor in a level 1 emergency room in Chicago, but I was wrong. The abuse I suffered over the past six years from men so depraved, they make psychopaths look normal, make every brutal night at the hospital back then a walk in the park.

I'll admit, the notion of suicide crossed my mind often. Especially in the beginning, when I was drugged and raped repeatedly by Dr. Rodriguez before he sold me to the cartel. The urge grew stronger with each man who used and abused my body for over a year before I was finally sold to the Triads to work as a sex slave. That's where Xiao, the Triad leader, noticed me one night and became obsessed, eventually imprisoning me here.

I still remember the night when I learned I was pregnant, and the idea of bringing a child, *his* child, into the world was too much. With the knife in hand, I was about to make twin cuts on my wrists when I suddenly felt Mei's movement. It was soft, like the gentle flapping of butterfly wings in my abdomen, and at that moment, I couldn't go through with it. Instead, I vowed to be there for my baby and raise them to be good because blood only makes up half of who they are.

"What's this word, Mommy?"

Mei points at a word on the page and then looks up at me expectantly. Somehow, she inherited my blue eyes, which contrast beautifully with her delicate oriental features. Another reason I can never leave her. There are men her father employs who love the exotic appeal of blue eyes. They find it makes them feel special to fuck one. But they're not special; they're disgusting pieces of human trash that don't deserve to walk this earth.

My eyes roam over the colorful pictures of my favorite fairy tale growing up. Only my beast will never turn into a handsome prince. "Haggard."

"Hag-gard," Mei enunciates. "What does that mean?"

A loud knock sounds through the room, and I glance at the clock on the wall. Right on time. Like always.

"Mei, my beautiful girl," Xiao announces as he walks in a second later because while I'm Mei's mother, I'm still a prisoner here. Something Xiao likes to remind me of often. "How are you this evening?"

Mei sets the book down and glances at me. I nod subtly and motion for her to say hello to her father, catching Xiao's disapproving glare. He hates it when Mei acts like she's seeking my permission because it makes him feel like a stranger in his daughter's life. Good. I wish he was just a stranger to her. But I'll still be punished for it later.

"I'm good, Bàba," Mei replies, using the Chinese word for Dad to please him.

Xiao, with all his flaws, truly loves Mei and has never laid a hand on her... yet.

"Bàba needs to talk to Mommy," Xiao says. "Can you be a big girl and go to bed on your own?"

"Yes," Mei answers.

I get off the bed and tuck Mei in, giving her a kiss on the forehead before leaving with Xiao. He guides me down the hall to his bedroom. The second the door closes behind us, Xiao slaps me hard across the face. Even though I expect it, the sudden impact catches me off guard, causing me to collapse onto the floor. My hand instinctively reaches up to cradle my stinging cheek.

Xiao sighs, as if hitting me somehow pains him. "How many times must I remind you? Mei is *my* daughter. She doesn't need your permission to say hi to her father."

He sends a kick directly to my rib cage. My mouth opens, but nothing comes out because my voice has been robbed of air. Curling in on myself, I try to crawl away, but he grabs my hair and pulls hard, forcing me to rise to my feet or risk my hair being ripped out.

"You should be thanking me that I even let you spend time

with her at all. If I killed you, she would eventually forget you even existed and move on. She would know no different."

He's right. The only thing that silences me and makes me obedient is the thought of what will happen to Mei if I'm not around. It's what keeps me capable of surrendering my body to this man whenever he wants it, however he wants it for the chance to spend time with Mei.

"I have been nothing but kind to you," Xiao continues as he drags me to the bed by my hair. "I could have easily disposed of you the moment she was born."

He tosses me on the bed before gripping my chin hard and forcing my face up to his. "You think because you're a doctor, that makes you special? I can get another one in a heartbeat. I don't even know why I keep you around." He shoves me away, and gravity forces me onto my back on the sheets. His furious expression flips like a switch to one of remorse, fast enough to give me whiplash. "Why do you make me do this to you, baby girl? Why do you make me hurt you?"

Xiao's narcissism is matched only by his insanity and bipolar disorder. If you were to look up the definition of a guy who habitually blames the girl for his angry outbursts, you would find his picture next to it.

"I love you, baby. You know this," he coos, running his hand down my sore cheek. "Don't you love me too?"

I want to shake my head. I want to spit in his face, kick him in the balls, rip his dick off, and shove it in a blender, but Mei's innocent face flashes in my mind, so instead, I nod and whisper, "Yes."

Xiao's lips curl into the sinister smile of a madman before he moves his hands to undo his belt clip. "Are you sorry?"

I nod again. "I'm sorry. Please forgive me."

He shoves his pants down and strokes his small, skinny dick. "That's right. Now show me how sorry you really are."

As I lower my head, my mind shifts to focus on the little girl waiting for me to come back to her. Xiao can hurt me, torment me, rape me, and threaten to kill me every chance he gets, but he will never break me. Because I know we'll escape this nightmare one day, and that small sliver of hope keeps me from falling into complete ruin.

3

RAPHAEL

I wait for her to scream. Honestly, I half expect it since there's a gun in her face. Only she simply stares up at me with a heaviness I can't identify in her eyes. Almost like she's ready for me to pull the trigger. Almost like she's hoping I do. But it would be a shame to do so and ruin such a pretty face.

"Who are you?" she asks, her voice barely more than a whisper.

Before I can respond, the blankets shift in front of her, revealing the dark-haired head of a small child. When my eyes snap back up to hers, a protective fire now swirls in those mesmerizing blue depths. The child is clearly important to her because she's prepared to defend her at all costs, like a lioness protecting her cub. Just like a mother would.

"Mommy?" A tiny voice breaks the silence, proving my assumption right.

As the dark head shifts toward me, I immediately lower my weapon. I'm not in the business of pointing a gun at a child, even those I don't know. The young child stares up at me with blue eyes similar to the woman holding her and blinks sleep away.

You would think the child would at least scream with a stranger standing in front of her. But just like her mother, she stares at me with a vacant look. Almost like my presence with a gun is a common situation in her life. A sick thought crosses my mind—perhaps a gun in their face is a regular occurrence for them, explaining their lack of surprise. The idea leaves me nauseous.

"Hi," the little girl says.

Without hesitation, I respond with a casual "Hi," unable to resist the magnetic pull of the child's voice and expression.

"Who are you?" the woman repeats her question, a little louder this time.

"My name is Raphael."

"Did he send you?" Her voice falters like she's afraid of my answer.

"Who?" I have a feeling I know the answer, but I need to hear it from her.

"Xiao."

I frown and shake my head. "No."

Her brow furrows. "Then why are you here?"

"I'm looking for Xiao." No use in lying because something in her tone tells me she's not interested in protecting him.

"Why are you looking for my daddy?" the little girl asks.

Her question throws me for a loop.

Holy shit.

Xiao has a kid and a baby momma? Evelyn found nothing of the sort during her research, but I'm not too surprised since finding what she did was hard enough. But if it's true, the daughter of Xiao and her mother lie in front of me. Of course, I'd rather it be Xiao himself, but having them is a close second. This changes things in a big way.

"Do you know where your dad is right now?"

The girl shakes her head.

I look at her mom. "Do you know where he is?"

She raises a hand and points at the door. "Last I saw him was two doors down."

Great. I searched that room and all the other ones upstairs and found no one.

"When?"

"I don't know...maybe a couple of hours ago?"

We confirmed he was on-site moments before we infiltrated. Where the fuck is he now? How did we miss him?

"Guys, you have less than a minute. Where the hell are you two?" Enzo demands in my earpiece.

"Downstairs is clear," Dominic announces.

I step back with a frown and say into the mic, "Xiao's not in the house."

"What?" Enzo says.

"Are you serious?" Dominic asks.

"Yes," I growl out the answer. "The upstairs is clear. He must have slipped out before we got inside."

"Or maybe he's still in here," Dominic suggests. "We should look around some more."

"You can't. You're out of time," Enzo declares. "Get out. Now."

I glance back at the girl and her mother and make a sudden decision. "Buy me a few minutes, then meet me outside with the car."

If I can't have Xiao, then his daughter and her mom will have to do. Maybe with them in hand, that'll be enough to tempt the rat out of hiding once and for all.

"Are you fucking serious?" Enzo snaps.

"It's important. I'll explain when I see you."

"Do you need help, Raphael?" Dominic offers.

"Just keep the escape route clear."

Kneeling in front of the bed, I look from the girl to her

mom. She's staring at me with the same strange expression from before, but this time, a layer of uncertainty laces it. "Something tells me you're not here by choice?"

The mom shakes her head. "We're not."

I assumed as much, which makes the next part easy to offer, and she'd be a fool to turn it down. "I can get you out of here, but we'd have to go right now."

She hesitates. A flicker of hope appears in her eyes, like she's ready to jump at the chance, before doubt snuffs it out. "We can't."

"And why's that?"

"He'll come after us and..."

She trails off and it doesn't take a genius to finish her sentence. Xiao will hurt her...or worse. "What if I tell you that you'll be safe?"

"You can't guarantee that."

Her doubt should annoy me, but it doesn't. Oddly enough, it calls to a strange part of me that stirs free a protective emotion. "No, I can't." I admit the fact honestly. "But anything would be better than staying here, yes? Don't you want the chance to get away? Be free?"

"In exchange for what?"

The woman's smart. I'll give her that. Her remark even makes the corner of my lips twitch. "Your help in taking Xiao down."

"I don't even know who you are."

"I can promise you I'm a better man than Xiao is."

Her eyes shift down to the gun stowed at my hip. Her brow rises in challenge when she looks at me like she doesn't believe a word I say.

"Look, I came here tonight for Xiao. To put an end to him. But I found you two instead. Let me help you, and in return, you help me." I shouldn't have to explain myself, nor do we have the time for it, but I need her to trust me in some way if she's going to help us take Xiao down.

With a visible gulp, she glances down at her daughter briefly before locking eyes with me again. The fire in her gaze has transformed into a blazing inferno, mesmerizing me by its raw beauty.

She nods. "Deal."

4

LILY

"Mommy?"

Mei stares up at me with a kind of innocent hope only a child could have.

She's only ever known this house. Xiao refuses to let her attend preschool or anywhere else, for that matter. She isn't aware of the dangers lurking outside these walls. She doesn't know that there are far worse things out there. To Mei, she sees Raphael as her rescuer, her hero like from one of her stories. But to me, he's just another man capable of the same evil as terrible as what I've experienced for years.

"Can I take Mr. Cuddles?"

"Of course, princess, go grab him."

Mei squirms out of bed and rushes over to the pile of toys in the corner. She digs through them, tossing aside the dozens of stuffed animals Xiao bought her until she finds her favorite one and the only toy she's ever received from me. It took more than money to buy, but the smile on Mei's face was worth the hours of suffering at the hands of Xiao and his men.

Raphael meets my eyes with a raised brow. "Mr. Cuddles?"

My daughter returns and holds up a purple-and-pink dragon with sparkly green wings. It's nothing fancy or anything, but it's special to her, which makes it priceless to me.

"Meet Mr. Cuddles! He gives the best hugs. Would you like one?"

Raphael peers down at my waiting daughter and her unique toy with surprise and shock. He tries to hide his smile but fails. There's a brief tug of his lips, and then it's gone in a heartbeat. If I hadn't been watching his handsome face, I would have missed it and—wait? Handsome face? I haven't thought of a single man as handsome in years. All I see when I look at each one is another bastard intent on hurting me.

I shake my head clear of the unwelcome thoughts and concentrate on the matter at hand.

"I would love one, but can I take a rain check?"

"Rain check?" Mei tilts her head.

"He means not right now but would like one later," I explain.

"Okay!" she chirps.

Raphael raises a finger to his ear as if he's listening to whoever is on the other end talking to him. "We'll be right there." He closes his eyes and frowns like he's annoyed by whatever they just said back. "Yes, I said we...I'll explain when we're out of the house." He lowers his hand and looks at me. "Pack a small bag of whatever you need as fast as possible. We need to go."

I follow his direction and toss in what little there is I want to take with us before bundling us up in jackets over our pajamas. December nights in Florida are just chilly enough to call for them.

As I move around the room, I can feel Raphael's watchful eyes on me. I'm familiar with having eyes on me. A side effect of being blond and blue-eyed with tits and an ass. But instead of a chill running down my spine, I'm warm wherever his eyes touch me. It's a peculiar sensation, neither pleasant nor unpleasant, and one that I struggle to identify.

I bend down and gather Mei into my arms. She squirms,

accidentally pushing against my ribs, and I hiss as the pain radiates through my chest. I don't think Xiao broke a rib. Not this time, at least. The pain isn't the same from the time he broke a few a couple of years ago. But he probably bruised one or two. Again, it's nothing I'm not used to.

"I'm sorry, Mommy," Mei apologizes.

"I'm okay," I tell her, swallowing down another wave of deep, throbbing pain.

"What happened?" Raphael demands, grabbing my attention right away. It's not aggressive but rapt curiosity.

He doesn't know me, and I don't know him, so I lie, "I fell...into my dresser."

Raphael hums low in his throat, fixing me with a doubtful expression. His eyes roam over my figure. Not sexually, but it's as if his eyes snag on every past bruise, cut, and broken bone I hide, and I hate how it strokes something deep inside me. I wait for him to push the subject, but when he glances at Mei, he decides against it and asks, "What are your names?"

"Lily," I answer. "And this is my daughter, Mei."

Raphael starts toward the door, and I follow him. Just before he twists the knob, he turns and suggests in a quiet voice, "You should cover her eyes for this next part."

I nod, understanding a gruesome sight awaits us out there. Cradling Mei closer to my chest, I tuck her face into my neck and give our "hero" a curt nod. I do my best to keep my eyes on Raphael's back as we navigate through the dark and silent empty house, but it's hard not to miss the many dead bodies scattered through the halls and rooms.

We reach the back door, and after he checks to make sure the coast is clear, Raphael holds his hand out to me. I stare at it like it's a bomb ready to go off, uncertainty and fear paralyzing me. All I want is to escape this prison, and Raphael offers me a way out. So why can't I take it?

"Hey," he says. "I know you're scared. And I know you don't know me, let alone trust me. I'd honestly be worried if you did. But I need your help too. In order to do that, you just need to take one step toward me. That's all it takes. Can you do that?"

I once lived my life with carefree abandon, never fully appreciating my freedom and independence until it was too late. That girl has long since been beaten down to the point where she hides behind walls I can't break through. But my daughter deserves to have the chance to live her life as she wants.

And maybe...maybe somewhere along the way, I'll find that girl again too.

5

RAPHAEL

Somewhere along the drive to the penthouse, Mei falls asleep curled up against her mother's side, but Lily remains quiet. Not surprising, really. Yes, I got her and her daughter out of Xiao's abusive hold, but I'm still a stranger to her. For all she knows, I'm as deadly and terrible as he is. Which, in a way...I am. I just like to think that I have better morals than Xiao. Morals that include not beating the mother of my child, for instance.

I have so many questions. Probably the same, if not more, than Enzo and Dominic. I saw them swirling in their eyes when we safely arrived outside to the cars. But they'll have to wait—even my father, who is currently blowing my phone up, will have to wait. At a red light, I shoot him off a text letting him know I'll come by tomorrow...or later today, I suppose, since the clock on the dashboard blinks 3:00 a.m. He's not happy, but after tonight's epic failure, who is?

Every step forward to catching Xiao results in two steps back, and I'm beyond frustrated. But now that we have Lily and Mei, Xiao's daughter, we may just get two steps ahead of the bastard. Finally.

My eyes flick to the rearview mirror...again, and passing streetlamps illuminate Lily's face...and her slightly swollen cheek. She can claim she fell into a dresser all day long, but I know the signs of abuse, and it's more likely she fell right into the path of Xiao's shoes instead and his hand shortly afterward.

Lily doesn't move when we pull into the underground parking garage. Dominic and Enzo pull up next to me, but they remain in the car, listening to my message to give Lily and her daughter some space for the night.

I twist around in my seat and meet Lily's piercing blue gaze. She's trying hard to look strong, but it's easy to see the uncertainty still lingering there, too. I don't know why, but I suddenly feel the need to ease her fears.

"We're here."

"Where is *here* exactly?"

"My home. I live in a penthouse upstairs. There's plenty of room for you to stretch out and have your privacy. But most importantly, it's safe."

"Who are you?" Before I can repeat my name, she continues. "Are you like former military or something?"

My lips twitch. "Something like that."

Lily bothers her bottom lip between her teeth before dropping her eyes to her daughter's sleeping face. "You don't know Xiao. He will kill anyone who stands in his way of getting to her."

She means his daughter. Their daughter. "That's kind of the point, Lily. Because when he comes for her, for you both, we'll be ready for him."

"And then what? What else do you want?"

It takes me a moment to decipher what she truly means. "I don't want anything else, Lily. No favors, no expectations, nothing like that. I only want to take your husband down."

"My husband?" She rears her head back as though I had slapped her, something that leaves me feeling uneasy.

"Xiao?"

"Xiao is not my husband. He is a cruel and evil, narcissistic man who enjoys abusing and raping women. Yes, he is Mei's sperm donor, but that is it. I told you I would help you take him down, and I meant that, but I don't care for the bastard. He can rot in hell for all I care."

The passionate intensity of her voice matches the blazing blue fire in her eyes. It's said that blue fire burns hotter than red, and it's easy to understand why. "Tell me how you really feel."

Lily huffs, her lips curling into the faintest hint of a smile. Leaving me to wonder how a genuine smile will transform her face, and what it will take to make one appear.

"You must be tired. Come on. Let's get you two inside."

Turning the car off, I climb out and open the door for Lily. She gathers her sleeping daughter's body in her arms and slides out of the car, when the briefest of winces pulls at her face.

"I can carry her, if you'd like," I offer before the words even register in my brain.

For a quick second, I think she actually considers it before she shakes her head. "That's okay. I've got her. She's not that heavy anyway."

Liar, liar, pants on fire. But if she wants to deny help and intentionally remain in pain, then fine. Let her be stubborn.

That resolve only lasts for half a minute. By the time we get to the elevator, it's clear from the way she clenches her jaw and carefully shifts Mei in her arms that she's in more pain than she expected to be.

When she leans back against the elevator wall, her face grows paler and clammier.

Alright. That's quite enough of this.

"Lily, please. You're hurt. Let me carry Mei for you."

Again, she considers it, but then she shakes her head once more. "No. I have her."

I cross my arms over my chest and look down at her. "You're a little stubborn, you know that?"

"I've been told," she mumbles, her voice barely audible as she pushes Mei up, relieving the pressure off her chest.

The elevator dings and opens to the foyer of my penthouse. Lily follows me out slowly. I peek behind my shoulder as I head further inside and find her staring around the space with wide eyes.

"There are two wings. The primary room is to the right, and the guest rooms are to the left." I gesture with my head in each direction.

I show her to a room I decided would be perfect for the pair on the drive over. A room that overlooks a beautiful outdoor terrace, softly lit by the warm glow of twinkling lights. To our left is the en suite bathroom, and the door beside it leads to a large closet.

"If you give me your sizes, I can have clothing and other necessities delivered to you by tomorrow," I casually mention as I head back to the door.

"You said you want to take down Xiao," Lily mentions after she places Mei down on the bed and turns toward me. "Does the truth about me not being his wife change things?"

I frown, my brow furrowing. "No. It doesn't change a single thing for me. Does it change things for you?"

"No," she answers right away.

"Alright then. Glad we got that out of the way."

The corner of her lips tugs up again, almost into another smile. She searches the room before spotting a notepad and pen on the desk in the corner. She writes their sizes down and includes a list of necessities. When she tears the note off and hands it to me, our fingers brush, causing a jolt of electricity to spark between us. She jumps back with a gasp.

I smile apologetically at her. "Sorry about that. I'll be more careful."

Lily simply nods and steps farther back, dropping her gaze to the floor.

"Good night, Lily." I turn to walk out but then stop to add, "Oh, and one more thing. The door locks."

Shutting the door behind me, I stand still, wait, and listen. Five seconds later, I hear the lock click softly, and it makes me smile.

6

LILY

I've always been the type of girl who carefully observes her surroundings, assessing every detail before making a decision. Those traits kept me alive through every minute of hell I endured over the past six years.

So then tell me why it only took one look into Raphael's light hazel eyes for those virtues to go flying right out the window.

I know leaving with Raphael was the right thing to do, but I fear I may not have thought everything through as I usually would. It's clear from his home and vehicles that he has money and power. He claims he wants to make Xiao pay for everything he's done, but I know the dark world Xiao deals business in...does that mean Raphael does too? For all I know, I'm merely swapping one devil for another, someone with similar intentions to Xiao. And if that's the case, then am I really any more free?

I lie down next to Mei, pulling her close to my chest before I curl around her small body. My body is tired, but my mind refuses to rest.

There was a time when falling asleep came easily and effortlessly to me. The significance of rest was deeply ingrained in us as doctors during residency. A vacant patient room, an old gurney abandoned in storage, or, embarrassingly, there was even that one time I dozed off on the toilet. Sleep was sleep. It didn't matter where so long as I got a few much-needed hours of rest.

That all changed the first night I was abused by Dr. Rodriguez. Too afraid to sleep, I would remain awake all night, catching every creak and rustle, finally surrendering to sleep when sheer exhaustion overcame me.

When Mei was born, it only got worse. The fear of something terrible happening to her was overwhelming, leaving me feeling like a zombie, only sleeping when I was certain I was alone. As time went on, the fears lessened, but the persistent feeling of unease never truly disappeared. I lived in a constant state of worry, bracing myself for the next outburst or attack, until I grew numb and concentrated on my only source of happiness. Mei.

When I first discovered I was pregnant with Mei, I seriously considered throwing myself down a flight of stairs. And then one night I dreamed about a dark-haired, blue-eyed little girl running through the water at the beach at sunset. I could hear her laugh, see her smile, and feel the warmth of her sun-kissed skin.

Mei's birth wasn't easy by any means and was probably the hardest thing I've ever done. In a bathtub with no drugs, I delivered my daughter all by myself. As soon as I held her tiny body, covered in blood and mucus, and heard her take her first cry, a wave of emotions washed over me: elation, love, hope, and guilt. How I could ever think of ending her life before she had the chance to live left me instantly feeling like the worst mother. I made a vow at that moment to always be there for her, to protect her, and to teach her.

Somehow, I reached my bed shortly afterward before passing out from blood loss and exertion. I'm not sure who found me, but when I woke up next, it was in one of Xiao's underground medical back rooms. Because despite being a perverted piece of shit human being who made his business in the trade of human flesh, Xiao made sure his...inventory...was well cared for medically. Apparently, victims don't sell as well when they're not in good shape.

The doctor who treated me after Mei's birth told Xiao I was lucky to be alive, but when we were alone, she praised me for delivering Mei on my own. I have my medical degree to thank and my instant maternal instinct for providing me with the skills to do so.

Then I did something perilous and begged the doctor to help me prevent another pregnancy. It's clear that the implant I had prior to being kidnapped had expired, or else Mei wouldn't have been conceived. But I wasn't ready to be a walking womb after her birth, either.

Reluctantly, the doctor agreed to insert an IUD and kept silent afterward. Something I will forever be thankful to her for.

But having Mei was only the first problem. Convincing Xiao to let me raise her took every ounce of respect I had for myself. I did things and said things I'm not proud of...anything it took to keep my daughter by my side. But that's what a mother does, what a mother should do. Sacrifice it all if it means the protection of their child.

Ultimately, I think that's why I took the chance and went with the devil I didn't know. Raphael can't do anything worse than what's already been done to me.

By the time I fall asleep, the sun is already caressing the night sky with its morning light and when I wake up in a bright room, it feels like no time has passed.

I turn over to check on Mei, but she's nowhere to be found.

I jolt out of bed and rush to the bathroom. With such a tiny bladder, she often gets up to use the restroom at night. Only the bathroom is empty, too. Where the hell is my daughter?

Flinging open the bedroom door, I don't even register the lock being undone before I'm out the door and running down the hallway.

"Mei!" I shout, the effort causing my ribs to protest.

The hall leads directly into a spacious main living area, filled with natural light, but my focus isn't on the beautiful, bright, and open space, but on something else. It's the little girl sitting on a stool at the kitchen island, happily swinging her legs as she eats a bowl of cereal.

Mei turns toward me with a big smile. "Hi, Mommy!"

7

RAPHAEL

"Note to self," I mumble while rummaging through my sparse and empty pantry. "Order a shit ton of groceries."

Cooking comes naturally to me as an Italian, but that doesn't mean I enjoy it. The prospect of cooking for just myself as a bachelor became dull, and the loneliness of eating alone was even worse. I'd sooner eat out or go to the estate to enjoy Mom's delicious cooking. She won't admit it, but with all the kids grown up and out of the house, she's constantly looking for an excuse to cook for someone more than her and Dad.

The fridge is no better. The eggs are past their expiration date by a week, and the cheese has a green and fuzzy growth. Surprisingly, the only thing that's still good is the milk. Which makes sense since I always pair it with my morning cup of coffee.

Just as I'm making a cup on the espresso machine, my phone rings, just as I expected it would sometime this morning.

"Good morning, Dad."

"*Buongiorno*, son. Michael will be by to pick you up shortly. We need to talk about last night."

And then he hangs up. That's fair, really, since neither of us got what we wanted last night. Like watching Xiao's miserable little life drain from his eyes.

"I'm hungry."

I turn away from the counter to see Mei perched on a barstool on the opposite side of the island. In the light of a new day, it's easier to see her unique physical features courtesy of her mixed blood. Her hair isn't quite jet black and falls past her shoulders with a slight wave to it. The shape of her eyes resembles her dad's, but they are the most striking blue, just like her mother's.

"Well, good morning, Mei. What are you hungry for?"

"I don't know."

My interaction with children is limited, especially given how my nephew isn't even crawling yet, but from what I've been told, kids rarely know what they want since it changes on a dime.

"Well, unfortunately, I'm all out of 'I don't know.' Maybe some cereal?" I remember spying a box in the sparse pantry.

"Yes, please!" As Mei starts on her second bowl of cereal, crashing sounds and running footsteps fill the penthouse, followed by a loud and frightened shout of "Mei!"

A second later, Lily comes barreling around the corner of the hallway and into the kitchen. Her eyes widen as she searches the open space for her daughter. When she finds Mei happily swinging her legs at the island and eating her breakfast, her alarm evaporates into immediate relief.

"Hi, Mommy," Mei greets through a mouthful of food, oblivious to her mother's anxiety.

My eyes track Lily's movements as she approaches. She runs her fingers through her tousled blond hair; the strands fall in a carefree manner, accenting her face's delicate bone structure. She's wearing a simple black shirt she must have found in the dresser that falls just above her knees, exposing a pair of toned, pale legs.

It leaves me suddenly dying to know what she's wearing

beneath. If she's wearing anything at all. And how those legs of hers would look over my shoulders while I—

Clearing my throat, I force myself to look away before Lily notices me gawking at her like a man with a one-track mind.

But she's so focused on Mei that she doesn't even look at me. "Why didn't you wake me up?"

Mei drops her shoulders, and her feet go still as she finally senses her mom's nerves. "Sorry, Mommy. I tried, but you were sleeping, and I was hungry."

Ah. Lily woke up to find Mei gone. Of course, she panicked. To find your daughter missing when you wake up somewhere strange and new is terrifying enough to scare any mom.

Lily sighs and then steps forward to hug her daughter. She kisses the crown of her dark head and mumbles, "That's okay, sweetheart."

"Did you get any sleep?" I ask over the rim of my coffee cup.

Lily looks at me for the first time. Her gaze lingers on my morning attire—gym shorts and a loose T-shirt that exposes my sculpted and tattooed arms. I always start my day with a workout whenever possible, and after last night, I had a lot to get off my chest.

Visibly swallowing, Lily looks away and clears her throat. "I did. Thank you."

Pleased, I gesture behind me. "Coffee is over there with sugar in the bowl next to it, and there's milk in the fridge. I don't have much in terms of groceries because I wasn't expecting...guests, but I'll have some delivered today. For now, all I can offer is cereal."

"Thanks," Lily murmurs.

Moving about the kitchen, she prepares a cup of black

coffee with a splash of milk and a spoonful of sugar but doesn't touch the cereal. Something I make a mental note of.

The entire time, I keep still, but my eyes follow her movements. She walks with a stiffness that isn't from fear but from pain. It seems her "dresser" injury is bothering her this morning.

I wait for her to sit, then open a cabinet and take out a plastic bottle of painkillers. I fill a glass with water and then place both items in front of Lily. She glances between them and my face before she murmurs another small thank you. Popping the top, she shakes out a couple before swallowing them with the glass of water.

The security panel chimes, letting me know someone punched in the code to my penthouse in the elevator and is on their way up. Lily's eyes shoot in the direction with heightened concern.

"Hey." I wait until she finally looks back at me before continuing. "Each penthouse has a unique security code. The doors won't open without it, and only a select few I trust know mine."

I grab my coffee and leave the kitchen to intercept my brother before she can say anything back.

"Rose," I greet, pleasantly surprised to see my future sister-in-law walk out of the elevator beside Michael with Liam strapped to her chest in one of those body wrap things designed for babies. "What are you doing here?"

"Michael brought me up to speed last night, and when his dad called this morning, I offered to keep Lily and her daughter company. If they'd like that, I mean."

"I'm sure they'll love the company."

"Is that coffee?" Michael begs. "Oh it is, thank the Lord,"

he groans, and before I know it, he steals the cup from my hands.

"Wha—"

Rose gives her husband a disapproving side-eye glance. "Liam's been fussy. We've barely slept for more than an hour."

"I'm sorry to hear that."

Michael snorts and grumbles, "Yeah, I'm sure you are."

"Aw, did someone not get enough beauty sleep?"

Rose lightly snorts. "That's better than what I said."

"What did you say?"

"That he woke up on the wrong side of the bed and to try again."

Michael mocks us in a muttering tone beneath his breath. And from the look on Rose's face, she's enjoying her fiancé's torment immensely. She's a kind and sweet woman with a heart of gold. But she's also incredibly strong and stubborn, with a tenacious spirit that matches Michael's headstrong and proud streak. She calls him out on his bullshit better than anyone else. Honestly, there's no one better for my brother, and I'm thrilled that they have found happiness together after everything they went through to get here.

"Come on, cranky. There's more coffee in the kitchen." I hook my brother around the neck and tug him along with me, laughing when he tries hard to land a blow to my side to break free.

Lily and Mei stare at us in equal parts of surprise and fright when we come around the corner. Her eyes shift between Michael and me. I sometimes forget that we're twins. Even though my tattoos and longer hairstyle set us apart, the initial look can be overwhelming.

"Lily, this is my twin brother, Michael, and his fiancée, Rose. The little one there is their son, Liam."

My rude-ass older brother grumbles a "good morning" and then turns away to fill a travel mug full of black coffee.

"Don't forget the sugar, dear," Rose reminds him with a condescending sweet smile.

Michael slowly spins around and returns the smile with narrowed eyes. If I know my brother, and I do, Rose just poked a furious bear who only knows how to fight back against sarcasm with more than his claws. "Oh, don't worry, *dear*. I got plenty of sugar this morning. Or did you forget about how you woke up with my mouth between—"

"Okay." I interrupt in a loud voice, remembering a young child present before I nod toward my guests. "Michael, Rose, this is Lily and her daughter, Mei."

"Good morning," Rose chirps cheerfully, making my brother groan and rub at his temples. Have I mentioned how much my brother hates mornings when he hasn't slept well? "It's really nice to meet you."

Lily offers Rose a tentative smile that doesn't look too forced. "It's nice to meet you too."

"I have to go with Michael to see our dad," I tell Lily, leaning one hip on the corner of the island before her. She shifts in her seat, tugging the shirt farther down her legs, but not before I get my answer to the question of what she's wearing beneath it. And it's not sleep shorts. It takes my brain a second to refocus and continue. "Rose has kindly offered to keep you two company. How does that sound?"

Hesitation is clear all over Lily's face, a sign that she's about to turn down the offer. My hope sinks more just before Rose steps in, having seen it too. "I know you don't know me, but I was hoping I could pick your brain about motherhood? Liam's been fussy lately, and I could use some advice. From one mom to another?"

I have to hand it to Rose. The woman knows how to tug at the heartstrings of anyone, even those that belong to a heart locked behind a steel door. Appeal to the mother in Lily and score one for Rose.

Lily nods sincerely, which pleases me because I want her to be comfortable. If Rose can help with even a fraction of that, then I'm more than happy for her to be here. "Of course. I'll try to help."

"Alright. On that note, we have to go," Michael announces before he steps forward and gathers Rose in his arms to kiss her. When she releases a tiny moan, I glance away to catch Lily watching them with a soft pink blush on her cheeks. When she notices me looking at her, her blush grows darker before she quickly looks away from the rising embarrassment. I'm not sure if it's from being caught or from something else, but I'm very curious to find out which.

8

LILY

"I'm sure this is probably all overwhelming," Rose says the moment we're alone.

That's putting it lightly. "Just a little."

"How are you feeling? Did you sleep well?"

I want to lie, but something about Rose makes me hesitate. Maybe it's how her eyes, a vibrant shade of green, are open and honest, with no trace of deceit. Or maybe it's because she's a mother, so we have that shared connection. Whatever it is, the words fail me.

"Look, I can't even begin to imagine what you've gone through," Rose admits solemnly, her eyes filled with compassion when I don't respond. Her eyes drop to the top of her coffee mug. Seeming lost in her thoughts, she runs her finger around the rim. "I guess I never really realized how lucky I was when Michael rescued me before anything more terrible happened. I know very well that it could have been worse."

"You were kidnapped?" I whisper, not expecting to hear that from her. What are the chances?

Rose takes a deep breath, like her next words are hard to say, and she needs a moment to compose herself. "I was sold into a sex trafficking ring by my father."

Yeah...that qualifies as something hard to say. "Your father?"

"Yes. Tell me, Lily, how much do you know about the High Table? Did Xiao ever mention it to you?"

When you're treated like you're invisible, it's surprising how much you can overhear. "It sounds vaguely familiar." Still, a bad feeling builds in the pit of my stomach.

"Three families make up the High Table. The DiAngelos, the O'Learys, and the Mikhailovs. Together, they oversee the crime world of Miami," Rose explains like she's reading the words off a piece of paper.

The bad feeling grows. "What does the High Table have to do with you?"

"My name is Rosaline O'Leary. Rose for short," she reveals. "My father was Patrick O'Leary, the previous Irish mob boss of the High Table. And Michael is the heir to the DiAngelo family."

As if I've just set my hand on a burning stovetop, I stand quickly and move away from Rose. My eyes land on Mei. Completely unaware of the danger we're in, my daughter continues to eat her cereal while fascinated by some picture book Rose brought.

Raphael is a DiAngelo. Just as I feared, I did, in fact, trade one hell for another. He's not just a part of the world I've been trapped in for the past six years, he leads it.

Rose approaches, and I can't help but feel a familiar sense of panic, like a deer caught in the blinding glare of oncoming headlights. Confusion fills her eyes when she speaks to me with concern. "Lily, what is it? What's wrong?"

"I won't go back," I tell her, quite proud of how steady my voice sounds. "I will not be abused and hurt again." I step forward into her space and drop my voice. "I would sooner die."

Rose's eyes transform from confused to panicked as my

words sink in. "Oh my God...no, Lily. That's–that's not what... we're not like Xiao. I swear. We're trying to stop him."

Raphael said the same thing, but now I'm not so sure.

"Sure, our families do business with illegal things, but human trafficking? Never. Not in a million years. Lily, we won't hurt you. Or Mei. I promise."

When she tries to touch me, I react instantly and withdraw my hands from her reach. The hurt that flashes across her face is too authentic to be fake, but I've been fooled before and will keep my distance until proven otherwise.

Still, there's a saying that curiosity killed the cat, and I'm the stupid cat because I'm inquisitive despite my apprehension.

"You said your father sold you? How? Why?"

"When I was twelve, my mother, little brother, and I were in a car accident. They didn't survive, but I did. And it destroyed my dad. So much so, he couldn't stand the sight of me and sent me away for ten years to live with my uncle in Ireland. When he brought me home for my sister's wedding, that's when he told me he had arranged a marriage for me. To a man more than twice my age."

If she's trying to make a positive case for the High Table families, she's not doing a very good job here. Her father sounds like a man Xiao would call a friend. Hell, maybe they are.

But...she can't mean Michael. Can she? There's no way he's over twice her age. "You don't mean Michael, right?"

Shaking her head, Rose gives a short laugh. "Oh, heavens no. When my father told me about my engagement, I ran off to a club where I met Michael for the first time. I had no idea who he was. I mean, how could I? We're ten years apart, and I was sent away before we ever had a chance to meet. But anyway, that night it was like...love at first sight." She smiles as if lost in the memory. "I know it sounds silly, but it was like I was meeting someone I've always known. Like I had finally found the second half of my soul."

Damn me and my stupid fairy tale-loving heart. "And then?"

Her face explodes in a red flush. "Well, as you can imagine. Our eyes met across the dance floor, and it was like something out of a romance book. The moment he touched me, I knew I was done for. I'll...spare you the details, but let's just say a certain employee bathroom at the club could tell a hell of a story."

Confusion grasps me. "I don't understand. I mean...I–I understand what you mean by details...I just mean how could your father...I'm sorry." I sigh, suddenly a bumbling idiot in front of Rose.

"You see this little baby right here?" she asks, gesturing to the sleeping infant beside her with a head full of beautiful red hair, and I nod. "Well, he's...kind of a miracle. You see, Michael was told he couldn't have kids, which was clearly a lie because a couple months later, I'm peeing on a stick and seeing two pink lines in return."

A scary thought forms. "Did your dad sell you because you got pregnant?" My father, God rest his soul, would have never done something so cruel.

"Sort of." Rose strokes her hand over her son's head, peering down at him like he's the greatest gift in the world. I understand the feeling. My greatest gift sits not far away from me. "I knew if my dad found out, he'd kill me, the baby, or hell, even us both. So my best friend Evie helped me escape to Italy. She's kind of a computer genius, and she gave me a new identity. I gave birth to Liam there, made friends, and was as happy as I could be. Until my father found me."

"And he sold you?"

"He did. I spent a week on a boat and then was brought to a warehouse, cleaned and dolled up to be sold like a pretty pig going to slaughter."

"Did someone buy you?"

"Yes," she answers softly, pulling her hand away from her son. She wrings her hands together like the pain serves as a reminder that she's here in the present and not lost in the past. I know the technique well because I use it too when the memories threaten to consume me.

"Michael saved me before he could...hurt me in the way. And then he made sure the sick bastard could never hurt anyone ever again." Rose straightens her spine, takes a deep breath, and meets my eyes with a shaky smile. "I'm thankful every day because I know it could have been worse. I could have..."

When she trails off, dropping her face again, I finish for her, "Ended up like me."

"I'm so sorry, Lily. I wasn't...I wasn't thinking."

She sounds so honest, so apologetic. Rose has never hurt me. If anything, she's opened up to me about a part of herself that is difficult to remember and even more difficult to share. Like she chose to put herself through that to make me feel better. A complete stranger.

Despite every instinct in my body saying no, I choose to follow my battered yet optimistic stupid heart and reach out to grab Rose's hand.

"Thank you for sharing that with me."

Rose smiles carefully, hearing the sincerity in my voice, and just like that, I think I've made a friend. My first in years.

Mei joins us on the couch, curling up beside me, and soon, her giggles fill the room. She's completely entranced by the kid show Rose helped me select on the television. Whenever Xiao indulged Mei with screen time, I was rarely included, and so much has changed.

Before I know it, hours have passed in comfortable company and friendly conversation. When Mei falls asleep, I carefully carry her to our bedroom and tuck her in. Hesitation fills me when I go to leave her alone, causing me to stop in the doorway and watch her. I don't know how long I stand there, but Rose eventually comes looking for me.

"She's a sweet girl," Rose says. "You raised her well."

"Thank you. I did my best. Tried to, at least. But Mei deserves to have a normal and happy childhood. We can't go back. I can't put her through anymore of that."

"You won't," Rose says adamantly enough that I glance away from my sleeping daughter. "You're not going back. I know we just met, Lily, but I want you to know you can be honest with me, and I'll be honest with you. Ask me anything."

No time like the present to test that.

"Am I safe here? Are we safe here?"

"Yes," she answers immediately. "One hundred percent, yes. Michael is fair and just in everything he does. He considers every detail and fact before making a decision. And yes, he's set to inherit the head seat of the High Table, but he's also a son, brother, and father. He is the most wonderful man and partner I could have ever asked for. Is he a little overbearing and protective sometimes? Absolutely. But when everything happened, when I learned who he really was, I asked myself one question. Do I feel safe with him? And the answer was yes. It still is. Even when he's grumpy as shit because he didn't get enough sleep."

I laugh softly, remembering how sour the man was this morning. The complete opposite of his brother. His twin. Michael's hair is styled with a shorter length on the sides and longer top, while Raphael's hair is more untamed, with longer locks that curl slightly at the ends, giving him an overall tousled look. Like someone ran their hands through it, maybe seconds before tugging him forward to capture those plump, sinful lips in a tantalizing kiss...

"Raphael is a good man, too." Rose's words break through the fog of attraction that shouldn't be there to begin with. "I owe him for so much and trust him with my life."

I want to believe her but I hardly know the man, and only time and his actions will prove her words to me.

"Do you think Raphael can really take down Xiao?"

"I do. I think with your help, we can stop him and put an end to his cruelty."

I nod before looking at Mei and seeing a dozen different girls all at once. Girls innocent like her, young like her...the perfect victim. How many girls can I help save? Because even if it's just one...that's one less life ruined.

9

RAPHAEL

"What is it with my sons bringing strange women home like lost puppies?"

Dominic chuckles into his coffee cup, and I quickly kick his shin beneath the table, causing him to choke on the hot liquid. He tosses me a dark look over the cup, and I return the look with a smirk.

"We're twins, Dad," Michael reminds our old man like he even needs it. "To be honest, I'm surprised she's not a redhead, but then again, Raphael has always had poor taste."

Don't get me wrong, Rose is a beautiful woman with gorgeous red hair and vibrant green eyes to match, but that's all she is to me. A beautiful woman.

I would do anything for my future sister-in-law because she's family, but I don't love her the same way Michael does. My brother worships the ground she walks on. He would burn the entire world for her if she asked. Hell, he would hand her the matches and watch her do it herself before fucking her senseless on the ashes.

I want that kind of passion in my life, that kind of devotion that consumes every inch of your heart, body, and soul. The kind of love you would go to war to protect.

Lily's face flashes across my mind. It's easy to see why Xiao kept her around. She's a beautiful woman, tortured soul and all. Blond hair frames her delicate and angled face with the most brilliant blue eyes I've ever seen. But she's in pain. She's lost and confused, with more weight on her shoulders than anyone should have to bear. And for some fucked-up reason, it calls to the protector in me, which is highly inconvenient given her past. Because a man is the last thing she needs trying to help her.

"Any updates on Xiao?" I ask, changing the subject before Michael's mouth gets us in too much trouble when Dad's already in a foul mood.

Dom shakes his head. "Nothing. I've had eyes on the house since last night, and it's been silent."

"Do you think he knew you were coming?" Dad asks.

Michael says what we're all thinking. "If he did, that means we have a mole in our ranks."

"And high up too," Uncle Leo adds.

Only a handful of our closest men knew about last night's mission. Each one arguably as close as family to us. If it is one of them, the betrayal will be terrible and the punishment even worse.

"Leo, look into the men," Dad orders his brother and waits for him to nod before looking at me. "This girl and child you took from Xiao. Is it true she's his wife and the girl their daughter?"

"She's not his wife, but the girl is their daughter."

"You're certain?"

"I am, and I think it's safe to say she hates the man."

"What makes you think that?" Dad asks.

"He was abusing her."

"Even husbands abuse their wives," Leo reminds the room solemnly. "She could be lying. You could have brought a snake into your home."

I turn a dark look to my uncle, not caring much for his tone or implication. "Then, it's a good thing it's my home."

Uncle Leo turns to Dad, gesturing to me with a hand. "Dante, we know nothing about this girl. She could be a spy planted by Xiao himself. Why else would he have kept her around for so long? You should throw her into—"

Dad holds his hand up to silence his brother. Uncle Leo does begrudgingly with a frown. He turns to me, and I meet his identical light hazel eyes, a strong family trait we all share. "What has she said to you?"

"She said that he is nothing but a narcissistic man who enjoys raping and abusing women," I recite her words out loud. "You didn't see the fear in her eyes, Dad. She genuinely hates him and has agreed to help in any way she can to take him down."

"How exactly does she expect to do that?" he asks.

"She said he'll come for them."

"And when he does, we'll be ready," Michael adds, having already heard the plan on the ride over. "We'll finally get rid of this rat."

"Do you think maybe she was trafficked?" Dominic tosses out the idea. "Some girl he got pregnant and then kept around for some reason?"

"If she is, then that would explain why we knew nothing about her," I add bitterly. "In all our research, neither of their names came up."

"Okay, fine. If everything she says is true, what does she want in return?" Leo asks with an edge of challenge lacing his tone. "What do we do with her when Xiao is gone?"

"I offered to help her and Mei start a new life once Xiao is dead," I answer his challenge with a steel look not to fuck with me.

Dad releases a hard breath before pushing back from his desk and standing. He rubs his eyes and runs a hand down his tired face. "Alright. Bring Lily and Mei here to the house. We can guard her better here. If Xiao doesn't already know we have them, we need to let it leak and—"

"No. She stays with me."

Dad swings his gaze to me. "And why is that, exactly?"

I struggle to come up with an answer, and my eyes flick to my brother for help. He sees my plea and glances at his phone like he's just received a message.

"Rose says Lily won't talk to her." Michael glances at me briefly, and I know right away that's a lie. "She says she'll only talk to Raphael."

Dad's lips form a tight line, revealing his annoyance, but he doesn't push the issue. "Fine. Do what you can, Raphael, but make it quick. Something tells me that Xiao won't take kindly to us having them, and he will retaliate. Soon."

THE ELEVATOR OPENS to the foyer of my penthouse. Except for the hum of a television show playing, it's quiet inside. When we round the corner, I immediately see why. Rose rests on the couch with Liam fast asleep on her chest.

And they're alone.

"Hey, where's Lily and Mei?" I quietly ask, aware of the sleeping baby.

Rose turns her head to look at us, her face breaking into a huge smile when she sees Michael. He leans over the couch to plant a kiss on her lips.

"Missed you," she whispers, reaching up to run her fingers

up his face and into his hair before tugging him back down for another kiss.

"Keep that up, and Liam won't be an only child for long," I muse leisurely.

"I wouldn't complain," Michael remarks.

"Oh my God, Michael, stop." Rose giggles, her face blushing a bright red, but the sinful smile on her lips and the sparkle in her eyes scream she is anything but embarrassed.

Igor stabbed Rose in the aftermath of their wedding, resulting in the loss of one of Rose's ovaries. The doctors froze the eggs they could salvage and had Michael fertilize the ones healthy enough. And while her other ovary survived the attack, it makes the ability to get pregnant naturally much more difficult.

"I've said it before, and I'll say it again. I want to see you pregnant," Michael growls against her mouth, kissing her once more. It's a sore spot for my brother knowing that he didn't get to be there for Rose during her pregnancy and the birth of his son.

"Moving on," I say, a tad bit louder this time. The two are like a pair of horny teenagers, and keeping them focused is just as bad. "Where are Lily and Mei?"

Rose helps hand a sleeping Liam off to Michael before sitting up. "It was time for Mei's nap, so they're resting in their room. Look, I need to tell you both something, though, before they wake up." Rose's tone is as serious as the look on her face.

"What is it?" I ask, immediately alarmed.

"Lily told me about how she came to be with Xiao. Six years ago, she was working as a relief doctor in Columbia. There was another doctor there, a creep...anyway, he drugged her and took advantage. After he got his fill, he sold her to some local drug lords. From there, she was sold several times until she was brought to Miami, where she ended up at an auction and was sold to the Triads. Xiao found her next at one of his whorehouses and was apparently entranced right away. He took her for his own."

"How the hell did she survive for so long?" The Triads are notorious for pumping their working girls with more drugs and alcohol than they can handle. It often leads them to overdose and death if something else doesn't take them first.

"I think it goes without saying that she did whatever she had to in order to survive. For her and Mei," Rose says.

I can only imagine what that included and shudder in anger at the thought of what Lily has endured these past six years.

"Do you think it was the same auction?" Michael wonders.

Rose fidgets with a lock of her hair. I've learned it's a sign of her nerves, so we wait her out. "I don't know. The way she described it to me...it seemed less sophisticated. But it could be."

Michael nods and runs his free hand down her back before drawing her in to kiss her forehead. "We'll look into it. I promised you I would end the one behind the auctions, and I will."

"Thank you," Rose murmurs, closing her eyes at his comforting touch. After a second, she opens them and stares directly at me. "Promise me you'll take it easy with Lily. With both of them, Raphael. I only suffered a couple of weeks of that abuse and was lucky nothing worse happened. But she has spent years drowning in it. That kind of trauma doesn't just disappear overnight."

"I know."

"So be patient. Because despite all that, somehow, she's still strong. I can see it. And maybe you can help show her?" Rose suggests, reminding me once again why she's the perfect match for my brother. Whenever Michael leaps off a cliff, Rose is always there, ensuring he's safely tethered to a sturdy tree before encouraging him to jump.

After they leave, concentrating on actual work for our various businesses is difficult when I know Lily's so close by, but there's no rest for the wicked to maintain our vast empire. As Michael's second, I'm responsible for the day-to-day, balancing the books and identifying any discrepancies that need further attention. On both the legal and illegal sides of our business.

The soft giggle of a young girl's voice floats through the air, and I glance up at the clock, realizing nearly an hour has passed. Rose's words echo through my mind, and I know I need to talk to Lily. Running a hand down my face, I close my computer and leave the office in search of my guests.

Just as I come around the corner to the kitchen, my phone rings. Digging it out of my pocket, I swipe the green button on Enzo's name and accidentally hit the speaker button.

"Hey, hold on, En—"

"Raphael! I was just fucking ambushed by the Triads," he rushes out, his tone laced with pain and adrenaline.

"What happened?"

From the corner of my eye, I notice Lily approach cautiously, leaving Mei behind to watch her show.

"They fucking T-boned my Land Rover and then started firing. Evie's with me, man, and she could have been killed. Those titty-sucking, motherfucking fuckers—"

"Enzo!" I shout, interrupting my friend to keep him focused. "Where are you?"

"The corner of Antonia and Fifth."

"Are you two okay?"

"We're a little banged up, but we're more alive than those pieces-of-shit, beady-eyed assholes. I killed every one of them," Enzo declares.

Of course he did.

I quickly glance up and catch Lily's worried expression, her wide eyes reflecting her concern. I don't know what she sees in mine, but whatever it is, it compels Lily to reach out and tightly grip my arm, and I remember Rose saying she was a Doctor. "Bring them to me. I can help them."

10

LILY

"What kind of doctor are you?" With a strong resemblance to a modern Viking, the large and imposing blond man raises an eyebrow as he voices his skepticism.

I don't blame him, considering the circumstances. He doesn't know me, and anyone with common sense would be cautious about allowing a stranger to take care of them. Especially someone who was part of a gunfight in broad daylight with a woman he obviously cares a lot for.

"I practiced as an emergency doctor at the leading level one trauma center in Chicago and also did a few tours in Columbia with Doctors Without Borders."

"Oh. So, you like...know your shit, then," Enzo praises me.

I quietly chuckle to myself. "I guess so."

Raphael strides over and shoves Enzo back into his chair, ignoring his shout of painful protest. "Just sit back, shut up, and let Lily help you two."

"Evie first," Enzo demands, ignoring the shut-up part.

"Absolutely not. You were shot!" Evie shouts back at the brooding Viking. "And you dislocated your shoulder. Lily needs to take care of you first. My wrist and cut can wait."

"The hell she will," Enzo growls. He narrows his piercing blue eyes on the blonde beside him, who is still a striking woman despite being a little banged up and bloody.

Raphael gave me a crash course on the pair before they arrived. Enzo is Raphael's oldest friend, and someone he trusts as much as his own brother. I already know that Evie is Rose's best friend and the one who helped her escape when she found out she was pregnant, but what I did not know is that Evie is also practically royalty, incredibly wealthy, and visually stunning.

"Stop being so bloody pig-headed, you big brut," Evie snaps, her British accent cutting through strong. "If you don't let Lily take care of you first, I won't shag you for a week."

The room goes silent, and I'm suddenly thankful that Mei is in the other room, preoccupied with a movie.

Enzo twists in his seat, pinning Evie with a look. He swallows down a grimace when the move pushes on his dislocated shoulder before he leans forward into her space. Evie visibly swallows but doesn't move away.

"And what do I get if I do behave?" Enzo's voice deepens, sending vibrations through the air, and Evie visibly shivers in response, her face blushing harder.

"A date," Evie answers after she composes herself. It's a simple answer for us, but it looks like Enzo's just won the lottery from the way he grins broadly.

"Deal."

It feels like I'm watching a highly erotic moment between the two, caught in their web of intimacy, and it's only when Raphael coughs do I realize how absorbed I am in it.

Enzo leans away, settling once again in his chair before looking at me. "I'm all yours, Doc. Just make it quick. Please."

I'm not sure if I should be impressed or concerned at the mini hospital Raphael brings me in the number of supplies. From simple Band-Aids to IV bags and everything between, he has every medical supply imaginable, covering all bases.

Michael arrives with Rose and Liam just as I'm cleaning off the blood around the wound to Enzo's lower leg. It's more of a graze than an actual gunshot, but it still requires medical attention, not just the few stitches I plan to add.

Rose hands Liam to his father before she rushes over to kneel beside Evie, her hands and eyes scanning every inch of her friend. "Oh my God, Evie. What happened? Is that blood? Where are you hurt? Show me."

Evie reaches out with her good hand to grab Rose's shoulder. She shakes her friend lightly as she repeats, "Hey, hey, look at me. I'm fine. Rose, look at me."

"No, she's not," Enzo grumbles before hissing between his teeth when I dab alcohol on the bullet graze.

Rose leans over and smacks Enzo's dislocated arm. Shouting from the jolt of pain, he forcefully pulls his entire body away from me in response.

I freeze at the sudden movement and close my eyes, fear shooting through me as I wait for him to lash out at me.

"Lily?" A large and warm hand falls on my shoulder. "You okay?"

I open my eyes and look up at Raphael. He stares down at me with concern swirling in those amber depths. Something about the sincerity in the emotion draws the truth from me. "Yeah. He just spooked me when he moved so quickly."

Raphael's eyes snap up to his injured friend. He's oblivious to our interaction, distracted by his argument with Rose. Before he can scold Enzo, I reach up and lightly place my hand on his. His eyes lower to me, and surprise replaces the annoyance there.

"Really. I'm fine."

Raphael hesitates for a moment before he finally nods and

steps back. I try hard not to notice how cold my shoulder feels after his hand slips away and focus back on the task at hand.

"You could have both been killed." Rose scolds Enzo like she's not a tiny redhead that he could snap like a twig. "What were you thinking?"

Enzo bares his teeth in Rose's face, but just like Evie, she doesn't back down. "I wasn't thinking. Is that what you want to hear? I was too busy—"

"Enzo!" Evie cuts in, and he stops midsentence.

"No, Evie. Let him explain. Too busy with what, Enzo? You put my best friend's life in danger. And for what? Because you were distracted? Are you kidding me?"

"Yes, I was distracted," Enzo snaps, ignoring Evie's attempt to stop him. "Distracted because your best friend had my dick in her hand."

Silence falls heavy over the room.

What the hell have I fallen into here? They're shouting and bickering at one another like they want to kill each other, but instead of feeling malice in the air, all I feel is...love. They genuinely care for one another enough to lash out and be honest with their feelings.

For so many years, I've kept my own feelings locked down, shoved so deep behind door after door that I don't even know which one hides them in the maze of my mind.

"Wh–what?" Rose stammers.

"My. Dick. Her. Hand." Enzo enunciates each word like it's even necessary. We all heard him clearly the first time. Hell, half of Miami probably heard him.

"Well, on that lovely note," Evie says, turning toward me with a bright smile. "Do you think the gash on my forehead will need stitches?"

Like a bucket of cold water thrown on a raging fire, the

room settles down. Rose only calms down once perched on Michael's lap with Liam in her arms. She holds Evie's uninjured hand but is otherwise quiet. I can only imagine what's going through her mind right now. Rose told me that Evie is like a second sister to her. But more than that, Rose literally owes Evie her life. Evie is the very reason she and Liam are alive and with Michael now.

Enzo stays silent too, borderline pouting as I finish treating him. With Raphael's help, we pop his shoulder back in and set it with a brace to keep the weight of his arm off the joint.

Evie's injuries are similar and easy to treat as well. The gash on her forehead won't scar and doesn't need stitches, but I add a couple of butterfly closures to be safe. Her wrist is lightly sprained, and I wrap it in an ACE bandage with strict instructions to ice it in intervals and to avoid...said extracurricular activities as much as possible until healed.

It's not until I'm putting supplies away and cleaning up my mess that I realize I voluntarily touched Raphael's hand and another man for the second time in twenty-four hours... without my mind venturing to a darker place. I even got close to Raphael when he helped me with Enzo. Close enough that I felt his breath fan hot across my neck.

And it felt good. The entire thing. Taking care of Enzo and Evie without being forced to has made me feel human again...I feel like a doctor again, and I like it.

"What happened again?" Michael asks.

Enzo leans back against the couch and pulls Evie to his side when she tries to shift away. At first, she struggles but then relents and curls up against him, resting her head on his uninjured shoulder. It won't take long for the pain meds I gave them to take effect as the adrenaline rush from the accident subsides.

"We were crossing the bridge when they surrounded us. We had nowhere to go except into the water. Evie got a hold of my gun and fired back. She took down two bikers, giving us time to get off the bridge. My girl here has quite the aim." Enzo smiles down at a blushing Evie.

"Grandad believed a lady should know how to shoot," Evie explains.

"Damn right he did. He taught us both," Rose adds. "I remember being so scared when Uncle James found out. I was worried he was going to tell my dad, but then he actually bought me my first gun."

"I knew I liked your uncle for a reason," Michael comments.

Rose softly laughs before she pushes up to kiss Michael on the cheek. He turns at the last second and captures her lips instead.

"Go on, Enzo," Raphael orders.

"When we got to the corner of Antonia and Fifth, a truck ran straight into us. When I came to, Evie was still out, and we were being fired on. I fired back."

"And you're sure they were Triads?"

"Positive."

"Any survivors?" Michael asks.

Enzo shakes his head. "I don't think so, but I can't be certain. Maybe one got away or something. I'm sorry, Michael."

Michael shakes his head. "Don't worry about it. Dominic's checking the cameras, and he'll report back any findings."

"You two just concentrate on getting better," Raphael adds.

"I'm so sorry," I spit out, the words finally breaking free

from my mind. "He attacked you because of me. Because I have Mei."

"None of this is your fault, Lily," Raphael insists.

"But it is. Because I left with you. I took Mei, his daughter, and now he's lashing out."

"Lily, we knew this could happen," Michael says. "We honestly expected it to."

"Kind of hoped it would," Enzo adds with a sly smile. The drugs are taking effect on him too. "Just preferably without Evie in the car."

Evie pats his thigh as if her touch will console him. He grabs her hand before she can pull it away.

"He won't stop," I warn them, a little annoyed that they're not taking this seriously enough. "Someone's going to get hurt worse than this, and that will be my fault."

This time Raphael says fuck it and grabs my hands between his. I try to pull them back, but he holds firm. "I'll say it again, Lily, and I need you to listen. Not a single bit of this is your fault. Xiao is responsible for his own actions, his own decisions. Do you understand?"

Not really...but yes, too. At least, I will. Maybe. We'll see.

"Mommy?"

Mei's voice draws my attention, and I twist to see my daughter standing in the hallway's mouth. She has Mr. Cuddles wrapped in her arms as she stares with big eyes at the crowd gathered in the room.

"Come here, princess." I gesture with my hand and hold my arms open when she runs to me.

Cradling her to my chest, I meet Raphael's striking eyes over her head. "Can you really stop him?"

"With your help...we can."

Call me crazy, but...I'm beginning to believe him.

11

LILY

A heavy darkness surrounds me, pressing down on me from all sides. There's no moon in the sky to light my way through the woods, no stars to guide me home. I may be running in circles and not even realize it.

I stumble, and my long nightdress catches on the branches. They tear through the fabric to scratch my skin. The forest is quiet, except for my breath coming in desperate heaves. Even the predators lurking have gone silent. As if whatever else is in these woods terrifies them more.

Collapsing against the giant tree trunk, I feel around and find a small alcove carved into the side of the wood. It's small, and it'll be tight, but I'm desperate. Because I need to hide. I have to hide.

With my back pressed against the mossy wood, I pull my knees to my chest and bury my face against them. My heart pounds against my chest. The sound of my blood rushing fills my ears. It's so loud, there's no way he won't hear it among the silence. And when he does, he will find me.

When he told me to run, I did. But I was stupid to think I stood any chance. Silly of me to believe I could get away. I never can. I never do.

A hand darts out from the dark, wraps around my bare ankle, and tugs hard. I scream as he pulls me from my hiding place. Dragged along on my stomach, I claw at the ground, grabbing at anything and everything I can to stop, but it's useless. The forest has turned against me. Or maybe it was never on my side at all. Maybe it whispered to him where I hid and showed him the path.

Firm hands grab my hips and effortlessly flip me on my back. His large body falls over me, his strong legs holding mine still as he settles on top of me. The warmth of his body is like a furnace, a fire that licks at my skin, branding me with his touch and scent. He leans forward, his face hidden by a mask of shadows, but his eyes glow like twin beacons in the dark.

"Oh my dear, sweet flower," he says in a guttural tone that reverberates deep in my bones. "You almost got away."

There's no use in struggling, but I try anyway. My pathetic attempts to buck him off my small body only make him chuckle.

"You should know that I like it when you fight back. Don't you feel what it does to me?"

The moment his hips press against mine, a gasp escapes my lips, overwhelmed by the intense feeling of his unyielding, dangerous body against mine. Moaning softly, I shudder as he grazes against the sensitive bundle of nerves that longs for his caress.

Something must be wrong with me. Something fucked up deep down inside that craves to be chased and caught and dominated. Or maybe there's nothing fucked up about it at all. Maybe it's everyone else who lacks the insight and desire for something so carnal and primal that the very idea of it scares them. Frightens them into believing it's wrong.

But to me...it's a reprieve. It's a relief. It's medicinal. It's necessary. To give up all the power, all my freedom, all sense of choice...is peaceful. It's putting my trust in someone else entirely. Knowing they realize exactly what I need at that moment. Believing that they recognize how far to push before it's too much.

Understanding when the line is crossed and where that line is to begin with.

"You're mine," he growls into my throat, nipping hard enough to leave marks. "I'm going to tear this flimsy dress off your body..." He moves down to snag one of the thin straps between his teeth and tears the fabric in half. "I'm going to claim every inch of this gorgeous body..." He bites down on my breast. Hard. And I cry out. "Scream all you like, sweet flower. No one can hear you. No one can save you." He laughs against my chest before moving farther down my body. "I'm going to fill your womb until your body has no choice but to swell with my child."

"Yes," I whisper. I want that too.

He tears what's left of my pathetic excuse of a nightgown before lowering his mouth to hover above my aching pussy. When I try to squirm and push the area where I ache closer to his mouth, he chuckles deep and low. His hot breath brushes against me, sending waves of electric sensations up and down my spine before leaving me in tears.

"Please," I beg, my voice breaking from sobs.

With a seductive smile, he murmurs, "Let's see how sweet you taste," before his tongue devours me with an intensity that leaves me trembling and unable to think of anything but the over-whelming pleasure. I'm being consumed by him, just like a predator would consume its innocent prey.

I arch my back and explode against his mouth, my eyes seeing the stars hidden in the black sky as my body shakes and quivers from my orgasm. Maybe it's the adrenaline of the hunt or the fear of being caught, but I've never come so hard in my life.

"Please..." I moan. "I need..."

"What do you need, sweet flower?"

"I need you, Raphael."

"Raphael?" He repeats, but his voice sounds different now.

No longer the voice of my savior...but of my torturer.

I look down and lock eyes with black instead of gold as the shadows retreat from his face.

"Xiao."

"Did you think you could escape me? That I wouldn't find you? You think he could keep you from me?"

Thrashing, I throw my body in every direction I can to break free. To fight. Because this is no longer a fantasy...but a nightmare.

WITH A SUDDEN JOLT, I sit up in bed, gasping for air. My heart pounds against my bruised ribs, causing a dull ache to pass through me. My skin is clammy from sweat, and tears have left my face swollen. I throw the blanket off my warm body and check on Mei next to me, relieved to see her still asleep. The child can sleep through a hurricane. And actually did last year.

Sliding out of bed, I tug at my top, desperate to cool down my flushed skin. It's useless, though. I'm still hot. My eyes wander around the room, finally fixating on the French doors that lead to the terrace. There's frost on the glass panes, and I move without even thinking. The freezing night air pierces my soul and cools my heated skin. It's a stark reminder of reality as the lingering nightmare fades.

I climb onto a round outdoor chair, cradle a pillow against my chest and curl my body around it, seeking comfort like a cat. I'm still warm and not ready to go inside yet.

In the distance, the lights of downtown Miami twinkle like a sea of stars, and the gentle sounds of the ocean waves crashing far below fill the air. Working together like a lullaby, they calm my exhausted soul and bring me peace when I close my eyes and drift into a dreamless sleep.

12

RAPHAEL

There's nothing quite like the rush of chasing your prey through the forest. The feeling that comes from the thrill of knowing how close you are to catching them. Every brief glimpse through the treeline, every crunch of leaves beneath her feet as she tries hard to escape me, fuels me forward. I'm eager to catch her. Eager to touch her, eager to savor the warmth of her soft skin beneath me as I devour her body and, ultimately, her soul.

She asked for this, and when I catch her, because I will, I'll remind her of that very fact.

"Raphael."

I turn my head to the left and follow the path, my steps as silent as a wolf stalking its prey. It's like an invisible string ties us together. When she's close, the string grows hot, and when she's farther away, it's cooler.

"Raphael."

This time, she's behind me. Only when I twist around, there's no one there.

"Raphael."

GENTLE HANDS FALL on my shoulders and shake me persistently. I close my eyes to the dark forest, and when I snap them open, a pair of blue eyes focus on me.

"Mei?"

The little girl's lip trembles as she stares at me with watery eyes. "I can't find my mommy."

"What?" I suddenly sit up, my sleep and vivid dream instantly fading away. I throw off my blankets and climb out of bed, mentally grateful that I wore sleeping pants tonight. Typically, I prefer to sleep nude.

Mei backs up, frightened by my quick reaction. "I want my mommy."

Crouching down, I try my best to soothe her. "Hey, it's okay. Sorry if I scared you. We're going to find her, alright?"

Nodding, she reaches out with her arms. It's clear what she wants, and without even thinking about it, I let her wrap her arms around my neck and then stand. Searching for her mother would be easier without her holding on to me like a sloth, but I understand she's scared and seeking comfort as best a child her age can.

We leave my room and check the spare rooms, the bathrooms, and hell, we even check the pantry, but Lily's nowhere to be found. She has to be inside somewhere...unless... I head toward the terrace doors. Unless she's outside.

Opening the door, I peer out. Soft lights cast a gentle glow on the stone floor and plant-decorated corners. At first glance, the terrace looks normal. Until I spy a small shape curled up on the couch. I set Mei down and hurry over to her mother.

"Lily!" I exclaim, kneeling in front of her. She's fast asleep and ice cold to the touch. "Lily?"

"Is Mommy okay?" Mei asks in a small and fragile voice.

"Yes, she just fell asleep out here," I tell her, hoping the forced smile I give her over my shoulder reassures her.

Mei giggles. "Silly Mommy."

Yes, silly Mommy.

I try shaking Lily's shoulder, first gently and then more forcefully, but she remains motionless. When I move to gather her in my arms, she still doesn't wake up. That, along with her blue-tinged lips, concerns me greatly. How long has she been out here? Why was she even out here to begin with? And without a blanket, too?

The foolish woman deserves to be placed over my knee for her carelessness. Her reservations and past abuse be damned.

As I gently place Lily on her bed, her whole body trembles. That's a good sign, right? Better than being deathly still, but I'm not a doctor. For all I know, she's about to have a seizure or something.

Climbing onto the bed, Mei snuggles next to her mom, and I cover them with a blanket before digging my phone out of my pocket.

"Mommy's cold."

"Yes, I know," I agree, fighting hard to keep annoyance and frustration out of my tone. I'm not mad at Mei but at her mother. Clicking on my sister's name, I hope to God she's awake at this hour.

Three long rings later, my sister answers, "Hello?" She sounds exhausted, and for a moment, I feel guilty about waking her. She graduates soon and has been working longer hours at the hospital, but then I watch Lily shake harder, and all guilt goes out the window.

"Gabriella, I need your help."

I hear shuffling in the background like she's climbing out of a bed and a low voice murmuring something before she responds with a muffled, "One second."

Just because it's not the eighteenth century doesn't mean I need to enjoy hearing the details of my sister's nightly activities over the phone. There was a moment when we suspected

Dimitri Volkov from the Russian Bratva to be more than a "friend," but that changed when Michael saw a woman on her knees sucking his cock at the Playground not too long ago.

"Must you answer the phone when in bed with someone?"

"Then don't call me when I'm in bed with someone," she bites back.

"Believe me, I'd rather not, but this is a medical emergency."

That garners her attention. "What is it? Are you hurt? Is it Michael? Rose? Oh, please tell me it's not Liam."

"No. Everyone's fine. It's actually about Lily."

"Oh, your new houseguest," she teases, her tone turning a little too gleeful for me. "Rose told me all about her. She sounds lovely, brother."

"Gabriella," I grind out between clenched molars. "Can you help or not?"

"Of course. What's wrong?" she asks, switching to doctor mode.

"Lily fell asleep outside, and she's cold to the touch. I brought her inside, but now she's shaking and won't wake up. What do I do?"

"I'm not even going to ask why she fell asleep outside unless she was trying to escape your ugly mug." She laughs when I growl out her name. "Do you know how long she was outside?"

"I don't."

"Shaking is actually a good thing. Okay. Listen carefully. You need to warm her up slowly. Blankets would be best and wrap her up like a burrito. It'll prevent any more body heat from escaping. If you can, change her clothes too. I recommend throwing some in the dryer for a minute to help give her body a quicker restart."

"And then?"

"Just monitor her. If she doesn't stop shaking or she grows colder, then she'll need a hospital and warm fluids."

"Okay." I pause, my eyes trailing over Lily's shaking figure and Mei's balled up small body next to her. "Thank you."

"Anytime. I look forward to meeting them, by the way. Maybe tomorrow? I can swing—"

"Good night, Gabriella." I hang up on my sister midsentence.

Mei remains curled up next to her mom as I follow my sister's instructions to the letter. A spare outfit warms in the dryer while I get more blankets from the closet and throw on a shirt myself. When I return to Lily's room with everything, she still trembles, and her lips appear bluer, but it could be my imagination.

"Lily? I have to get you out of your cold clothes and into some warmer ones." It seems silly to tell her what's about to happen aloud when she's not even awake, but it makes me feel better, like I'm not a complete perverted asshole. She would be awake to give me her permission in a perfect world, but it's life and death here. I don't have a choice. "I'll be quick, I promise."

Lifting Lily against my shoulder, I try hard to ignore how she instinctively turns into my neck, as if subconsciously seeking my warmth. Grabbing the bottom of her shirt, I drag it up and over her shoulders, pulling back just enough to tug it off her head.

When she nearly topples over, I instinctively wrap my arms around her bare back to stop her.

And...fuck.

Her skin is cold and smooth to the touch, and I can feel the firmness of her nipples pressing against my chest. I fight the irresistible urge to pull her closer, my longing to bring her to the bed and possess her body overwhelming. But no...I'm not like Xiao. I prefer my women to enjoy their time with me. I never have to force them.

Somehow, without seeing or touching a single thing of note, I pull the fresh shirt down her body and place her back against the bed. She scrunches her face up in the most adorable way, almost like she's upset her heat source is suddenly gone, making me chuckle.

My eyes fall next to her pants, and I pray to everything holy that she's wearing underwear of some kind. She is. Much to my delight...and disappointment. Really, I should get a damn reward for being this...virtuous.

Once changed, I tuck a plush blanket around her like a burrito and then tug a thick comforter up to her chin. Mei curls up beside her mom once I'm done, and I cover her in a spare blanket before grabbing another one for myself. Pulling an oversized chair up close to the bed, I settle in for the night. It's only after Lily stops shivering and a hint of pink returns to her cheeks that I finally fall back asleep.

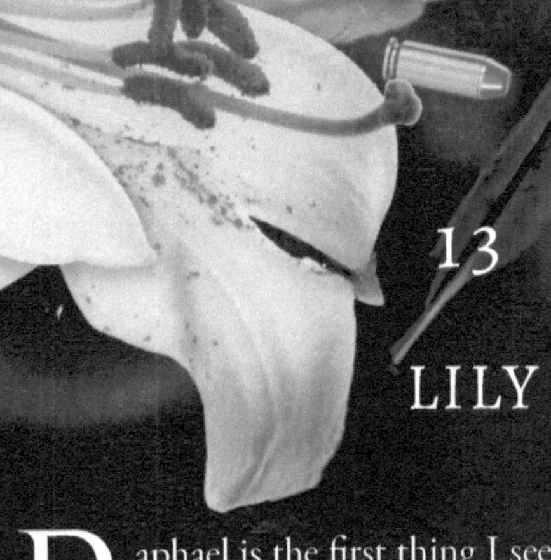

13

LILY

Raphael is the first thing I see when I open my eyes. He rests his head on his arms, right in front of me on the edge of the bed. He's so close that I can feel his warm breath gently brushing against the back of my hand that he holds.

I wait for the panic that a man's touch brings me...but it doesn't come. Strangely enough, his touch is comforting, like a warm blanket fresh out of the dryer or finally putting on that old T-shirt after a long day in scrubs.

His face is softer, less intimidating, and more vulnerable in sleep. Before my kidnapping and abuse, Raphael was precisely the kind of man I found myself attracted to. Tall, dark-haired, tattoos, with a killer body. Raphael checks every box and more.

And the thought terrifies me. Because I can see myself falling for him. It would be so easy. But that can never happen. It won't. Raphael lives in the world I've grown to hate and want to be free from. And I'm too damaged to be loved. Too lost. And that's okay. Because when this is all over, I will have Mei, and she's enough for me.

From the second I stared into my daughter's eyes, my life belonged to her. The moment she took her first breath, she became the center of my world. My sole purpose in life transformed into ensuring she grew up happy, safe, and loved.

Granted, I'm two for three there, but I'm working on it now that I'm free of Xiao. I'm not sure how…but I'll figure it out.

Raphael shifts and raises his head like he senses I'm awake and watching him. Groggy, sleep-hazy amber eyes meet mine before a lazy smile pulls on his lips. "Good morning."

"Morning," I whisper back, my voice small and cautious.

"How are you feeling?" Raphael sits up, and I brace myself for him to let go of my hand, but he surprises me instead by keeping a firm grip, and I don't resist his touch.

"I'm fine," I instinctively reply, the words slipping out without a second thought. How come is it so easy to talk to him? "Why are you here?"

"You fell asleep outside last night."

"I did?"

"Yes. Want to tell me why?"

I steal a look at our still tightly clasped hands. It doesn't seem like either of us is ready to let go.

"I couldn't sleep."

"Why not?"

"I had a nightmare." Partially true. My dream started out lovely enough until it shifted into something worse.

"Do you want to talk about it?"

A trace of hope lines his question. I want to tell him, but I also remember calling out his name before the man between my legs turned into Xiao. My face heats at the memory. No. I can't tell him.

I shake my head. "Not right now. How did I get back inside?"

A brief look of disappointment flutters across his face, but it's gone within a heartbeat, and he doesn't push the issue. "Mei woke me up when she couldn't find you."

I glance over my shoulder, expecting to see my daughter behind me, but the bed is empty. "Where is Mei?"

Raphael gestures with his head toward the pullout couch across the room where my daughter's small body rests. Her arms and legs are spread wide like a monkey, and her mouth is open in the cutest little "o" with Mr. Cuddles beside her.

It must have been terrifying for her to wake up and find me gone, and then have to explore a strange place on her own to find help... If there's a Worst Mother of the Year award, I definitely win by a landslide.

"We found you passed out on the terrace. You were freezing and shaking. Even your lips were blue." I notice a subtle trace of disappointment in his tone.

"I'm so sorry. I didn't mean to burden you." Dropping my eyes, I try to extract my hand from his, but he refuses to let go.

Raphael's hold is just strong enough to prevent panic from setting in. If I really wanted to, I could still pull free...but I don't. His thumb ever so slightly brushes over the top of my hand, and surprise comes over me at the calming feeling his touch brings.

"You're not a burden." His voice is firm and confident, but doubt still lingers in my mind.

Out of the corner of my eye, he extends his free hand and lifts my chin with two fingers. Warm amber eyes search mine, pulling me in like a bee to his honey trap as he continues. "Look, Lily, I know you have no reason to trust me, but you need to know my family is not like Xiao. *I'm* not like Xiao. I hope you can see that or will one day."

His words echo Rose's. All I've ever known is pain in this dark world he lives in. It would be insane to trust him, insane to believe what Rose said, but I guess that makes me insane.

Because...

"I'm trying to," I whisper and draw my bottom lip between my teeth. It's a bad habit of mine when I'm nervous. Raphael's eyes flick to them and something predatory flashes across his face. When he looks back up at me, honey transforms into a darker shade of amber. Heat skirts down my spine, pooling between my legs.

Before Dr. Rodriguez, before Xiao and the years of torment and abuse, I enjoyed sex. A lot. As any red-blooded woman would. That all changed the first time I was raped. But God, how I want to go back to the woman I was before. And she's there. For the first time since my hell started six years ago, I can feel her hovering beneath the surface, trying to break free. And I think it's because of Raphael. For whatever reason, she trusts him to save her. Again, that stupid heart of mine.

Raphael clears his throat and drops my chin. He releases my hand, and I miss the contact immediately. He sits back, looking ashamed, if that's even possible for a man as bold as he is. "If we're being honest here, I have something else to confess."

"What is it?"

"Your clothes were cold and a little damp from being outside. I had no choice but to change you."

I glance down, and sure enough, I'm not wearing what I wore when I went to bed last night. "You...changed my clothes?"

"Yes, but I saw nothing, touched nothing, I swear." He holds his hands up in defense like he expects me to go off the rails and yell at him.

I should be angry and lash out at him. I should accuse him of being as narrow-minded as Xiao and his men...but something in the way he looks and sounds prevents me from getting the words out.

"It was that or let you freeze and die," he continues.

I snort softly. "You're being dramatic. I wouldn't have died."

"Maybe not, but you would have gotten more sick."

"I'm not sick either."

Raphael picks up a thermometer from the nightstand before swiping it over my forehead. When it beeps, he turns it around to show me a low-grade fever of 99.8. As a doctor, I know that doesn't classify as being really sick. But it is enough to warrant some medication at least.

As if he heard my thoughts, a pair of pills appear in my vision, along with a glass of water, and I follow the hand up to his face to see a smirk playing on his lips. "I asked my sister what you should take when you woke up. She recommended Tylenol."

I accept the pills and water, taking the medicine before asking, "Your sister?"

"She graduates in the spring with her nurse practitioner license."

"That's impressive." I hope the sincerity is clear in my voice. I had the privilege of working with incredible nurse practitioners in Chicago. In my opinion, with their experience in bedside nursing, they have a unique perspective that gives them an advantage over doctors.

"Do you mind if I ask you how long you were a doctor before you were kidnapped?"

It's painful to remember the memories even now, but trust is a two-way street. "Right out of med school, I started working in an emergency room in Chicago for a couple of years. I was on my third trip down to Columbia when a doctor I worked with drugged me. He raped me, and abused me, and when he was finally done with me, he sold me to a group of men who did the same."

Raphael reaches out his hand, palm up, and places it on the bed close to mine. He's offering me a comforting hand...literally. I slowly slide my hand into his, and he engulfs mine with a gentle squeeze.

"I meant it when I said you're safe here, Lily. Xiao can't get to you."

I want to believe him, but he doesn't know Xiao like I do. The moment I took Mei, I signed my death warrant. And doomed anyone else who helped us to the same fate.

"But he can get to you...and to the others," I argue. "Enzo and Evie have already suffered at the hands of his anger."

What if next time it's Raphael? Or Rose? Or innocent little Liam? I can't handle the guilt if someone gets hurt or worse... dies because of me.

"Remember when I asked you to help us take down Xiao?"

"Yes."

"We've spent the past year searching for him, and just when we think have him, he slips through our fingers. But in less than a single day, you just being here has brought the bastard out of hiding."

Unable to look him in the eyes, I study our clasped hands and say, "Rose told me about her family and yours...that your family leads the High Table and everything that goes with that."

"Yes." He must catch on to my fear. "Does that scare you?"

Honesty goes hand in hand with trust. Raphael hasn't lied to me, nor has he given me a reason to doubt him. He deserves the truth from me. "I'd be lying if I said no."

Raphael remains quiet for so long that I finally glance up.

He's looking at me with a quizzical, almost humorous expression. "I'd be worried if you said no."

"What else can I do to help?"

"Right now?"

"Yes."

"All I want is for you to concentrate on getting better."

"Why? How does that help you against Xiao?"

"I know how men like Xiao think, Lily. In his mind, you and Mei have been kidnapped, not rescued. So when he sees that you two are doing fine and are even happy, it'll piss him off."

"Make him angry enough to lash out. Like you want him to. Like he's already done," I conclude.

"Exactly. Now you're getting it."

"Raphael," I sigh. "Why do you even care if we're okay or happy? You don't know us. You don't owe us anything."

"That's true," Raphael agrees. "Maybe it's because you're both innocent in all of this, and if I can do anything to help you get back the life that was stolen from you, I will. It's the least I can do for you after you agreed to help."

Yep. I'm in danger of falling, alright.

14

RAPHAEL

I once heard that doctors make the worst patients. Whoever coined the idea was one hundred and fifty percent right because this damn woman is testing my patience.

"How about you just sit there and relax? Hmm?" I suggest, my tone heavy with sarcasm since this is my fifth time I'm telling her the exact same thing.

Lily groans and rests her head back on the sofa. "But I need to check on Enzo and Evie."

"And you will get the chance when you're no longer running a fever," I remind her once again.

"But I'm not running a fever."

"A fever is anything higher than 100 degrees, right?"

She narrows her blue eyes at me, knowing full well that I'm right. "Yes."

"And what was your temperature fifteen minutes ago?"

"It was 100.8," she mumbles before tacking on, "which is not even that high."

"It's higher than it was this morning, and we don't want to risk Enzo or Evie getting sick while they're recovering. Do we?" I ask, compelling to her doctor's side.

"No." She pouts.

"Or Mei?" I sent her daughter upstairs to spend the day

with Rose while her mom focused on getting better. The only reason Lily agreed is because deep down, she knows I'm right.

"Well, what about you?" she counters, a little rebellious fire sparking in those captivating blue eyes of hers. I'm instantly transfixed by the sight. "What if you get sick?"

I pick up the tray of tea, medicine, and food and bring it over to the couch. "Someone had to make the sacrifice. I volunteered."

Lily raises a brow. "You volunteered?"

"Yes."

"Bullshit."

Her single word makes me pause in the middle of pouring her a glass. I glance over and meet her feverish gaze. "Bullshit?"

"Yeah." She shrugs a single shoulder clumsily. The fever is affecting her motor movements in a way that makes her almost appear drunk in a cute way. "It's not like you'd let anyone else watch me."

Her walls appear to be crumbling, and I can't help but wonder if it's the fever or something deeper that's causing her to be more open with me. Either way, it's quite a sight to see and I want more.

"I can't trust anyone else with you."

"Why?"

Her question is simple but heavy. I don't know how to answer yet because it's too complicated to put into words how she makes me feel when I'm not even sure of it myself.

I finish pouring her drink and hand her a cup. "Here, drink this. It'll help break the fever."

Lily obeys and drinks the entire cup in one go. She burps and immediately covers her mouth with a cute giggle before her cheeks explode with more color, and she averts my eyes. "Oh my God. That's so embarrassing."

I actually find it endearing. The women I spend time with are always impeccably dressed like Barbie dolls and behave like robots. It gets so tiresome and dull that even as delirious as Lily is right now, she's far more interesting.

Lily leans back against the couch, turning her head toward me. I feel her eyes on me like twin blue flames, burning every inch they touch, and wait her out because whatever is on her mind, she needs to say it in her own time.

"I wish you would have met me before..." She waves her hand in the air. "You know...before everything. I think you would have liked me."

"I like you now." The honest admission slips so easily from my lips. .

Lily blushes hard and tucks her face into the couch cushion. Once again, I wait her out. When she raises her head, the blush lingers, but now shadows haunt her eyes. "You don't mean that. You *can't* mean that."

"I don't say things I don't mean, Lily."

"I'm not good for you."

"If you don't mind, I'll be the judge of what's good for me."

Lily drops her eyes, nibbling on her bottom lip before releasing it with a pop to whisper, "I'm scared, Raphael."

"Of what?"

"Of everything," she says, inching a little closer to me. I hold my breath, afraid to move. If I do, she's surely going to bolt. "I'm scared Xiao will find me and what he'll do when he does. And I'm scared for Mei. Scared that if I'm not there to protect her, she'll become a victim like me." She reaches out, nearly touching my hand, and then pauses. Her eyes drop to the cushion like she's just now noticing her actions. "But more than anything, I'm scared that when everything is said and done...I won't be the same person I was before."

This may backfire spectacularly in my face, but I'm willing to risk it. I slide my pinky out and carefully hook my finger over hers. It feels like I wait forever before she copies me and wraps her finger around mine. I lift my eyes to her face and meet her turbulent ocean gaze. Emotions crash and spin like a hurricane in the blue depths. Pain, anger, hope, and...lust? No, that last one can't be right.

"You're right. You can never go back to being the person you were before." I push my luck, extending my other hand to gently brush the back of my finger along her soft cheek. Her eyes flutter shut, and a slight smile appears on her lips as she gives in to my touch. I know it has to be the first time a man has touched her with such tenderness in years. "You'll be better."

"I hope so," she whispers.

Between the tea and the medicine, Lily falls asleep, nestled in soft, warm blankets beside me on the couch. She moves from holding my pinky to slipping her entire hand into mine while she dreams. Her simple touch makes me feel like a raging hormonal teenager, which is pathetic because she's just holding my hand. I'm sure if she climbed on my lap right now, I'd embarrass myself by blowing my load immediately. Good thing that won't happen.

My phone buzzes. I tasked Dominic with finding this Dr. Rodriguez from Lily's past and have been anxiously awaiting news.

DOMINIC: I found the doctor.
Me: Where is he?

Dominic: He just flew back to New York. He was helping orphaned and sick children in Africa.

Me: I don't care if he's the fucking Pope himself. He drugged, kidnapped, and raped Lily. Who knows how many others have suffered the same fate? Bring me the bastard.

Dominic: I'm already on my way.

IN LESS THAN A DAY, I'll have my hands on the man responsible for Lily's every nightmare, and when I do, I'll make sure he feels every second of the past six years of her pain.

Lily shifts in her sleep and fully turns into me. She snuggles against me like a cat seeking warmth and comfort. The way she sighs when she finds it makes my pants suddenly grow uncomfortable.

Jesus. I need to get laid. But the very thought of finding pleasure between the legs of any other woman fills me with nausea, especially since the one I desire can't offer me the comfort I want.

Flipping on a hockey game to distract my complicated thoughts, I also take advantage of the quiet moment to check in with my brother. Michael's on the verge of losing his mind due to his recent houseguest additions. Rose's suggestion was more of a demand as she asked Evie to stay with her while she recovered from the accident. Which, of course, meant that along with Evie came Enzo too. Because the two are a couple, but not a couple. It's a strange dynamic that hurts my head just thinking about it.

"No...stop," Lily mumbles, twisting her head from side to side like she's trying to escape something...or someone. "Please. No more."

"Lily?"

"It hurts," she cries. "Please, stop. I can't—please. I can't take it anymore."

Okay, that's enough of this. I reach over and firmly shake her shoulder. "Lily, wake up. You're dreaming. It's not real."

"Raphael…"

"Yes, I'm right here."

"Please…help me."

This time, I reach farther down and carefully pull her slumbering body onto my lap. At least here, cradled in my arms, she can't move around too much, which will force her to stay still and break free of her nightmare.

"Lily, I'm here," I murmur into the crown of her head. "Wake up."

All at once, her movements cease. A moment later, her breathing shifts, and I know she's awake. "Raphael?"

"It's me."

I wait for her to freak out. Wait for her to fight against being in my arms, fight against resting on my lap, cradled like a baby against my chest. But she doesn't. Maybe she feels what I do. That this is natural somehow, that my arms, my touch will never harm her.

"What happened?"

"You were having a nightmare." I don't push for more detail, though I hope she offers them up on her own. She can only keep quiet for so long.

"It was Xiao," she says after a long pause, her voice laced with a weariness, like she's finally releasing a heavy burden. "He was hurting me in front of Mei. He's never done that before. He saves his abuse for when Mei is not around, so he can portray the image of being a loving father and a good man. I've tried so hard to hide it from her, but I think she knows. To some degree, at least. What kind of mother does that make me? She's so young. She doesn't deserve any of this."

"It's a blessing that she's so young. She may remember now, but she won't forever. The good memories you create from here on will eventually replace the bad until only the good remains."

"What about my memories? No amount of good can ever erase them."

"In time, they'll fade into the background of your mind. The good will outweigh the bad. It just takes time."

"I hope so," she whispers so softly that her words almost escape me, if she wasn't so close already.

Hearing her talk about her concerns and worries reminds me of my father's suggestion.

"I've been thinking," I say, and Lily immediately sits up, bracing herself with one hand against my chest. When she notices, she shifts off my lap, much to my disappointment, and settles on the cushion next to me. Her gaze is filled with curiosity and hesitance as she looks at me. "About taking you and Mei to my family's estate."

"What? Why?"

"It's safer for you both there."

She frowns. "I thought your penthouse was safe? Isn't that what you said?"

"I did, and I meant it, but my family home is a fortress on an island. No one gets on or off it without approval."

"Sounds more like a prison," she mutters under her breath before realizing I can hear her. Flushing, she adds, "Sorry. I didn't mean that."

"Yes, you did." I laugh, and she peers up at me through her lashes. "It's okay. You're right. It pretty much is, but you're not a prisoner there, Lily. I promise."

Lily chews on the side of her bottom lip, and I fight back the urge to tug it free. As much as I want this to be her choice, it also isn't. Eventually, I'll need to take her to the estate, but I'd much rather her be happy about it than feel forced.

"Okay, we'll go, but on one condition."

I smirk, finding it adorable that she's making a demand. "Which is what?"

"That you come with us."

My smirk transforms into a smile. I can tell her I never planned on sending her and Mei alone, but where's the fun in that?

"I guess I can make that work."

15

LILY

"Wow! Mommy, look! It's like a castle from one of our books!" As Raphael pulls the car around, Mei strains her neck to get a better look at the DiAngelo estate.

When we drove over the bridge to the private island, it felt like we had been transported through a portal, escaping Miami's industrial views for a beautiful oasis. And I'll admit, the house is quite impressive. It looks like a scene straight out of a magazine or a movie, with its picturesque beauty and impressive grand scale and style. "I have a surprise for you two," Raphael says when he turns the car off.

I twist in the passenger seat and look at him. "You do? What is it?"

"It wouldn't be a surprise if I told you."

Mei giggles and swings her legs in her booster seat in the back. Something he surprised me with this morning before admitting it was Rose who bought it. "I hope it's a pony!"

I turn and fix my daughter with a look. "It's not a pony. Right?" I glance at Raphael for confirmation. He smirks like a cheeky devil, and I'm concerned for a moment that Mei's right, but then he shakes his head in silent answer. "You'll just have to wait, Mei. You don't want to spoil the surprise."

"Okay," she whines.

Raphael exits the car and hurries around to open my door

before I even have my seat belt off. He extends his hand with a raised brow. I glance between it and him before placing my hand on his. "Well, aren't you a gentleman?"

He tugs me up gently, being mindful of my sore ribs. I don't know what's changed since yesterday to explain it, but I'm no longer scared that his touch will hurt me. Maybe it's because his touch has only brought me comfort, or perhaps it's because of the sincerity I see in his eyes when he does, or maybe it's a combination of both. But whatever it is, it's as frightening as it is exciting.

I raise my eyes to his face. The flecks of green in his amber eyes dance, and I suddenly know exactly what it feels like for a bug to be hypnotized by an electric zapper.

"I am far from a gentleman, Lily," Raphael whispers, the deep rumble of his voice vibrating in my chest.

Raphael looks like he's about to say something more before he stops and shuts his mouth. Stepping back, he releases me to help Mei out of the car just as another car pulls into the circular drive.

"It's Rose!" Mei shouts before she rushes over to hug the redhead's legs. After spending the day with her, it seems Rose is Mei's new best friend.

Rose pats her back and glances down at her lovingly. "Hi, little one. Are you excited about Christmas?"

"Yes, but I'm afraid Santa won't find me here." Mei's precious face falls, and so does my heart.

Last night, I expressed to Raphael how I had nothing for Christmas once I realized just how close it was. We spent the next hour talking about gift ideas and all the things I'd want to give Mei if I could. It was nice to dream and imagine, but in the light of a new day, I still have nothing to give her, and neither does Santa.

"Well, that's easy to fix," Rose says, gathering Liam in her arms when Michael hands him over. "We'll just write him a letter to let him know where to bring all your gifts. Come on, if we go write it now while we bake cookies, there's plenty of time. How does that sound?" Rose looks at me. "If it's okay with your mom, of course."

Mei swings around so fast, she's a flurry of dark hair and pink colors from her dress. "Can I, Mommy?"

"Go ahead. But behave and listen to Rose. I'll be right behind you."

"The island is safe, remember?" Raphael reassures me as they disappear into the house ahead. "She'll be okay."

"I know." I sigh. "It's just hard to have her out of my sight."

"I understand. Come on, let's go introduce you to my dad and then see what kind of mess they've made in the kitchen."

<hr>

EVEN IN A NORMAL SITUATION, meeting the parents is a terrifying event. But when one parent leads a trio of crime families in Miami, it makes the meeting just a little more intense. But Raphael swears his father will behave. Which also tells me he sometimes doesn't. Not very reassuring, if you ask me.

Stepping into the DiAngelo house is like being transported to a magical winter wonderland. At the center of a dual staircase, a towering Christmas tree is decked out in a dazzling display of sparkling lights and ornaments, creating a mesmerizing sight that stretches toward the ceiling. The soothing melodies of the holidays and the aroma of cinnamon and pine fill the air. The warm and inviting atmosphere instantly transports me back to the cherished memories of every happy Christmas from my youth with my parents.

The dozens of presents under the tree serve as a somber reminder that a certain young girl will be let down on Christmas morning. Stepping closer, I read Raphael's name, Rose, and Liam's, Dante and Alice and…wait, does that say Mei? And there's another one that says Lily.

"Raphael, what is this?" I ask, turning to find the man smiling like he's proud of himself for whatever this is.

"I may have sent a list of the items you mentioned yesterday to my mother." He shrugs a single shoulder as his eyes roam over the many presents. "She works fast."

"Raphael—" My mouth opens and closes several times as my brain tries hard to work through its jumbled thoughts. "Raphael, I…I can't—"

"You can and you will," he says firmly. "It's the least we can do."

"You're already doing so much for us," I argue. "You rescued us and have given us a place to stay. Anything more is unnecessary."

"Do you really want Mei to be let down when Santa doesn't come on Christmas morning?"

Well, ouch. He knows exactly where to poke me, right in a sore spot labeled *Everything Mei*.

"Fine," I cave reluctantly. "But I didn't get you or anyone else anything."

He smiles like the Cheshire cat. He's up to something more.

"What are you planning now?"

"I'm not planning anything."

"That's a very vague answer."

Raphael laughs like he's won a game, and he probably has. "Come on. My dad's waiting."

DANTE DiANGELO IS every bit what I imagine a Mafia leader to look like. His rugged features command attention, creating an air of power around him I feel the moment I step inside.

"Lily." His deep voice carries across the office space, sending a chill down my spine. This must be how a deer feels when cornered by a bear.

"It's nice to finally meet you." And then he smiles, and suddenly, the air lifts in the office.

Releasing a breath, I smile back and remember my manners before saying, "Thank you. You have a beautiful home."

"I'll have to tell Alice. She'll be thrilled to hear it." The way he smiles reminds me so much of Raphael. Which makes sense, of course. It's like looking at an older version of him, with the same amber-colored eyes and dark brown hair graying around the edges.

Raphael shows me to a seat before claiming the one beside me. With a quick look around the room, I see dozens of pictures adorning the walls and bookshelves. Moments of happy memories like graduations, birthdays, holidays, and more. If I didn't know any better, I'd argue that I'm in the office of a regular family man and not one belonging to arguably the most dangerous man in Miami.

"Is there anyone we can reach out to for you?" Dante's question pulls my attention back to him.

I shake my head. "It's just me."

"Raphael told me about how you ended up with Xiao."

There's a question hidden there. One he doesn't have to ask. "But you want to know why he kept me around? And why he still did after Mei too?"

"In gentler terms, yes."

"At first, it was about infatuation. And then I got pregnant. He learned about my medical skills and decided to keep me around to be a doctor for the Triads. After Mei was born, he changed. His infatuation turned to obsession and his obsession turned to aggression and abuse"

"So it's safe to assume you hate him?"

"If you're wondering if I suffer from Stockholm Syndrome, the answer is no. He's just Mei's sperm donor to me."

The corner of Dante's lips twitch. "Good to know. I was wondering if you could tell me more about Xiao and—"

A loud rhythmic knock interrupts Dante, and as one, we all turn to the large cherrywood door.

"Yes?" Dante calls.

The door opens, and a young, pretty brunette woman walks in.

"Hi! I'm Emilia, and I was told my fiancé is in here?"

"Fiancé?" The word escapes my lips.

"Yes. Raphael DiAngelo."

16

RAPHAEL

In all the craziness over the past few days, Emilia's pending arrival completely slipped my mind. And her timing can not have been any worse.

"Fiancé?" Lily repeats, and she sounds almost devastated.

"Yes. Raphael DiAngelo."

Lily turns to me, her wide blue eyes reflecting a whirlwind of emotions, sadness casting the deepest shadow. I feel compelled to tell her the truth because it seems like if I don't, I might lose her. The idea of her believing Emilia feels like a knife to the gut.

Right as I prepare to counter Emilia's statement, Dad interrupts.

"Emilia, what a wonderful surprise. We weren't expecting you until tomorrow."

"Well, I just couldn't wait to come visit and meet Raphael." Her eyes dart to me before she blushes. "My fiancé."

I'm uncertain what about my face makes her feel welcome. Seems like she needs to be reminded. "We're not engaged."

"Officially, not anymore, but—"

"No buts. We are not engaged, so I am not your fiancé."

The pout she sends my way screams her young age. "I hoped that after we spent some time together, that could change back."

"It won't."

"Emilia." Dad steps in, and she drags her attention to him. "Your father and I dissolved the contract of marriage between you and my son because it was no longer—"

"I didn't agree to that." She stomps her foot, once again acting like the child she is.

Dad narrows his eyes, clearly annoyed by her interruption. That Emilia is a guest here is probably the only reason he doesn't lash out. "Because it was not up to you. I graciously agreed to allow you to visit Miami out of respect for my friendship with your father. Do not make me regret that decision."

"Dante?" Mom announces a moment before she enters Dad's office. She surveys the crowd, discerning the tense and uncomfortable atmosphere permeating the space.

"Maybe I should go find Mei and the others," Lily suggests, making ready to stand.

My hand shoots out automatically and grabs her arm. "Stay." I urge. At first, she tenses under my touch, but then she surrenders and stays seated. "I was not aware we had company," Alice says politely, focusing on Emilia.

"Alice, this is Emilia. Emilia, this is my wife, Alice." Dante introduces the two.

Emilia holds her hand out. "It's wonderful to meet you, Mrs. DiAngelo, or may I call you Alice?"

"Thank you, and Mrs. DiAngelo is fine," Alice replies, ignoring the disappointment clear on the girl's face. "We were not expecting you until tomorrow. Your room is not ready."

Emilia drops her hand. "Oh. I can wait."

Alice inhales deep and slaps the most fake smile I've ever seen on her face. "Of course. I'll get right on that." Before Emilia can say another word, Mom turns to me, and her smile transforms into a real one. "And you must be Lily."

Lily stands, walks closer to my mom, and sticks her hand

out, but instead of accepting it, Alice gathers Lily in her arms for a quick hug. "I've been so excited to meet you."

"Uh, me too, Mrs. DiAngelo."

"Oh please, there's no need to be so formal. You may call me Alice."

I've got to hand it to my mother—she's the queen of passive aggression and no fucks given. She once stormed in during an important meeting of Dad's, pregnant with Gabriella, demanding to know why he missed their ultrasound appointment. When he blamed his mistake on his phone, she took the device and threw it against a wall, missing his head by mere inches. Mom also refused to prepare the wedding bouquet for Sophia when she married Michael. An Italian tradition she claimed wasn't necessary since the bride was Russian.

"Okay...Alice, thank you for having us," Lily says gratefully.

"Of course. Your daughter is the most adorable little girl."

"Hey Raphael, are you still in here?"

Michael walks into the already crowded office. Dad drops his head and sighs, mumbling something about *the damn holidays and needing a larger house.*

Mom kisses her eldest son's cheek before turning to her husband. "I'll get the girls out of your hair, darling."

"Much appreciated, dear."

Alice ushers a simmering angry Emilia out. Lily looks back at me over her shoulder and smiles softly before following.

"Was that Emilia?" Michael asks as soon as the office door shuts.

"Yes," Dad answers.

"She's early."

"She is," I answer this time.

Michael raises a brow at me. "You want to talk about it?"

"No," I bite out.

Michael chuckles, apparently amused by my predicament. Bastard. "Well, maybe what I have to share will cheer you up. Dominic's at Sinners with the doctor."

"WHAT ARE you getting Lily and Mei?" Michael asks as he navigates the car through the city streets toward Sinners.

After the shit show in Dad's office, I'm itching to get my hands on the man and shed some blood.

"I don't know yet." I haven't given it much thought until last night when I sent the list we made to Mom. "What are you getting Rose and Liam?"

Michael groans and runs a hand through his hair. "It's not just our first Christmas, it's the one Rose will always remember. If I fuck this up, I'll never live it down."

I stare at my brother in wonder. He's actually freaking out about this. "I'm sure it'll be fine. You could give the woman a brown potato sac and she'd be happy."

"What do you think about a pair of emerald earrings? They'll bring out her green eyes. No. I can't do earrings. Liam will just grab them. He's already pulled a pair off the other day. What about a new ring? I could do Liam's birthstone," Michael rambles. "What's the birthstone for September, anyway?"

"Emerald," Enzo supplies from the back seat. "Evie was born in September too."

Michael peers at Enzo in the rearview mirror. "What are you getting Evie?"

Enzo pushes harder into his seat, rotating his sore shoulder to ease the discomfort. Poor guy, just as he was recovering from the bullet wound he suffered while shielding Rose, he gets into a car accident. He's lucky all he ended up with was a dislocated shoulder and a bullet graze.

Frowning, Enzo stares out the window. "No idea. If the woman wants something, she just goes out and buys the damn thing. Can't surprise her with anything."

Sounds like there's more to unpack there, but we pull up to Sinners before Enzo can elaborate.

Dom looks up from his phone when I walk into the white room downstairs. He holds the device up with a quizzical look. "Why did Michael create a group chat freaking out about Christmas?"

Jesus. I left the man alone for less than a minute. "Don't ask. How's our friend?"

Dom waves his hand toward the doctor tied up in a chair while his eyes remain glued to his phone. "He passed out somewhere around the fifth toenail being pulled off."

The bloody evidence litters the tile floor. The doctor's head hangs forward heavy against his chest.

Looks uncomfortable.

Good.

While I'm busy filling a bucket of water, Michael and Enzo enter the room, arguing about how a bracelet is better than a necklace. Sighing hard, I bow my head at the sink and wonder what I can say or do to convince everyone to just leave me alone with the doctor.

Once satisfied with the water level, I turn around, aim, and promptly toss the entire contents onto Dr. Rodriguez. He wakes up immediately and starts yelling. It won't do him any good, though. The room is completely soundproof.

"What the hell?" he shouts. "Let me go! You sick mother-fuckers."

"Such language is ill becoming of a doctor," I comment.

"I don't give a fuck! Who in their right mind kidnaps a man and tortures him? What do you want?"

"And what kind of man drugs and rapes an innocent woman before selling her?"

Dr. Rodriguez looks at me in confusion and pain. "What—what are you talking about, man? I already told the other one, I haven't ever done something like that."

"Come on, Joe. The more you lie, the more painful things are going to become."

"I'm serious! I'm a doctor, for God's sake!" he cries out. "We save lives."

"That's interesting." I glance at the others, who are finally more interested in what's going on than picking out gifts. "Have you guys ever heard of a doctor who treats their patients by selling them?"

Michael shakes his head. "Can't say I have."

"Nope," Dom adds.

"Nada," Enzo says.

Looking back at the doctor, just the very idea of this bastard touching Lily, using her, abusing her over and over against her sends a hot surge of anger rushing through me until all I see is red.

Pulling my knife out, I bury it in his hand, effectively pinning it to the chair armrest. Then, with another knife, I slice off his pinky. The sight of blood squirting and the sound of his agony brings me pleasure deep in my dark soul, pleasing the devil on my shoulder. So I slice off his thumb too.

"Kind of hard to be a doctor without a thumb. Don't you think so?" I comment casually while I study the severed digit before I flick it into the doctor's screaming face. It falls to his lap and then the tile with a sick, wet sound.

"Help! Someone help me!"

The most annoying part of torture is the screaming. It hurts the ears and interrupts necessary conversation. If we didn't need him able to talk, I would have poured battery acid down his throat already just to shut him up.

I drag a chair forward and plop down in front of the doctor. "So. Let's get back to it then, Doc. Tell me about your time in Columbia six years ago."

Joe tosses his head back and sobs. His face is wet from sweat and tears, growing pale from the pain and blood loss.

"What are you talking about?"

"Maybe all the drugs have damaged his brain over the years," Michael suggests.

I wouldn't doubt it. "Let me refresh your memory." I pull my phone out and open a picture of Lily dressed in her professional white coat. Evie sent it to me the other day when she ran a background check on her. Something I hated to do but understood was necessary. Turning it around, I ask, "Remember her?"

It takes a second, but then his eyes light up in recognition, and his pale face grows a sick gray.

"Yeah," I say, putting my phone away. "That's what I thought."

"I don't know what she told you, man, but she asked for it. She wanted me to fuck her. She begged me for it."

"Man, give this guy an Oscar." Enzo snorts. "That's the best acting I've ever seen."

"I'm serious! I didn't drug her, and I definitely didn't rape her. She wanted it. I swear."

"You keep saying that, but I don't think you understand

what consent looks like," I say. "Didn't your parents teach you that no means no?"

"That's rich, coming from a maniac who has me tied up and torturing me."

Finally. Now, we're getting somewhere.

A sick smile stretches across my face as I lock eyes with him, letting him see the unsettling sight of a devil sharpening its claws in my gaze. A devil excited to come out and play.

"What kind of doctor did you say he was again, Dom?" I ask, my eyes never leaving the shaking man.

"He switched from emergency medicine to plastics a few years ago. Must be all that guilt weighing on his mind from all the women and, who knows, maybe men too, he sold." Dom replies.

"I've never fucked a man, you sick bastard."

"Oh, well, thank God for small miracles, I guess," Dom snaps back.

I run the cold steel of my blade down one of his three remaining fingers on his hand. "What happened, Doc? The women in emergency med no longer doing it for you? So you switch to plastics, where you just have free access to them all the time?"

"Don't tell me you molest them while they're under," Michael growls.

Joe's face falls as more tears fall freely from his eyes. We have our answer, and it drives me to grab his uninjured hand and sever it completely right above the wrist joint. Blood pours out and gathers quickly on the tile.

"Shit." Oops. I stand and turn to the table.

"I got it." Dominic sighs, annoyed with me for cutting the doctor's hand off. He steps forward with a towel to cover the bloody stump and a tourniquet to slow the bleeding.

I lean forward against the steel table and focus on taking deep breaths to bring my anger back under control before I snap his fucking neck.

"We need him alive," Michael reprimands me as if reading my mind.

"I know that."

"For now, at least. Get what you need and then kill him."

Reminded of my goal, I feel the devil settle down before turning back around, composed and ready to continue.

"Who did you sell Lily to?" I ask, twirling my knife in my hand.

"I don't know...it was some local guys," Joe cries. "I swear. It was the first time I ever dealt with them, and I never saw them again."

Sounds like teams were rotated to collect the "goods." It's sickening to think that we do the same in our various businesses, but it's a common tactic. "And who did they work for?"

"I never saw their faces or talked to them personally."

"I'm sure you heard something." I slap his pale, damp cheek a few times. "Come on. Think, Joe. Use that doctor brain of yours."

He groans deep from the radiating pain. I really shouldn't have cut his hand off. But I loathe the man with a level of hatred I never thought possible. Maybe not as much as Xiao, but I still want to send him to the deepest pits of hell where he can spend his days tortured over and over by the devil himself. Until I arrive to continue at least.

"The Los...Renegados," he whispers. "I swear...that's all I know."

I believe him. And we have what we need.

"What else does Rose like? Maybe a day away from Liam at like the spa or something?" Enzo asks, switching back to the earlier conversation since our time with the good doc is ending.

Michael snorts. "A day away from our son is the last thing she wants, but a spa day does sound nice."

"What about you, Raphael? Are you going to get Lily and Mei something?" Dom asks.

My eyes roam over the dying doctor, and the devil on my shoulder whispers something dark and delicious in my ear.

"I think I have the perfect gift."

17

LILY

"The cut looks great," I tell Evie, gently running my fingers over the healing gash on her forehead. "Keep it covered for the next few days to be safe."

"You're positive it won't scar?" Evie asks with hesitation in her voice.

"I'm sure. How's your wrist?"

She holds up her brace-covered wrist. "Sore but I haven't had to take painkillers today."

"That's good."

"Speaking of, how are you feeling?" Rose asks as she multitasks, feeding Liam with one hand and cutting Christmas shapes out of cookie dough with the other.

My eyes shift to where Mei is busy combining ingredients for more dough with Alice at the counter. Raphael's words about making good memories to replace the bad echo in my mind. A smile spreads across my face as I watch her create new and happy memories.

I turn back to Rose and Evie. "I'm fine. It was barely a fever."

"That's not what your nurse said." Rose winks.

Evie grabs a bottle of orange liquid and pours a glass for herself. "And what a handsome nurse you had, too." She pours another glass and pushes it toward me.

Picking up the glass, I sniff the drink and recognize the

sweet and crisp scents of orange and champagne. I can't even remember the last time I had alcohol, let alone a mimosa. Whenever Xiao forced me to drink, it was always straight tequila or vodka. Anything that rendered my senses useless and left me defenseless for him and his men to take advantage.

I start with a gentle sip, and when the flavor explodes on my tongue, I take another larger sip. Then I force myself to set it down because if I'm not careful, the alcohol will go straight to my head.

"Careful, Evie," Rose warns her best friend with a laugh. "You don't want Enzo hearing you say such things."

Evie leans back in her chair and smiles coyly. "Maybe I do. Jealous sex is almost as good as angry sex."

"Who's having sex now?" A beautiful woman with tan skin, hazel eyes, and thick dark hair piled high in a messy bun asks as she enters the open kitchen. She's the type of gorgeous that even dressed in scrubs with little to no makeup on, she just draws your eye immediately.

"Gabriella," Alice greets the woman. So this is the elusive little sister. "Are you all done for the holidays, my dear?"

"Yes, I'm all yours, Mom."

"Excellent. Have you met Lily and her daughter, Mei?"

Gabriella turns to me with a bright smile. "No, but I've been really looking forward to meeting you. I hope you're feeling better."

"I am. Thank you for your help. Raphael told me you're about to graduate as a nurse practitioner?"

"That's right."

"Do you know what specialty you want to go into?"

"I was thinking pediatrics." Her eyes drift between the kids, her features softening as she watches them. "I want to help give them a voice. Protect them. You know?"

"That's honorable." I admire.

Evie offers a glass of mimosa to Gabriella, who shakes her head. The Brit narrows her eyes and says, "What are you, pregnant?"

"Who's pregnant?" Alice asks abruptly, the one word snagged her attention in an instant.

"No one, Mom," Gabriella calls over her shoulder. She turns back to Evie and says, "I'm just exhausted and don't need any alcohol helping that along."

Evie shrugs and then tops her glass off with the amount she poured for Gabriella.

"Hi! I'm Mei, and you're really pretty," my daughter announces as she literally pops up next to the table.

Gabriella smiles at Mei, leaning down to get eye level with her. "Well, hello there, Mei. I'm Gabriella, Raphael and Michael's little sister, and thank you for the compliment. You are very gorgeous yourself."

"Thanks! Bye!" she chirps and runs off back to the counter where Alice waits. From the looks of it, my daughter has been taking advantage of the free cookies and is now on a sugar high. Which means she's going to crash and crash hard soon. Hopefully, by then, I'll know where we're staying too.

"Oh, my gosh...I love her," Gabriella gushes, watching her bounce away. "You'd never know, looking at her..."

"That she's Xiao's daughter?" I finish her thought.

Gabriella looks at me, horrified. "Oh no. I didn't mean it like that."

I know she didn't, but that doesn't make it any less true. "It's okay. He's just her sperm donor."

Rose snorts, still finding the line funny even though she's heard it before.

"Well, look, he only makes up half of who she is. And she has a fierce mama bear protecting the other half of her."

"Thanks, Gabriella."

"A bangin'-hot mama," Evie compliments with a heavy English accent. I have an idea. The boys will be gone all day, and I've been dying for a spa day. I'm talking about hair, nails, facials...the whole nine yards. We need it, ladies."

Rose sighs, picking Liam up to burp the baby over her shoulder. "I guess it would be nice."

Gabriella shrugs and looks around with a half smile. "I'm not against it. I've had a hard few days at the hospital."

The offer is tempting, but I can't shake my hesitation to get close to any of them while Xiao remains a threat. His presence is like a dark cloud hanging over my excitement. And I want to get close to them. I really do. But if I do... if I open that door and let them in, the thought of losing them and being dragged back into that unbearable hell feels like a death sentence. Not just for me but for Mei, too.

"What do you say, Lily?" Rose asks, wiggling her eyebrows at me.

I gaze around the room, catching on each of their expectant faces. Even Alice meets my eyes with an encouraging smile. Raphael's words echo through my mind, reminding me I'm safe here. Reminding me to fight for the girl buried beneath the lingering pain and layers of scars. And the only way I can do that is to stop living in the past and focus on the future. One day, one step, one new memory at a time.

"Well, I have had a rough six years," I say, enjoying how each of their faces falls in surprise before I crack a smile and laugh. "Do you think there's a facial that can erase that amount of time?"

"...AND so the girl opened the window and stared out at the grand forest like she's done so many times before. Only now was she about to see it from below. She gathered her long lock of golden hair and threw it out the window and over a hook before watching it fall to the green ground below. She climbed up on the railing, took one giant breath, and jumped—"

"Like this, Mommy?" Mei asks, demonstrating the book scene as best she can. She takes a deep breath and jumps on the bed, collapsing in a fit of laughter next to me.

"Just like that! Good job." I praise her. She often likes to act out scenes from her stories, and I encourage her imagination. "Now get back here, wiggle worm, and listen to the rest."

Mei settles in for the rest of her story, and before the secret princess even reaches the castle, my own little princess is fast asleep. I make sure she's tucked in and kiss her forehead, whispering sweet dreams before sliding off the bed. My bruised ribs feel better each day and only twinge painfully when I twist a certain way.

I turn to the door and nearly have a heart attack, slamming my hand over my mouth to buffer the scream from escaping. Raphael leans against the doorjamb with one shoulder, his arms crossed over his chest. He runs his eyes over my body in a lazy motion with a teasing half smile.

I take him in too, blaming the ache it causes between my legs on the ridiculous amount of drinks this afternoon into dinner.

"I like the new haircut," he admires as I walk closer.

I shift my hair to the side, exposing the light pink highlights underneath. "Really? I don't know about the color. Gabriella suggested it, and then Rose insisted, and then Evie guilt-tripped me, and then…" I sigh hard, looking down at the color. "And then they got Mei involved. And how can I say no to my daughter? She even got a haircut and has some cute pink extensions."

"I think it looks great." Raphael's deep timbre sends a shiver down my spine, forcing me to look up into his face. His eyes blaze in the shadows his hair creates around his face. I watch him lift his hand in my periphery but don't break contact with his eyes as it draws closer. His hand brushes down my hair, snagging a lock of the pink strands around his fingers. The hitch of my breath turns his eyes from a bright hazel to a dark amber. He gazes at me with a distant look as if grappling with his thoughts, uncertain of his next step or words to utter.

"Thank you." My whispered gratitude breaks the moment between us.

Raphael drops his hand and steps back, clearing his throat as he does.

An awkward moment of silence envelops us. Raphael looks like he's about to turn and leave, and the stupid part of my heart still alive after years of abuse forces my mouth open.

"Your clothes are different, and your hair is wet," I observe and take a step closer, grabbing the door handle as I do. Mei has just fallen asleep, and I don't want our conversation to wake her.

His lips bloom into a small smile as he steps back to give me room to close the bedroom door.

"Follow me." He heads down the hall, and I follow without question.

Raphael leads me to an outdoor seating area, where the glow of a gas fireplace fills the air with a comforting warmth against the chilly night air.

"Well?"

"Well, what?" He repeats, and if I didn't know any better, I'd say his tone is borderline playful.

"Your clothes and hair. Are you going to answer me?"

"You didn't ask a question."

I open my mouth, ready to argue...but pause because he's right. Raphael meets my glower look with a wink, and now I know he's being playful on purpose.

"Fine. Why are your clothes different and your hair wet?"

"I took a shower." He answers like it should have been obvious.

"You took...a shower," I repeat. "Why?"

Raphael chuckles low, and the vibrating sound reignites that foreign ache in me. "You're very curious tonight."

"I'm a doctor. It's what I do."

Raphael laughs again and reaches behind him. "I enjoy hearing you say you're a doctor."

I do too. It's a truth I've long since buried under years of abusing my license, abusing what medicine stands for. It got to a point where I started to consider myself as someone with a knowledge of medicine, and that's it. Because I didn't deserve to carry the title.

Raphael brings his hand back, holding a wrapped box I don't remember seeing before. He sets it in front of me, and I glance down at the black wrapping paper and cute bright red bow in the corner.

"What is this?"

"What does it look like?" Again with that playful tone.

"A gift."

"Ding, ding," he singsongs.

"But Christmas is in a couple of days. Don't you want to wait?"

"You're stalling." He calls me out. "Besides, it's not really a gift you should open around others."

I frown and narrow my eyes at his cryptic clue. "Why?"

"Just open it."

I pull the bow off and playfully stick it to the top of my head. Whoever wrapped it did a wonderful job. The corners are even and tight and better than anything I've ever wrapped before. The perfection and attention to detail almost makes me feel guilty about ripping into it, but I'm too curious to wait.

The wrapping paper falls away to reveal a simple white box with a lid. Pulling it off, I find a layer of tissue beneath it. I lift it away to see...

"Is–is that—" I pause because maybe the dark is playing tricks on me. But no...what lies on the tissue is very real. "Is that a...dick in a box?"

18

LILY

Look, I've received various levels of gifts throughout my life. Gag gifts, like a two-foot-long, four-inch-wide dildo with a suction cup on the bottom to sentimental gifts and everything in between. But I've never been given a dick in a box. Not even a fake one. And this one is very...*very* real. I don't need to be a doctor to know that. The bloody end where it was once attached is too realistic to be fake.

"Yes."

I close my eyes briefly at his honest admission.

"Why is there a dick in a box?" I turn to look at him. "If this is some kind of sick joke of yours—"

"It's not. It belongs to Dr. Joe Rodriguez. Well, it *belonged* to the late Dr. Joe Rodriguez."

"The late," I repeat, the definition of the word dawning on me slowly. "You mean he's dead?"

"He is."

"How?" There's only one way his dick ended up in a box, but I need to hear him say it.

"By my hand."

I release a hard breath before leaning forward to place my head between my knees. Black shadows threaten my vision as the sound of my blood floods my ears in time with my pounding heart. It feels like a panic attack closing in from all sides, but it's not that. It's something different.

For so long, that man has lingered in the shadows at the very back of my mind. Every cruel and terrible man who came after him was because of him. Because he couldn't handle the rejection of being told no by a woman. Because he was a coward and a monster, my life was forever changed.

Over the years, I sometimes imagined seeing him again. Imagined shoving my thumbs into his eyes so that he could never lay his seedy gaze on another woman again. Imagined cutting out his tongue so he could never speak to another woman again. Imagined cutting off his dick so he could never hurt another woman like he did me.

But now I don't have to. The bastard is dead, and his dick lies in front of me, resting on the tissue paper like a gift. Thanks to Raphael and his completely unhinged, borderline psychopathic ways, he slayed a monster who has long since not deserved to breathe another second of air. He recognized my deep yearning for revenge and selflessly took it upon himself to fulfill my deepest desires...so that I didn't have to. So I didn't have to further taint my already damaged soul with more darkness.

My mom used to call me her little miracle. That I was blessed by the angels. And maybe she was right. Maybe I do have a special guardian angel watching over me and protecting me after all. Only mine is not bound by laws or rules. He does what he must to keep me safe.

"Lily?" Worry laces his tone. Like he's concerned I'm angry with him or disgusted by the gift.

I'm not.

All at once, my heart slows as my vision returns and my hearing clears. It wasn't a panic attack. It was a wall coming down. It was relief flooding my system as light returned to destroy the shadows that the monster once occupied.

I sit up and give the shriveled-up piece of flesh one last look. It no longer has any power over me. Dr. Rodriguez no longer holds power over me. He's dead while I'm still here, still alive. He tried to break me, and for a while, he succeeded, but the woman I once was is still there and coming back stronger than ever, surging even.

"Lily?" Raphael tries again.

I turn to meet his concerned face and smile. Sliding off my seat, I fall to my knees between his legs, never once breaking eye contact.

I can tell I'm taking him by surprise from the way his eyes widen. For a second, I wonder if I'm making a mistake, reading too much into whatever this is between us, but the hope in those warm honey depths encourages me to continue.

Raphael's hands jerk toward my arms like he's fighting every impulse to pull me forward and take control like he wants to. But he's letting me take the reins here. I'm calling the shots. And right now...I want to see if he's as skilled with his tongue as he is with his words.

His breath rushes forward, skirting across my lips as I inch closer. His eyes drop to my mouth, and lust darkens his eyes. We're merely centimeters apart, and I know it's killing him how he could just lean forward, but he still waits. The rush of power that gives me pushes me to close the distance.

Our lips crash together, and both of us inhale at the same time as if the kiss is a breath of fresh air. His mouth is all-consuming, his lips soft and firm as he guides the kiss. He brings one hand to cup my chin and maneuvers me into an angle that gives him even more access to my mouth. It's like he's a starving man and I'm the first glass of water, the first meal he's had in so long that he can't help but devour every inch.

Our tongues move together naturally, like we've been doing this dance all our lives. And maybe we have, but only in our dreams.

My hands slide up his hard chest to bury in his messy locks. I tug lightly, pulling a deep groan free from his chest that reverberates down to my throbbing clit. I push forward, seeking more, but Raphael keeps one hand on my face and the other firmly placed between my shoulder blades.

He pulls away but only far enough to press his forehead against mine. The air between us mingles with our breath as our chests heave for air.

"I want nothing more than to strip you naked, lay you out on this lounge, and feast on your pussy like it's my personal fucking nirvana."

I shudder at the image he creates. "Do it."

He growls, pushing his head harder against mine like he's fighting back his desire.

"You say that now, but Lily, you need to know that once I've buried myself inside you, there is no running away. Ever. Do you understand?"

I nod mutely because his words and actions have left me dizzy and overstimulated. He's right. It's not my mind controlling my mouth. It's my body or, more accurately, the greedy, horny bitch between my legs. I wish I could say I won't regret it in the morning, but I likely will, and if we have any hope for something to grow between us, he deserves to have me all in.

After a long second, Raphael brings his other hand to cup my face before he leans up to press a long kiss to my forehead.

"Good night, *la mia ninfea*," he whispers. "My sweet Lily pad."

19

RAPHAEL

I'm finding it hard to concentrate on my run when thoughts of Lily's soft lips from last night keep distracting me. I wasn't lying when I voiced my intentions, when I told her how badly I wanted to lay her out and bury my face in her pussy until I suffocated in her pleasure.

And God, when she said do it…how ready I was to take her up on her permission. But the dumb angel on my shoulder shouted louder than the devil's encouragement that her approval was because of passion fueling her brain and not logic.

I also wasn't lying when I told her that when we cross that bridge, and we will, that's it. There will be no turning back, no second-guessing decisions, no hiding from a chance to heal. Because I'll help her heal. With every kiss, every gentle stroke of my tongue, every tender caress of my hands, and every passionate thrust of my body inside hers will wash away the pain she's endured until she only knows me and my touch.

The door to the indoor gym opens, and Enzo struts in with a slightly noticeable limp. His one arm rests in a sling while he waves a tablet in the other. I turn off the treadmill, grab a towel to wipe the sweat from my face, and take a big swig of water.

"Evie found this late last night," he says as he hands me the tablet. "Let me tell you. That woman does her best hacking after a couple of mind-blowing orgasms. She does this one move that—"

"Enzo." I interrupt with a quick look. "I'm not really in the mood to hear about your sex life with Evie."

Enzo smirks, and I realize my mistake too late. "Someone got a bad case of the blue balls today?"

"Someone want to lose their balls?"

"And here I thought killing the doctor would have put you in a good mood. Did Lily not like her gift?"

"She liked it."

"Then what's wrong?"

"We kissed and—"

"You kissed? Whoa! Hold up. First off, Dominic owes me a hundred bucks. I can't wait to shove this in his face. He's going to flip—"

I tune the big idiot out and instead focus on the report in my hand. I hate to admit it, but if sleeping with Enzo gets this level of intel, Evie's welcome to spend every second in the big blond man's bed. Hell, I'll offer to chain him to the bedpost if it helps.

The Los Renegados was a large cartel controlling nearly all of Columbia, but when their leader was killed in a war among cartels, they dissolved. That was nearly five years ago, not long after they bought and sold Lily. It leaves me wondering if she had been taken after their war...if the Los Renegados weren't around to sell her too, where would she have gone? I hate to admit it, but while there's no denying her past is terrible, it could have been worse. She could have died.

The very idea makes me sick to my stomach. In less than a week, Lily and Mei have become such an integral part of my life that I can no longer imagine one without them in it. I always felt like something was missing but could never put my finger on it. So I just ignored it or filled the hole with other vices, like alcohol and women, until I no longer felt it.

When Michael made the choice to pursue a life with Rose and Liam, before we knew who she was, I accepted my fate. I accepted that whatever was supposed to fill that hole would never come. And I was fine with that. Or at least I was after a night I drank myself into a blacked-out slumber.

The relief I felt when Rose's true identity came out and I was relieved of my duties as the heir wasn't as freeing as I thought it would be. The hole remained. That feeling of something missing grew larger. So once again, I threw myself into distractions, anything to numb the feeling. Until a pair of blue eyes opened in a dark room and filled the void.

"So no one is left who harmed her except Xiao?" I conclude, handing the tablet back to my friend.

"Yeah. No one that Evie could find, anyway."

"Dom sent me a text last night that he's looking into a possible Triad hideout. Have you heard anything more from him?" It's beyond frustrating knowing the last man to pay for hurting Lily keeps evading us.

"He checked in earlier this morning. Said not to worry, that he won't be late for Christmas Eve dinner tomorrow. He knows Aunt Alice will kill him if he's not there."

It's not uncommon for Dominic to go off on his own to track down a lead. But Xiao's silence about Lily and his daughter being with us is concerning. Especially after his failed attack on Enzo. I don't like for any of us to be unaccounted for. Because from the way Lily describes the Triad leader, his daughter is his most prized possession, and he's just crazy enough to do whatever it takes to get her back.

Enzo's phone beeps, and he glances at it before softly smiling. "Got to go. Duty calls."

"Is that Evie's nickname now?" I laugh while I walk over to the bench press.

As he leaves the gym, Enzo mimics my laughter in a mocking tone, telling me I touched a sore spot.

I'm sliding weights onto the barbell and getting ready to do a set when there's a soft knock on the door.

"Lily," I say her name with a smile when I see her standing in the doorway.

"Hi." She's been a little shy all morning, which is kind of cute in an endearing sort of way.

"Did you need something?" I consider reaching for my discarded shirt but throw the thought out when I catch her eyes running down the length of my chiseled and slightly damp chest. The gray sweatpants I'm wearing hide little, not that I'm little in *that* way, so when her eyes snag on the outline of my dick, her face explodes red as she bites on her bottom lip. Which only makes my dick jerk in my pants.

Jesus. The hold this woman has on me. I'm very sure that the moment she touches my cock, I'll come like a teenage boy being touched for the very first time. It'll be embarrassing as hell, but nothing I can't fix with a mind-blowing orgasm. Or three.

"Um, I still have nothing for Christmas, and I don't want to arrive empty-handed. Especially since your family has gone out of their way to buy presents for Mei and me...and then there's your...gift from last night." Lily shrugs, trying her damnedest to avoid my eyes and body. "I don't know. I just want to do something nice after...I don't know, something normal I guess."

I can think of a few nice things she can give me, but I'll keep those thoughts to myself...for now.

"How about this?" I wait until she looks up at me and

smile reassuringly at her. "After I finish my workout, we can order whatever you want."

"Are you sure? I don't have any money to give you or anything—" She stops abruptly and wrings her hands together.

"If you are about to offer your body to me, I don't want that either," I tell her. "Not in exchange for a favor at least...as tempting as that is."

She blushes hard. "I-I...Raphael, I—"

An idea comes to mind, and I interrupt her. "Actually, there is something you can give me."

"Okay," she says hesitantly.

"A kiss under the mistletoe?"

Lily smiles softly. "I can do that."

"Good. Now, will you come over here and spot me?"

She raises a brow. "Spot you?"

"Yes. You stand behind me and be there in case I need help."

Her eyes take in the number of weights on the bar. "Raphael, isn't a spotter supposed to be able to lift the same weight? There's no way I could help you if you needed it."

She's not wrong. And to be honest, I didn't need a spotter. I'm lifting a weight I'm comfortable with, but it's giving me an excuse to keep her near.

"Then how about you act as inspiration?"

Lily shakes her head with an exasperated sigh but pushes off the doorway anyway and approaches. I lean back and slide beneath the silver barbell as Lily comes around to stand behind me. She stares down at me, fighting back a smile, but I don't because it feels like I've won.

Feeding off the energy between us, I wink up at her, which breaks through her defenses. The most beautiful smile stretches across her face, framed by her blond hair. From this angle, with the room's light behind her, she looks like an angel.

"You're trouble, aren't you, Raphael?" She whispers on a breath. It's there in the depths of her ocean-blue eyes that reveal the woman fighting to return, and I can't wait to meet her when she does.

"Sweetheart, you have no idea."

20

LILY

"I don't know about this," I share uncertainly while I take in the sight before me.

Gabriella hears me and waves away my concern. "Relax. I know my brother, and he'll love this."

I hold up a roll of festive red-and-white wrapping paper adorned with cute stocking designs. "Something tells me this isn't Raphael's style."

"I know, right?" Gabriella reaches over the table and snags the roll of paper from my hand. "The man has no sense of style."

"I think he looks great." The words are out of my mouth before I can stop them, and it takes me a solid three seconds to realize Gabriella, Rose, and Evie have gone still. Glancing up, I take in their stunned faces and wait.

"I meant how he styles his home for the holidays," Gabriella explains with a teasing smile. "Not what he wears."

Shit.

"But clearly you do," Evie concludes with an equally teasing smile.

"That—that's not what I meant." I can feel my face turning warm from the growing embarrassment. "I just meant—that, you know...he—he dresses nice." My voice drops as I mumble that last bit.

"There's nothing to be embarrassed about here, Lily. Not

with us," Rose assures me. "What you're feeling is completely normal, and we would never judge you for that."

A spike of anger stabs at my chest, causing me to pick at the cut end of a ribbon, which only makes the edges more frayed. "I know, I just—" I sigh in frustration and toss the piece of fabric on top of the table. "I hate feeling like this."

"Feeling like what?" Gabriella asks. "Like it's wrong to like someone?"

"Yeah," I mumble. My eyes focus on the damaged ribbon. How much it resembles me is symbolic in a way. A little torn and uneven round the edges, flawed and unable to ever be put back together the same as it was before. "Raphael is too good for me. And I know that's like an oxymoron because he has just the same amount of blood on his hands as Xiao does. But... even though he does, even though it should send me running for the hills, I'm not scared of him. I want to be near him; I want to know him. I want to feel his touch against my skin and his arms around me. I want to kiss him again, but it feels wrong to want that because I'm not worthy of him. Raphael deserves to be with someone who is not damaged and fucked up in the head. It wouldn't be fair of me to ask him to wait because what if I never recover? What if I'm too broken beyond repair?"

The familiar burn of tears pricks at my eyes. I hate crying. I always have. I'm sure some therapist somewhere would argue that it's healthy to cry and that it's the body's way of healing from trauma. If that's so, then how many buckets do I need to fill up before I'm healed?

Gabriella moves from the other side of the table and sits right across from me.

"Lily." She leans forward and takes my hands in hers. I look up and meet her eyes. They're so eerily familiar that, for a moment, my heart squeezes because it's like Raphael sits in front of me. "I wish I could say that it would have been nice to have met you before everything happened. But I'd be lying because I get to know the woman you are now...and the woman you're becoming, and she's stronger than anyone I've ever known. There's this power inside you, this raw strength that has been beaten down and locked away for years, but I can see it growing stronger and stronger every second. And when it finally breaks free, it will be amazing."

Rose kneels beside Gabriella and places her hand over our clasped ones. "You may think you're too broken, but Raphael is too. And I think that, together, your broken pieces fit. You just have to be willing to take a little bit of that strength we see in you to try and trust again."

I know they're right. Just like how a wound will never heal if left untreated, my battered soul will never heal if I don't take that first step. But I'm not afraid to admit that the idea terrifies me. At the same time, the vision of the woman I could be standing on the other side of this is worth fighting for.

"Thanks." I don't know what else to say, feeling over-whelmed by their support and reassurances.

"I'm sorry," Evie speaks up. "But can we circle back to this kiss you mentioned?"

Rose's and Gabriella's faces light up with wicked smiles, like cats that got into the milk.

"Oh yes, you said kiss again. What kiss?" Rose asks.

"And when did this happen? Tell us everything." Gabriella urges.

It feels like I'm suddenly back in high school, gossiping in the cafeteria with my girlfriends about the first boy who ever kissed me in the hallway.

"Last night. After he got back to the house." I look away and pick up the wrapping paper to give my hands and brain something to distract them while my heart talks. "He liked my hair, and then I followed him outside, where he gave me an early Christmas present. I was so overwhelmed by it I couldn't stop myself. I had to kiss him."

"You kissed him?" Rose's smile widens, and pride shines in her green eyes.

"I did."

"And then what?" Evie asks.

"He kissed me back, and then that was it."

"What a gentleman," Evie admires before smacking Rose's upper arm. "Looks like you picked the wrong brother."

Rose rolls her eyes and snorts. "Not even close. Raphael is every bit as great as Michael, but he's not Michael. Besides, Raphael is completely infatuated with Lily."

"We barely know each other."

"Look, I met Michael at a club, and within five minutes, we were having sex in the bathroom." Rose shrugs. "Sometimes you just know right away. There's no explaining it."

"What was the gift that drove you to kiss him?" Gabriella asks.

Rose's soft chuckle and glance at Evie tell me they already know. Michael and Enzo must have shared the details.

"There was this doctor in Columbia. He was the one responsible for everything. He drugged and raped me before selling me to the local cartel. Well, anyway, I guess Raphael tracked him down and presented his severed penis to me in a gift box."

Gabriella goes silent and still while Rose and Evie fall into a fit of laughter.

"He gave her a dick in a box," Rose jokes between fits of laughter.

"Wrong dick, though," Evie comments back.

"Holy...shit," Gabriella finally says. "That's...a unique gift and one hundred percent my brother." She laughs too, and before I know it, I join in, enjoying myself because I don't feel any judgment or pressure around these girls. They understand what I'm feeling because they live in this life and understand it better than anyone I knew from before ever could.

"Knock, knock," Alice sings before she appears in the doorway with Mei and Liam. She volunteered to watch the kids while we wrapped the many presents that arrived this morning. Much against my annoyance. But Raphael pressed the checkout button last night on the online cart we packed before I could get a word in otherwise.

"Mommy!" Mei cries out before she sprints forward to collide with me.

"Hi, princess. Did you have fun with Alice?" I smooth her dark hair away from her flawless, porcelain skin and stare into her blue eyes, sparkling with joy.

"Yep! We made bread with fruit in it!"

I glance up at Alice for clarification.

"Panettone. Think of it like fruit cake but better," she answers.

Liam squeals when Rose reaches for him. I watch him and see Mei at that age in my mind's eye. When she was a baby, Xiao often used her to control me. If I behaved at one of his parties, I got to spend the night with her. If I pleased his men, I got her for a day. Xiao spoiled her as she grew older, and I'm not proud to say this...but I used it to my advantage. So when she wanted her mommy, Xiao eagerly complied. Still, he kept using her whenever I misbehaved. A constant dark storm cloud of threats hanging over my head, always forcing me to seek shelter.

Rose bounces Liam on her knee while she talks with Evie.

He sees me and gurgles some baby nonsense, waving his chubby arms around in the air. If I didn't know any better, his cuteness makes my ovaries flip with need.

"Mommy, when can I have a little brother?" Mei asks.

All conversation ceases, and we're suddenly in the spotlight.

I reach for Mei and cup her arms, bringing her close enough to look up at me. "We've talked about this, honey. Not now."

Mei pouts and stomps her foot. She always does the same thing whenever we have this conversation. "But I want one now!"

"Mei, that is enough," I say sternly. "We are guests here, and you will behave. Do you understand me?"

Mei drops her face and mumbles, "Yes, Mommy."

I sigh and lean forward to kiss the crown of her head. "I love you, Mei."

"Love you too."

"Do you want to watch *Beauty and the Beast*, Mei?" Alice asks.

All thoughts of a sibling slip from her mind at the sound of watching what has quickly become her favorite movie as she chirps, "Yes, please!" And then she's gone to the other side of the room, where Alice turns the TV on and starts the movie before sitting on the couch next to her.

"Lily, can I ask you a question?" Rose asks. "It may be sensitive, so if you don't want to answer, that's fine. No offense taken."

"Okay," I answer, wary of her question.

"Why haven't you had more kids with Xiao...or anyone else, for that matter?" She's careful with the words she uses and asks her question slowly and quietly.

"I have an IUD," I explain.

"Xiao allowed that?" Gabriella asks incredulously.

I shake my head. "No. But he doesn't know either. The doctor who helped deliver Mei worked for him but took pity on me. You see, as sick as it is, Xiao takes care of the girls who work for him. He doesn't like to see them pregnant because, at a certain point, they can't work, and if they can't work, they're not making him money. So he has them all on birth control. So the doctor inserted an IUD and told Xiao that I suffered a rare complication that could make conceiving more difficult in the future. It's how I've been able to avoid getting pregnant again despite Xiao's efforts."

"Wow," Rose breathes out.

Evie leans back in her chair. "Bloody hell, that's intense."

"Did you ever see the doctor again?" Gabriella asks.

"No. And I wish I could thank her, but I didn't. I wish I could tell her how she saved my life and the lives of any further children born."

"I lied earlier," Gabriella confesses. "You're not just strong. You're incredible."

My eyes land on the ribbon resting on the table. I reach out for it and a pair of scissors. With one quick and decisive snip, I cut off the damaged end and watch it fall to the floor in small frayed pieces.

I may be frayed around the edges like this ribbon, but you know what? I too will cut my broken ends off to reveal the person left whole and new behind.

21

RAPHAEL

"Any news from Dominic?" Michael asks as we jog along the trail that weaves around the island.

I match his pace, my rapid breaths creating tiny white puffs in the morning air. "He checked in last night that his search was a dead end."

Michael curses under his breath. "That was the last lead we had on Xiao."

"I know."

"Raphael, I hate to ask, but..." He trails off, and from the corner of my eye, I catch his hesitant glance my way.

I sigh, knowing exactly what he wants to say. "I'll ask Lily if she knows anything more."

"Maybe we should consider Dad's suggestion?"

I come to an abrupt halt.

When Michael notices, he too stops and turns around to face me. He holds his hands up and pants out an apology when he sees my expression. "Sorry."

"I am not using Lily and Mei as bait," I tell him. My tone is hard, and my words are final. It was an option at first, but not anymore.

Michael wipes sweat from his brow and frowns. "I figured you would say that."

"Then why even ask?" I demand, pushing past him to continue down the trail.

Michael catches up and puts his hand on my shoulder, forcing me to stop and face him. "I didn't mean it like that, brother."

I wait him out, and eventually, he sighs. "I'm only asking you to think about the idea."

"No. Their presence here is more than enough. He thinks I kidnapped them, but when he sees that wasn't the case, he'll fuck up when he comes for them." I know I'm being unreasonable, but he has to understand where I'm coming from. If I was asking him to do the same with Rose and Liam, he'd be saying no, too.

"How will he see that if you keep them hidden?" Michael argues, earning a glare from me. "We can brainstorm a way to ensure their safety but still draw the bastard out."

I cross my arms over my chest and take a deep breath through my nostrils, then exhale hard.

"Raphael, please."

My eyes shift to my brother, and the misery there on his identical face makes my heart sink and my resolve falter.

"I need him gone, and I know you need the same even more."

"Rose is still having nightmares?" I assume.

Michael drops his eyes and kicks at a pebble. "Yeah."

"Fine." I cave.

My brother looks up with expectant hope. "Fine?"

"I'll talk to Lily." Michael's mouth drops open, but I continue before he can say a single word. "But I'm not guaranteeing anything."

"I'll take it." Michael smiles and reaches out to clap my shoulder before he turns away to continue back down the trail.

I catch up to him, and as we round the last corner, the main house comes into full view. I wonder if Lily's awake yet.

She spent all damn day yesterday with the other women in the house, and when dinner came around, Dad pulled Michael and me away for a meeting downtown. By the time I got back, she was fast asleep, curled up with Mei. I desperately wanted to wake her up, but I couldn't imagine disturbing her sleep when she looked so peaceful. I hate the idea of bringing Xiao up even more when she's working so hard to move on, but Michael's right. This is bigger than her tortured past and my anger.

Speaking of. "Have you confirmed if Lily came from the same auction as Rose?"

"Nothing yet," Michael answers with a hard sigh.

"What about Connor?"

Michael shakes his head. "He's exhausted all of his contacts related to the auction Patrick sold Rose to. They're dead, or they've disappeared, or they know nothing of worth."

"I'll ask Lily if she remembers anything else about the auction too."

Michael clasps my shoulder as he passes by me into the house foyer. "Thank you, Raphael."

I watch him jog up the stairs before heading toward the kitchen at the back of the house. This early in the morning, I expect to find the room empty, but it's not. Instead, a pretty little flower sits on a barstool, reading the newspaper while sipping on a cup of tea from the smell of it.

Leaning against the doorframe, I cross my arms over my chest. "Good morning, Lily."

As I expect, she jumps in her seat and nearly spills her tea with a startled gasp. Spinning around, Lily levels me with a glare I suppose is meant to be intimidating.

"You scared me, Raphael," she snaps with little heat behind it.

My eyes drink the sight of her in the morning light. Pleasure skirts down my spine to gather in my groin when she does the same, her brilliant blue eyes snagging on every swell and dip of my muscles on display.

I run my tongue over my bottom lip when she meets my eyes. When her lips fall open and her tongue flicks out to lick them, I have to fight back the immediate urge to storm over and devour her mouth for breakfast.

Lily clears her throat and stammers, "Wha-what are you doing up...so early?"

"I was out for a run with Michael," I answer. "What are you doing up so early?"

"I couldn't sleep."

"You couldn't sleep? So your first thought is to come downstairs, make yourself a cup of tea, and read the newspaper?"

"No. My first thought was to come find you, but you weren't in your room."

"You went to my room?"

"Yes. I thought you could—" She stops midsentence, her cheeks exploding red before she jumps off the stool and hurries toward the first open door she sees, which leads to the pantry.

I follow her before she can turn back around.

When she realizes her mistake, Lily spins around and runs straight into me. She bounces off my chest and bumps into a shelf. Almost as if in slow motion, I watch the sack of flour teeter and then tip over, covering Lily from head to toe in white powder.

With a tiny little shriek, she freezes as the cloud settles over her. She's a mess, but the most adorable one at that, and the sight makes me snort in humor.

"It's not funny," Lily snaps, her attempt to sound angry just as cute as her appearance right now.

"It's a little funny." I disagree, enjoying how she scowls up at me. "Now tell me, what did you think I could do for you?"

"Nothing," she mumbles, averting her eyes as she tries to wipe flour from her shirt. "It's not important now."

"Try again," I advise her. "Whatever it is made you run from me."

My accusation makes her eyes snap up to me and narrow. "I didn't run from you."

"No?" I raise my brow while I bring my hand up to brush some flour from her hair.

"No." She doesn't pull away from my touch but seems to subconsciously lean into it.

"Funny, because it feels like you've been running from me ever since we kissed the other night."

Lily pulls back and frowns up at me. "I haven't. We've both just been so busy."

It's cute how flustered she's growing over an assumption I don't mean. But I care about how I'm no longer touching her. I can't explain it, let alone define it, but I want...no, I need to touch her. Constantly. It's like an addiction I have no desire to fight.

I just need to remain patient, which is a virtue I struggle with, to be honest, but I will do it for her. Because I think it's safe to assume Lily feels the same for me. Only she's struggling to bury years of abuse and pain before she can finally accept what's here between us is real and worth fighting for.

"I know."

Lily's frown deepens before it dawns on her that I'm joking. "Then why would you say that?"

"Because you're cute when you're angry."

The woman enjoys keeping me on my toes. I never know what she's going to do next, so when she grabs some flour collected in a pile on the shelf and throws it at me, my mouth drops open in shock as the white powder cascades down my front.

"How's that for cute?"

A light, teasing note in her voice calls to the dark in me, and I step closer.

Lily shivers from lust and not from fear by the way her blue eyes glaze over as she meets my gaze.

Raising my hand, I trace down her face before cupping her chin. She gasps and then sighs from the pleasure my touch brings her.

"How's this?"

She knows what's coming and doesn't fight me when I descend and cover her lips with my own. She moans into my mouth as my tongue dives in to explore every inch of her mouth, claiming every torture space for my own.

Lily places her hands on my chest and slowly explores her way up to tangle in my hair, spreading flour among the dark strands. She giggles against my lips, telling me the devious vixen knows exactly what she's doing. So I reach back and grab her tiny wrists with one hand and shove them above her head, all the while pushing more into her until she's trapped between the shelves and me.

Her giggle dissolves into another moan when she feels how hard I am for her. She rolls her hips, pushing against my cock, and I growl into her mouth at the sensation gathering at the base of my spine.

"Tell me you want me," I whisper.

Lily pulls to free her hands half-heartedly, but I refuse to let go. Not until I hear her say those magic little words.

"Tell me you want me to make you feel good."

She bucks against me, practically dry humping my lap to seek relief from the ache between her legs.

"Please, Raphael," she begs. "Erase their touch. Erase every memory of pain. Make me feel good again. Please."

Like a key, her consent unlocks my hesitation and frees the beast in me.

Dropping her hands, I lower mine to skim over her thin shirt. Her taunt nipples strain against the fabric, and I purposely flick one as my hand moves farther down. She hisses from the shock of pleasure and buries her hands in my hair, pulling my face to hers. She nips at my bottom lip as if she means to pay me back for my behavior before crushing her lips to mine, her tongue diving in to trace every inch of my mouth.

The devil on my shoulder purrs in approval at the domineering move because it means she's letting go of her darkness to play in mine, and I'm more than eager to show her exactly how well I play.

I wrap one hand around her back, securing it between her shoulder blades to hold her in place while my other dances along the hem of her loose pajama pants. Lily rolls against me again when my hand slips beneath the waistband and brushes against her center. My fingers explore, sliding between her slit, pleased when she instinctively opens more for me. She's so wet and ready for me, I practically come in my pants from the mere thought of how she'll feel wrapped around my cock. Her tight, slick heat envelops my finger as I sink one into her while I swipe my thumb over her pulsing and swollen clit.

"Holy fu—" she moans, unable to finish her sentence before I cover her mouth. The pantry door may be closed, but that doesn't mean the house lacks listening ears.

"You need to be quiet, Lily pad," I whisper when I finally let her up for air. "No one else will hear your pleasure but me."

Her response is to grab my face and capture my lip between her teeth, nibbling and sucking on the flesh. I add another finger and increase the pressure on her clit. When she bites down harder, the taste of copper explodes in my mouth, and I know she has broken my skin. But before she can try to pull away, I push forward so she tastes my blood. I'll happily bleed for her if it means she never has to.

I feel her tighten, her walls enveloping my fingers in a vise-like grip I know is going to feel like heaven around my cock. She shudders, and I know she's close. I move from her lips to spread open-mouthed, teeth-nibbling kisses down her jaw when the door suddenly opens, and a voice I forgot existed snaps out.

"What the hell is going on here?"

22

LILY

"It's a good thing you're getting these behaviors out of your system now, Raphael," Emilia remarks in a snarky tone.

I hastily try to pull away from Raphael, winning against him when he fights to hold on. Hiding behind him, I straighten my clothes in an attempt to compose myself. Silly to do when we were caught with our hands in the cookie jar... literally.

"And what exactly do you mean by that?" Raphael demands.

"Well, I expect our marriage not to just be on paper. I won't tolerate you straying. Even to one as...old as she is."

I freeze. Raphael assured me they were not engaged. That it was a marriage arranged when Michael was believed sterile. He's never even seen or met Emilia. When the truth about Michael and Rose was revealed, Raphael's father did the right thing and dissolved the engagement. Only Emilia doesn't seem to understand or accept that. For whatever reason, she believes that this little trip of hers will ignite some feelings between them. But calling me old? That's not only rude, it's also unacceptable.

Raphael must feel the same because he doesn't hide his disdain when he says, "Old? I'd rather be with her than tied down to a child like you."

I don't need to see Emilia to know she's mad, but a loud alarm rings through the house before she can say anything back.

"What is that?" I have to shout for Raphael to hear me.

Raphael turns around and bends close to my ear. "I need you to go get Mei, then find Rose or my sister and stay with them."

"Why? What's going on?"

"That alarm means someone has breached the island security. Come on, I'll take you to the stairs."

Raphael grabs my hand and pulls me after him, brushing past Emilia, who's standing there with her mouth opening and closing like a fish out of water. We hurry through the house to the foyer. Michael and Enzo are already there at the base of the stairs. Enzo is talking to someone on the phone but acknowledges us with a nod in our direction.

"What happened?" Raphael demands.

"All I know is a body has been dropped off at the gate," Michael replies before his eyes fall on me behind Raphael.

Raphael turns to me. "Hurry upstairs and find Mei and the others."

"I will, but—"

"No buts, Lily. This is dangerous. Go now."

"I know, but—"

"Lily," he warns in a gravelly tone. "Do not make me throw you over my shoulder, and—"

"Stop," Enzo snaps, his deep voice echoing in the house foyer. "We need her."

Raphael and I turn our attention to the modern Viking. He holds his phone away from his ear, but his face is pale, his eyes wide and terrified.

"It's Dominic."

I'LL NEVER FORGET the day I lost my first patient.

It was a Tuesday afternoon. Nothing special about it. I had already treated a few broken bones, several colds, and was wrapping up my last case of a particularly nasty rash when the ambulance arrived with a car accident survivor.

Mr. John Ruthledge. I'll never forget his name.

Upon first assessment, he appeared in good spirits and even made a few dad jokes. His labs looked good, and his x-rays were normal. His only complaint was lower stomach pain. My head resident and I both agreed to treat his symptoms and kept him under observation. The last time I checked on him, he was sleeping, a side effect of the pain meds, and assumed nothing worse.

We soon grew busy with a rush of patients, and before I knew it, a couple of hours passed. I expected Mr. Ruthledge to be awake, maybe even slightly angry with my long absence. But I never predicted I'd find him writhing in pain.

His pain was actually from a liver laceration that went undetected in his tests. Though it was small at first, it only grew larger until he was bleeding out inside of his abdomen.

We tried to save him. We rushed him into surgery, but it was too late. He was too far gone. The damage was already done.

The moment he went started bleeding out on the operating table, I knew the fight was over. There's no coming back from multiple organ failure when blood pours from every hole in your body. In the end, his death was no one's fault. A freak accident, as they say, but it didn't make the reality of his death any easier to accept.

The guards bring Dominic inside the house and lay him on the dining room table. He's been beaten to the point where he's nearly unrecognizable. There's so much blood that I can't even tell where it's coming from.

"Is he breathing?" Enzo asks from behind me.

Without a second thought, I press two fingers to his neck, searching for the precious beats of life. I close my eyes and concentrate, trying hard to ignore the chaos around me.

"What the fuck happened?" Michael demands.

"The guards said a car barreled through the gates and threw his body out. They fired on the car, but whoever it was, they got away," Enzo answers.

"It was Xiao," Raphael says. "Had to be."

Thump...thump.

There it is. Barely, but there.

"He's alive," I announce to the room, all talk ceasing at my words.

Raphael rushes to my side. "What do you need?"

"Anything and everything you have."

While he leaves to gather supplies with Michael, Enzo helps me peel away Dominic's bloodied and soiled clothes, revealing several wounds in various states. I'm familiar with the sight, having seen countless wounds like these on Xiao's men.

"He was tortured," I say.

Enzo freezes and meets my eyes. "You're certain?"

I nod grimly.

"What happened?" a new voice bellows, and Enzo wraps his hand around my arm and quickly pulls me away from Dominic's body before the newcomer pushes me away.

"We're still trying to figure that out," Dante assures the stranger, having followed him in. He walks over to place his hand on the man's shoulder and squeezes. "Let Lily work on him, brother. She's a doctor and can help."

The stranger I now know is Dante's brother, swings toward me. Enzo still has a solid hold on my arm, his touch tense, like he's ready to move me again if needed.

"You're Lily?"

"I am." I don't know why, but something about him rubs me the wrong way. Call it intuition or a gut feeling or whatever, but he doesn't share the same kindness in his eyes as his brother. Don't get me wrong, Dante is a scary man, but in the brief time I've gotten to know him, I've seen how much family means to him and how it drives him.

But this man? There's something hard in his expression. Something I can't quite define but see.

"Save my son. Now," he orders in a firm tone, stepping closer.

Enzo's hand tightens on my arm, and I back up toward him, as if seeking the safety his large presence provides.

"Leo," Dante warns. "Back off. Let Lily work."

Leo sneers at his brother before glaring at me one last time and turning away. Enzo releases me a moment before Raphael and Michael return, their arms heavy with supplies.

"What can I do?" Raphael asks when I step over to grab what I need.

"Just be ready to hand me things when I ask for them."

The way Dominic's body has been stabbed, beaten, and broken is terrible and cruel. I can only imagine the pain he went through. He's missing a finger on both hands, and one ear is so badly burned, it may need to be amputated altogether. He's missing teeth while others are broken. The bottoms of his feet have been shredded like they took a cheese grater to the skin. His knees don't look right, and if I had to guess, I'd say his kneecaps are shattered. The number of stab wounds decorating his body is too many to count. Some are scabbed over, and some are still fresh enough to be bleeding.

If he survives this, his recovery will be long and painful. And that's a big if.

I glance at Raphael and see the question in his eyes. He's wondering the very same thing. I could lie to him. I probably should. But he deserves to know the odds. And they're not good.

I shake my head slowly, and my heart sinks when I watch his face fall at the news.

"We need to take him to the hospital," Leo says to his brother.

"You know he won't survive the trip, Leo," Dante replies.

Leo whirls around and swipes his arm over a side table, sending a vase of flowers to scatter all over the floor. I jump back to avoid the mess and bump into Raphael.

"Knock it off, Uncle!" Raphael shouts over me. "Your anger is not helping."

"My son, your cousin, is dying. He should be at the hospital receiving the proper medical care, not second-rate care from the doctor of the man surely responsible for this," Leo snaps back. "For all we know, she's killing him right now."

Raphael moves toward his uncle, but before he can get to him, Dante steps in front of him, places his hand on his chest, and yells, "That's enough! Both of you."

"Once he's stabilized, we can move him to the hospital," I say, hoping to ease the tension in the room. It's nothing I'm not used to. In times of crisis, family members often react strongly, especially when they feel powerless.

The room falls silent enough for me to refocus on

Dominic. For a minute, I have hope. Hope that there's really a chance. And then his blood pressure tanks.

"What's happening?" Raphael asks.

"He's crashing," I reply. "Start CPR, and I need a syringe and the bottle of epinephrine."

Raphael starts compressions while Michael hands me a syringe and a glass bottle. I draw up the amount I need, and once administered, I check his pulse and curse when I feel an erratic rhythm.

"Keep going," I tell Raphael as I prepare another syringe. "Do you have a defibrillator?"

Dante nods and disappears down a hall, returning less than ten seconds later with a bright red and clear box. I need to shock his heart now before I lose his pulse.

Once hooked up, I shout out, "Clear!" and press the paddles down on Dominic's bare chest, sending a strong current of electricity directly to his heart.

Dominic's body lurches upward, and I drop one paddle to press my fingers to his neck. Still not regular.

Increasing the level of electricity, I shock Dominic again. Only after the third round does his heart finally restart into a normal rhythm.

Setting the paddles down, I breathe a deep sigh of relief. Raphael places a comforting hand on my damp back, and I practically melt at his touch.

"We should get him to the hospital now," I advise them.

"I'll get the car," Enzo says before he leaves out the front door.

Raphael kisses the side of my head and whispers, "You did amazing."

"Thanks." I'm exhausted, the rush of adrenaline fading quickly from my body.

Opening my eyes, I focus on Dominic's broken body. It felt strangely therapeutic to care for someone innocent. Well, maybe not *that* innocent, considering what he does for a living, but Dominic's only been kind to me during the few times we've exchanged words. Compared to Xiao and his men, Dominic and the others are saints.

"How could you let this happen to my son?" Leo accuses, directing his harsh question to his brother.

"I didn't *let* anything happen," Dante snaps.

"You sent him to look into that lead because you didn't want to risk your sons. But you will happily risk mine."

"That's not true, Leo," Dante urges. "You know that. Dominic is my nephew, and I love him like a son."

"But he's not your son. Is he?" Leo hisses, pushing away from his brother to pace along the wall.

Dante exhales hard and looks at Raphael. "When did you hear from Dominic last?"

"Early this morning. He sent a text that the lead was a dead end," Raphael answers.

One glance at Dominic and anyone can tell the torture he received didn't happen in a few short hours.

"It wasn't Dominic who sent that text," Dante concludes in a grim tone before he turns to Michael. "Can you trace where his phone has been?"

The eldest DiAngelo nods. "Yes."

"When was the last time anyone spoke to Dominic or saw him in person?" Dante asks before looking at his brother. "Leo?"

The angry man pauses long enough to answer. "It's been a few days."

Michael and Raphael confirm the same, and that timeline aligns more with Dominic's wounds.

I narrow my eyes when a thin trickle of blood leaks from Dominic's nose and falls down his face. Maybe it's a trick of the light causing me to see things, but either way, I step out of Raphael's hold and approach the table.

And that's when I watch it happen. Blood begins to pour heavier from his nose, his eyes, and his mouth. And then his entire body shakes and thrashes from the seizure his brain is suffering from due to the lack of blood.

Chaos falls over the room, but I know it's too late. It's like I'm back in that emergency room all those years ago, and all I see is Mr. Ruthledge.

"Help him!" Leo hollers, and I jump at the fury in his voice.

Raphael looks at me, and I meet his eyes with defeat and sorrow. He sees my answer and drops his head, reaching for Dominic's hand to hold so he's not alone.

Michael watches the exchange and, like his twin, grabs Dominic's other hand.

"What are you doing? Why aren't you helping him?" Leo demands.

He pushes his nephews aside and gathers his son's body to his chest. Dominic's head flops, and his face grows paler by the second.

Bleeding out is a gruesome sight, but it's actually quite peaceful. As the blood leaves the body, your mind shuts down as each of your organs fail, until finally, your heart slows to a final stop. I've heard it be compared to falling asleep after spending all day in the sun.

The blood slows, and I don't need a heart monitor to know Dominic's dead. A second later, when his father goes still and silent, I'm sure of it.

"I'm so sorry," I say mournfully. "There was nothing more I could do."

Leo slowly lowers his son's body to the table and touches his face lovingly. His eyes meet mine, and the only thing I see is a fiery, intense hatred.

Before I even see it, before any of us sees it, he raises his hand and slaps me hard. Pain explodes across my face, and the taste of copper is instant on my tongue. I raise a hand to my lips and draw back to see bright red blood on my fingers.

Raphael steps around me and immediately goes for his uncle, landing a punch to the jaw before the heartbroken man can stop it. He lands another two before Michael is there, pulling him back to my side.

Dante reaches for his brother and stops him from retaliating, shoving him away like he weighs nothing. "That's enough, Leo. We do not strike women."

Pointing a finger at me, he growls, "This is your fault. If you weren't here, Xiao wouldn't have gone after my son. Because of you, my son is dead! You killed him!"

"Uncle Leo—"

"No!" He interrupts Raphael with a shout. "Dominic's death is on you as well. You should have killed her and that wretched child the night you found them. Instead of thinking with your cock and taking her like some grand prize to be won."

"Leo, that's uncalled for. The only one to blame here is Xiao. Focus on that, brother," Dante urges. "We will make the bastard pay for what he has done."

Leo shoves his brother off him, and with one last angry look at us and then his son, he storms out of the room, shoving past Enzo who stands like a statue in the doorway. The front door slams open and closed a second later as he leaves the house.

Since Mr. Ruthledge, I've lost my fair share of patients. And maybe it's horrible to say, but death became a regular occurrence afterward until, eventually, I grew numb to it. Some were harder than others, but few stuck around as much as the first.

And something tells me that this moment will stay with me forever.

23

RAPHAEL

The scalding water pounds down on my skin as if the flames of hell are trying to take my soul. And I'm tempted to let the devil have it.

My cousin didn't deserve to die. And when I get my hands on those responsible, I'll make sure they feel the same pain ten times over.

In our line of business, we play with death every day. We never know when our last day could be. It's why we do everything to the extreme—why we hate so hard and love even harder. It's the reason we don't let go when we find that special one.

I bow my head and watch my cousin's blood flow down the drain until the water runs clear. The rhythmic patter of the water against the tile is interrupted by the opening of the shower stall door.

I already know who it is without turning around. We're connected in a way that I would recognize her presence instantly.

"You shouldn't be here," I warn her, my voice devoid of emotion, though my heart and body scream the opposite. I crave her touch. I need it to remind me that I'm alive.

She's quiet for a long moment, and it's only because of our connection that I know she waits behind me.

"Do you hate me?"

Her question is so soft, I nearly miss it over the rushing water.

I turn immediately, then slam to a halt at the sight before me.

Lily stands naked as the day she was born in front of me. She's shivering, but I know she's not cold because the space is near boiling hot. She shakes because of how vulnerable she is at this very moment. Standing there, completely exposed, with every physical scar and mark on display for judgment.

And what a fucking sight she is.

My eyes trace over every inch of her bare skin, lingering on the subtle silver stretch marks left by pregnancy and the faint pink scars that tell the story of the past six years of torment and pain she's endured. Breasts just the right size to suffocate in with perky pink nipples. Nipples I remember feeling against my chest the night she fell asleep outside.

My eyes drop to her bare pussy, and I about fall to my knees. Because I'm ready to worship at this woman's feet. She's it for me. She has been since the second she opened her eyes that night with my gun pointed at her. The moment her blue and my gold clashed and mixed into something beautiful, I was hers.

Lily drops her head, mistaking my silence as an answer. "I tried to save him, but there must have been something else I couldn't see. I'm so sorry. Please don't hate me."

I reach out to lift her chin, witnessing the pain and sorrow storming in her brilliant blue eyes. "I could never hate you. My uncle was wrong. None of this is your fault—" She opens her mouth to argue, but my fingers holding her chin move to her lips, silencing her. "And I know you may think it is because of Xiao, but like I've said before. He is a grown man capable of making his own decisions. And his decision today has guaranteed his death."

Lily slowly nods, but I'm no fool. It will take the bastard's head at her feet to prove my words to her. Just like how Dr. Rodriguez's severed cock showed her that he would never hurt anyone ever again.

Actions speak louder than words.

"How's your face?" I ask, tilting her head to the side so I can get a proper look at where my uncle slapped her and the small red cut splitting her bottom lip.

"It's sore, but nothing I can't handle," she answers solemnly, reminding me she has, in fact, suffered worse.

I drop my hand to my side. "I told you I'd keep you safe and—"

Lily reaches out and grasps my face between her hands, forcing me to look directly at her. "You are keeping me safe. I am safe. Right here. With you."

I rest my forehead on hers and close my eyes. "Tell me what you want, Lily," I practically beg her because I need to hear her say the words out loud. "Tell me what you need."

Lily hesitantly reaches out to place her hands on my pecs. The cool of her touch against my heated skin makes me hiss, and the pleasure causes my cock to twitch. She looks at me with pleading eyes, desperation shining in her endless blue depths. "I need to feel something. Something real. I want to forget all the bad and replace it with something good." A sinful smile graces her lips. "I need you to finish what you started in that pantry."

Stepping back, I enjoy how her eyes lower to my partially erect cock, widening slightly at its size and thickness. Her eyes follow every hard ridge of muscle up, tracing the curves and lines of the tattoos decorating my skin. From the way her chest blushes as red as her cheeks, I know she likes what she sees.

"I need that too...but are you sure?" She nods, so I continue. "You control every second of this, Lily. You control me. Understand?"

Skating my fingers up the sides of her smooth, flawless skin, I graze over her breasts and circle her nipples, enjoying the deep moan it draws from her throat before moving down to cup her sex. Only an hour ago, my hand was buried between her folds, driving an orgasm from her before we were so rudely interrupted.

Leaning forward, I nuzzle her neck and whisper, "You're gorgeous. Every inch of you is perfect."

Lily pushes back, grabs my face, and captures my mouth in a languid kiss that causes goose bumps to explode along my arms before shooting down to make my cock twitch. When she feels it, Lily hums into my mouth and sashays against me like a naughty little minx.

Nipping at her bottom lip, I pull her flush against me before releasing her mouth.

"If we do this, that's it, Lily," I tell her, hoping she can hear the certainty in my voice. "You're it for me. Do you understand me?"

Lily shudders in my arms before she places a chaste kiss over my heart. "Yes."

24

LILY

Raphael cups my face between his two large hands and kisses me, the taste of water mingling with the gentleness of his kiss. Such tenderness coming from a hard man sends my heart racing and turns my breath ragged.

For so long, pleasure has escaped me, as men used me for only their satisfaction.

But Raphael isn't like that. He wants to make me feel good. It's almost like my pleasure is his greatest desire. And I want the same for him. Something I haven't felt in quite some time. I want to feel the touch of someone I *want*. Not someone I'm forced to be with.

In the steamy warmth of the shower, my hands roam freely over his chest, tracing each tattoo and feeling his muscles jump beneath my touch.

"What does this one mean?" I ask him, transfixed by the image of an angel bursting free from flames branding a sword.

"My surname means from the angels. So it's a tradition in our family that we're named after angels. When Michael and I were born, our father gave us the names of God's strongest archangels and soldiers," Raphael explains. He brings his hand up to mine and follows the path I trace. His eyes glance down at the tattoo. "There are many interpretations of what the archangel looks like, but this is my favorite one."

"I like it," I reveal honestly. "And I like the tradition. The name Raphael suits you."

"How so?"

"In Bible class, we learned Raphael was the archangel responsible for healing Earth after the fallen angels destroyed it," I recite what I remember from those Sunday Bible classes my parents signed me up for during the summers of my youth.

Raphael's chest shakes with laughter beneath my touch. I raise my eyes to see a small smile on his lips. "You see me as a healer?"

I shrug, suddenly feeling very self-conscious standing here naked in front of him reciting silly facts. Dropping my eyes, I mumble, "It's just something I remember. It's nothing really. Forget I said anything."

Raphael reaches for my chin and guides my face to peer up at him. "It's not nothing to me, Lily. I'm just surprised because I am the last thing from a healer."

"But to me, you are," I confess, the truth escaping me easily. "In your own unique way, you've healed me and continue to do so."

Raphael's eyes widen and his nostrils flare, as if my admission surprises him. I have little warning before his mouth descends on mine. The momentum pushes me backward against the tile wall, water cascading over us like a waterfall.

"You are too good for me," he growls against my mouth between kisses.

"Then show me how to be bad," I beg.

With a guttural groan, he bends slightly enough to grip under my thighs and pull me up. Instinctively, I wrap my legs around his waist. His cock presses against my aching core. No barriers between us.

I lock my wrists behind his neck and tug him closer,

rocking against him, needing, seeking the relief I crave. He groans deep when I rub against him.

"Lily, if you don't stop, I will end up in you bare," he rasps against my lips, giving me a quick but brutal kiss that leaves me tingling. "I should get a condom from the bedroom."

"I have an IUD," I blurt out. "And Gabriella said my tests were clean." A request I made to her the day we met because I had to be sure everything was okay before I went too far down the rabbit hole with Raphael. "I mean, if you don't want to, I understand. I don't want you to feel pressured." I'm babbling, but I'm also on the verge of tears from the primal desperation to feel him inside me.

"I'm good there too," he says in a restrained voice as he presses his forehead against mine. "But are you sure? Because once I take you bare, that's the only option going forward."

Hearing his intention that this is not a one-time thing makes my heart do a little flip, filling me with excitement. "Yes."

To prove my point, I work a hand between our slick bodies and grasp his impressive cock, directing the crown to my center and nudging forward. All he has to do is take a step forward. "No foreplay. Fuck the bad away and then love me with the good."

"God, you're fucking perfect," Raphael hisses against my mouth. "If you need me to stop, I will stop. Tell me. Hit me, slap me, push me, I don't care. Do something, anything, and I'll stop. Okay?"

I won't, but I nod all the same and then press forward to kiss him hard, our tongues dueling before I relinquish the fight.

"This is going to hurt," he warns me as he pushes forward an inch. I can feel the stretch already and the burn that comes with it. It's fair to say that Raphael is packing a weapon much larger than Xiao or any of the men he allowed to force themselves on me. And if any man is going to claim me after years of abuse, I'm happy it's Raphael because only a real man can erase every tainted inch left behind.

"Do it. All at once. Please."

Raphael's mouth covers mine just as he thrusts inside me. A borderline scream tears free from my throat, but he swallows the sound.

He waits, his mouth wandering from my mouth to my jaw, nosing my face up so he can have easier access to the space behind my ear. He kisses the erotic spot before nipping at my earlobe. The sharp pain there pulls my attention away from the stinging stretch between my legs. I adjust my hips, gaining a new angle, appreciating that he's giving me time to adjust with a distraction.

"Are you okay?" He breathes into my ear.

"I'm perfect."

Raphael moves, slow and steady. I can feel him everywhere. Like a missing puzzle piece, he fills me completely in a way I never imagined possible but always wished for. And just as I asked, Raphael heals another wound with every thrust until nothing but the feeling of him is left.

Raphael buries one hand in the nape of my neck to prevent me from banging into the wall as he thrusts harder. With his other hand, he brings his thumb to my clit, rubbing in time with his thrusts.

"You're so fucking tight," he bites out in a strained voice. Like he's actually struggling. "So fucking perfect. My perfect Lily pad."

My orgasm builds at the base of my spine. A sensation I've long since forgotten and missed dearly.

"I can feel you tightening. Your pussy is squeezing my

cock," Raphael groans, his words guttural and harsh, like a growl. "You're close."

I bite down on the inside of my cheek to prevent it. I'm not ready. Not yet. I want more of this. More of him.

"Come for me, Lily. Be my good girl, and come now."

His order is all it takes to send me over the edge. An orgasm so strong, my toes curl and my spine arches as it violently consumes me. Like a tidal wave, it crashes over me, washing away the pain of yesterday and leaving me ready for a better tomorrow.

Raphael presses into me, his mouth claiming mine as he swallows every one of my moans. His entire body shudders a second later, and with a deep groan, he comes inside me, and the feeling of warm liquid fills me.

His face falls to my neck, and I bring my hands up to cradle his head there, running one hand over his wet locks. We're panting hard, but neither of us is ready to let the other go yet.

Raphael kisses a trail of wet, open-mouthed kisses up my neck and along my jaw before placing a chaste kiss on my lips. His light hazel eyes have transformed into a darker hue of amber, and I bring one hand forward to trace his brow, entranced by the color.

"We should finish cleaning up so I can make love to you." He smiles devilishly at me. "I have a name to live up to after all."

25

RAPHAEL

It's strange how peaceful I feel right now, even with all the grief and misery that waits outside my bedroom door. Eventually, I will need to leave this bubble of sereneness and return to the world outside, but I have no desire to move from this bed.

Lily rests with her head on my chest, giving me the perfect angle to run my fingers through her damp blond hair. The way she nuzzles into me, practically purring like a kitten, makes me wonder when she last experienced such intimate affection. To be touched for no other reason than the need to touch her.

"How are you feeling?" I ask.

Lily shifts her head to look up at me. A shadow in her eyes makes her blues darker, like the ocean's depths. She furrows her brow. "I honestly don't know."

My heart picks up in growing concern. Is she second-guessing this connection between us? Worrying she may have made a mistake?

"Is it wrong to feel happy?" she asks. "After...what happened to Dominic?"

She's seeking affirmation of her feelings, and I cannot disagree with her. Maybe that makes me a terrible cousin for agreeing when a man I've known all my life was brutally tortured and killed a mere few hours ago. But being here together will not change the past, so why not enjoy this moment?

"It's okay to be happy, Lily," I tell her, my fingers tracing her face. "This life is dangerous and deadly. We never know when our last day could be. So I try to focus on the things that remind me I'm alive and make me feel happy. They give me something to fight for."

"Mei has been my happiness. The thing I fight for," she admits with a small smile. "I think if she hadn't been born, I would have died long ago. I'm certain of it, actually."

I shift in bed, needing to face her better. She slips off my chest and gathers the sheet to her naked chest when she turns to face me. I'm tempted to pull the sheet away and burn the damn thing, but then her gorgeous breasts will be on display, there to distract me.

"Don't say such things."

Lily drops her eyes. "It's the truth, though, Raphael. I considered ending it all dozens of times, but when Mei came along, I couldn't stand the idea of leaving her alone with that man, her father, and in that dark world. A world he could sell her into if he really wanted to in a heartbeat."

"My world is just as dark," I remind her.

She shakes her head. "I thought so too, but it's not. There are several shades of gray after all."

I lean forward and kiss her. When I cup her face, she winces and hisses against my lips. I pull away and study the slight discoloration forming on her cheek and her swollen lip, only aggravated more by our activities. "I'm sorry again for my uncle."

"He had just lost his son, Raphael. I'm not justifying what he did, but as a parent, I can understand the pain he's feeling."

"Still, I'll make sure he apologizes when he returns."

"It's unnecessary, but I appreciate the offer."

I reach out and slide a hand along her side toward her back, gathering her to my chest. She squeals in the most adorable way, gifting me with a brilliant smile that I will never grow tired of seeing. Her core brushes against my cock, and I push back, earning a deep moan from Lily. One thrust and I'd slip inside.

"When did you get an IUD?" I ask.

"The doctor who delivered Mei. I begged her to put one in. They're good for about five years."

I hate to imagine what she would have done after those five years. I don't want to consider it or even ask her. Because the what-ifs mean nothing now. She will never be in a position to need them.

"Would you ever want more children?"

Lily studies my face quizzically. "I never considered it because of Xiao."

"And now?"

She blushes, seeming to have caught on to my true intention. "I could be persuaded."

With a smile, I cup the back of her head and kiss her deeply until I leave her breathless. Now's not the time with Xiao still out there, a threat to us both, but afterward? I intend to be very persuasive.

Lily rocks against my cock and looks at me with fuck-me eyes, shrouded in lust.

"Ride me, Lily," I encourage her, thrusting my hips up, desperate to feel her slick heat surround my cock. "Do it. Take your pleasure."

Balancing one hand on my chest, she slides the other between our bodies, grips my cock, and lines it up to her entrance. Her beautiful eyes never leave mine as she sinks down slowly, only closing them when I'm fully seated inside her.

"You feel incredible." I groan, my hands moving to rest on her hips. "So perfect. So fucking good."

My words seem to spur her on. Leaning forward, she kisses me, her tongue diving in to battle with mine. It's a fight I surrender to quickly, my mind too blown by the gorgeous woman riding my cock like she's at the fucking rodeo on a bucking bronco.

"I've missed this," Lily confesses with a quiver. "I forgot how good it can feel."

"Holy *fuck*." I sit up and capture her mouth, keeping my cock buried inside her. She wraps her legs around me and locks her hands behind my neck, kissing me back with just as much passion. Grinding my pelvis to hers, I brush against her swollen and needy clit with every thrust.

"You're already close," I groan against her mouth. "I can feel it. Fuck. Your pussy is squeezing my cock so hard."

Sliding my hand from her hip to between us, I only need to swipe twice over her clit before she shudders in my arms, the breaths jagged. It doesn't take me long to follow. She's barely come down from her orgasm before I explode inside her, filling her with so much cum that if she didn't have the IUD, I'd wager it was enough to get her pregnant. A vision of her heavily pregnant on the beach, holding Mei's hand during sunset, comes to my mind, and it's so realistic. It's almost like I just saw the future.

Lily collapses against my chest, our sweaty bodies fusing as one with me still buried inside of her. Neither of us is willing or eager to move.

"We need to take another shower," Lily observes with a soft laugh.

Chuckling, I wrap my arms around her waist and, in one fluid motion, flip her onto her back, driving my already hardening cock back into her.

"How are you ready to go again?" Lily moans even as she wraps her legs around my back and pulls my face down for a kiss that claims my dark soul.

26

LILY

"**R**aphael is just using you. You know that, right?" a voice asks from behind me. I already know who it is without even turning around, and I'm not in the mood for her. "He's never going to marry you."

I turn around and look directly into Emilia's arrogant face. "That's funny because from what I know, you're the only one not marrying Raphael."

Emilia crosses her arms over her chest, appearing smug. "We'll see."

Either the girl is delusional or desperate, and there's no use arguing with her over a marriage that will only ever occur in her crazy mind.

Raphael explained Emilia to me in more detail after her unexpected arrival the other day. The girl is delusional in thinking she can somehow gain Raphael's affection. He has no desire to marry a girl her age any more than he did when his father initially made the marriage deal months ago. A contract he quickly dissolved with Emilia's father when Michael was declared heir once again.

Emilia looks at her perfectly manicured nails, flicking invisible dirt off them before her eyes rise to meet mine. "Enjoy Raphael while you can. Because when he's done with you, you'll still be nothing but a dirty and washed-up, used slut."

I'm tired of her mean-girl attitude and delusional thoughts.

"Continue to dream all you want, but it was my pants he had his hand down and my pussy his fingers were buried in. Remember that."

The furious expression on Emilia's face as I walk by brings a ray of sunshine to an otherwise gloomy day.

Leaving her behind, I continue down the hall toward the room Mei and I share. She's just starting to stir when I walk in.

"Hi, Mommy," she says with a large yawn.

"Morning, Princess," I greet her before bending down to kiss her forehead. "Are you hungry?"

"Yep!"

We get dressed and head downstairs, or more accurately, Mei bounces down the stairs, and I simply follow.

When we pass the room Dominic died in, I pause in the doorway. The smell of antiseptic and bleach lingers in the air, the table gone along with his body. It's almost like it never happened...but it did. I may not have known Dominic well or very long, but he was Raphael's family, his cousin, and a built-in lifelong friend taken too soon and in the cruelest way.

Voices float through the air, coming from the direction of the kitchen, and we follow the sound. Alice stands at the island, stirring a bowl of some mixture. When she notices us, she looks up with red-rimmed eyes and a sad expression.

"Look who's awake," she says, trying hard to smile.

"Morning, Alice."

Mei stands next to Alice, rising on her tippy-toes to try and peer inside the bowl. "What are you making?"

"French toast, dear. Would you like to help? I warn you, though, it gets messy."

Mei smiles big. "I like messy!"

Alice peers up at me. "Would you be a dear and grab the flour for me? It should be in the pantry."

Oh...shit. My eyes snap to the open door, and before I know it, I'm inside the room, staring at the white powder mess on the shelves and floor. We really did a number in here.

"Did you find it, Lily?" Alice calls.

I zero in on an unopened bag of all-purpose flour and leave the pantry quickly. I'm hoping Alice doesn't know about the mess in the pantry, but when I meet her eyes as I hand over the bag, the spark in her dark eyes answers my question.

"There's a broom in the room over there," she says casually, pointing at a closed door.

"Thanks," I mumble as my face burns hot from embarrassment.

"Don't worry, dear," Alice calls after me once I'm back in the pantry, sweeping up Raphael's and my mess. "The DiAngelo men are very passionate lovers."

Oh my God. Kill me now. Rose walks in with Liam just as I finish cleaning the pantry.

"Morning, Lily," she says as I approach and take a seat beside her. From the shadows darkening her green eyes, it's clear she knows about Dominic. I doubt Michael would have kept something like that from her anyhow. "How are you feeling?"

I sigh, staring down at my hands. If I look hard enough, I can still see his blood on my skin and under my nails. "It's hard anytime I lose someone. Especially when I couldn't do anything to save him. It's even harder knowing that his death was intentional and not an accident. That Xiao planned this in retaliation for Mei and me."

"Which doesn't make any of it your fault, remember?" Rose stresses. "It's terrible what happened, but you didn't drive Xiao to do this. He chose to do it himself."

"So I keep hearing," I mumble. "How are you doing? You had to have known Dominic better than me."

Rose kisses the top of Liam's redhead, tugging him a little closer as if she needs the reassurance that he's really there. "Dominic brought Liam back from Italy after Michael rescued me. I'll always owe him for that, but after that, we only met a handful of times, mostly when he'd come to the penthouse."

"Sounds like he was a good guy."

"The best cousin a girl could ask for." Gabriella's voice interrupts us.

Rose and I turn to see the youngest DiAngelo standing in the open kitchen doorway. Her eyes are red, and her face is splotchy like she's been crying.

Alice turns off the stove's griddle and then helps Mei down from her stool. My daughter runs over to me while Alice goes to hers.

"Hi, sweetheart," Alice says softly into her youngest's hair while she caresses it. "It's not fair, Mom," Gabriella cries, breaking down in her mother's arms.

"I know. But we'll get the one responsible for this. Your father, uncle, and brothers will not let Dominic's death go unanswered."

Gabriella pulls away from her mom with a hard sniff and rubs at her eyes. Alice kisses her daughter's cheek and gives her a sad, comforting smile before turning back to the stove.

The feeling of responsibility and guilt continues to hang heavy on my shoulders. I know it's not my fault, but just because I didn't pull the trigger doesn't mean I didn't hand Xiao the gun when I left.

"Mommy, can I have extra syrup?" Mei asks, completely unaware of the heavy atmosphere in the room.

I squeeze her tiny body closer, needing the reassurance of

her presence, just like Rose did with Liam. "Of course, princess."

Mei jumps off my lap and hurries back to her stool, where Alice meets her.

When Gabriella sits beside me, I drop my eyes, unsure of what to say. She bumps my shoulder. "Hey."

I raise my eyes to meet hers. She doesn't look angry, just sad.

"I heard what happened. I know you did everything you could. You did everything right. So thank you for trying."

I nod mutely.

"I also heard about what my uncle did. It was uncalled for."

"He was grieving." I give her the same lame excuse I gave Raphael.

"That's no excuse for his behavior," she continues, calling me out just like her brother did. "He needs to apologize to you."

"He doesn't have to," I insist. "Really. It's fine."

Gabriella hums low in her throat, like she doesn't believe a word I'm saying, before sharing a side-eye with Rose. Thankfully, they don't push the subject anymore.

"Who needs coffee?" Rose asks.

"Can I have it in an IV line?" Gabriella jokes.

A dark cloud still hangs in the kitchen's atmosphere, but it's significantly lighter now. Laughter can be wonderful medicine in times of pain and loss. Serving as a gentle reminder to savor the good moments and appreciate the gift of life. Because you never know when everything could suddenly end.

27

RAPHAEL

The overcast gray sky in Miami matches the somber tone of the event. It's almost like Mother Nature is aware of the sad occasion and refuses to let the sun come out.

Today is the day we bury my cousin.

Dominic's autopsy revealed that there really was nothing Lily could have done differently, or any doctor for that matter. His body was damaged beyond repair. A fact I'm confident Xiao knew. That is why, after he brutally tortured Dominic, he dumped him at our front gates like a broken toy no longer of any value.

It's been three days since Dominic's death, and Xiao has disappeared, leaving us all on edge. It feels like we've been left in the dark, and it's unnerving.

The DiAngelo home has been on lockdown for three days now, and if Dad had his way, we'd continue, but I can see Lily is growing uncomfortable. It doesn't matter how large the estate is or how often I assure her she is not a prisoner, her past lingers, and the feelings continue to haunt her.

It doesn't help either that the lockdown includes Emilia. The girl is frustrating beyond compare and actively searches for any moment to corner me or catch Lily off guard enough to torment her. But my little Lily pad has thorns hidden beneath the surface. She doesn't stand for Emilia's mind games and gives it back ten times over, but like I said…it's starting to weigh on her. Which means it's weighing on me. And with how I'm feeling already from Dominic's unaccounted for death, I'm close to tossing the damn girl in the ocean with a concrete block tied to her fucking ankle if she doesn't leave us the hell alone.

Needless to say, after today is done, I'm taking Lily and Mei back to the penthouse. Dad can get upset all he wants, but Michael and Enzo feel the same way and are ready to leave.

A small raindrop lands on my forehead, and I silently curse as the priest continues his Bible readings. If he doesn't hurry, we're all going to be soaked.

"But the just man, though he die early, shall be at rest.
For the age that is honorable
comes not with the passing of time,
nor can it be measured in terms of years.
Rather, understanding is the hoary crown for men,
and an unsullied life, the attainment of old age.
He who pleased God was loved;
he who lived among sinners was transported—
Snatched away, lest wickedness pervert his mind
or deceit beguile his soul;
For the witchery of paltry things obscures what is right
and the whirl of desire transforms the innocent mind.
Having become perfect in a short while,
he reached the fullness of a long career;
for his soul was pleasing to the Lord,
therefore he sped him out of the midst of wickedness.
But the people saw and did not understand,
nor did they take this into account.

Because grace and mercy are with God's holy ones,
and God's care is with the elect."

CLOSE BY, Aunt Mary, Dominic's mom, cries behind her black veil. She flew in yesterday for the funeral and has been a mess since. Uncle Leo's been no help either. In fact, I've barely seen the man, and when I do, he's drunk off his ass. He hasn't apologized to Lily yet, which has left me and the others extremely upset with my uncle. It doesn't matter what the autopsy report says, he still believes his son's death is her fault.

Seeing him standing next to his estranged wife is honestly a surprise. I half expected him to skip the funeral in favor of the bottom of a bottle. But there he is, swaying ever so slightly beside my father. He's wearing dark sunglasses, probably to hide his bloodshot eyes from a combination of crying and no sleep.

Meanwhile, Dad stands rigid beside his younger brother as if he's prepared to grab his arm at a moment's hesitation. Gabriella and Mom stand behind Dad, the perfect examples of composure and grace.

Something Emilia is not. She didn't even know Dominic yet came to the funeral for appearance's sake. Enzo's been playing referee all morning, keeping her from Michael and me. Because while the ocean idea is nice...so is a six-foot-deep empty grave, and the girl is tempting my patience. To top it off, she's been sobbing next to my aunt, who is so lost in her grief, she simply latched on to the first person who offered her any resemblance of comfort.

My gaze roams over the intimate crowd and snags on Connor's eyes. He gives me a small nod that I return, appreciating his support today. Ever since the events last month at the church with the previous Irish mob boss, his wife's late father, Patrick O'Leary, relations between the Irish and Italians have been uneventful. Being the brother-in-law of Michael's fiancée helps.

However, I wish I could say the same about the Russians. The Irish weren't the only ones who lost someone that night in the church. Igor Mikailhov was shot and killed by Patrick. The current Bratva leader lost his younger brother, and he's been grieving ever since.

He says he doesn't blame the families for what happened. He claims his brother had gone crazy and lost his mind over a young girl. But as a brother myself, I know how strong that bond is. Even if Michael went borderline crazy like Igor had, I would still be angry over his death, with a need to take revenge on those responsible.

My eyes fall on Dimitri, the stoic Russian captain and the only leader in attendance, along with a handful of his men. It shouldn't bother me that Sergei is absent, but it does. Grief or not, he should be here to show support. Had he chosen to do a public funeral for Igor, we would have shown our support, too. Another small thing that has me feeling on edge about the Bratva leader.

By the time we make it back to the DiAngelo estate for the wake, the sky opens up and cries the tears I'm unable to shed for my cousin. It's not that I don't want to or that I'm unable to. It's just that...I can't. There will be time to grieve after his death is avenged. Right now, that's all I choose to focus on.

"I'll go check on the girls and kids," Enzo offers before the car even comes to a stop, and he's gone before either Michael or I can halt him. We were blood with Dominic, but he was

Enzo's best friend. The grief he must be feeling right now is as terrible as we feel.

Enzo disappears, and I fight back the urge to follow. I'd enjoy nothing more than to be buried between Lily's succulent thighs, worshipping her pussy until she forgets her name, and I forget the pain of the day. But that'll have to wait, as much as I hate the idea.

"Hey." Micheal nudges my shoulder. "Connor wants to talk to us."

Curious about what the Irish leader has to say, I follow Michael to Dad's office. It's empty of the man himself since he's conversing with those who came to pay their respects.

Connor stands beside the liquor cart, helping himself to a bottle. Normally, I'd make a witty remark, but the second person in the room grabs my attention instead.

"Dimitri?"

The dark-haired Russian turns from the bookcase he'd been inspecting, his blue eyes as sharp as the ice they resemble. Michael closes the door behind us and then directs his attention to the Russian. "How's that eye of yours?"

Sure enough, if I look closely, the pale skin around his left eye is slightly bruised. Like a black eye healing.

"How's the jaw?" Dimitri snaps back.

A couple of weeks ago, the pair got into an altercation at our club Sinners. I'm not sure what sparked the argument since I wasn't there, but it escalated to a physical confrontation. Michael has remained quiet about the incident. And if Rose is aware, she's not saying anything either.

"Will one of you finally explain what the hell happened between the two of you?" I demand, glancing back and forth between the men.

As far as I know, it had nothing to do with Gabriella.

Following the incident at the hospital, Dimitri assured our dad that he really was only friends with our baby sister, and he has since kept his distance from Gabriella.

Still, I can't shake the lingering feeling that something is going on between them or did at the very least. Both options make me uneasy. Because I don't really know how I feel about the Russian. He's quiet. Too quiet. And in my experience, quiet equals mysterious, which often leads to dangerous. And I don't care about people or things I don't understand.

"A simple misunderstanding," Dimitri replies in his usual cryptic style.

Michael crosses his arms over his chest, leveling the Russian with an unamused look. "Yeah. A misunderstanding."

Rolling my eyes with a hard sigh, I turn toward Connor. The blond Irish watches the exchange with intrigue. He must feel the same way I do. That they're both fucking lying through their teeth.

"What did you want to talk about?" I ask him before I put my brother in a headlock and force whatever bullshit he's hiding free.

"Not me," Connor admits. "Dimitri wanted to talk—"

"What?" Michael barks.

"—and he knew you wouldn't agree to it if he had asked," Connor finishes.

"He's right," Michael says.

The Russian closes his eyes slowly and his chest expands, like he's trying hard to stay calm.

Connor sighs. "Will you just listen to him, please?"

Michael meets my eyes, and I give him an exasperated look. I'm done with today and just want to spend the rest of it with Lily.

Grumbling under his breath, Michael leans against a bookcase and nods begrudgingly.

"I've noticed something strange happening in our sex clubs the past few weeks. People have been disappearing," Dimitri explains.

"There's nothing strange about that, Dimitri," Michael points out. "Your line of business doesn't really scream long-term career."

"True. But it's not just the employees. It's the patrons too."

I frown. Now, that's not normal. As different as the Russian sex clubs are, they're still considered safe for those who enter their dens of inequity. The employees are there by choice and not force. "Are you sure?"

Dimitri nods. "Yes. Whoever it is, they're only taking a few at a time. And I've identified a pattern. They usually look physically the same. All brunettes one time, and then all blonds the next."

"And you think they're being kidnapped?" Connor guesses.

"It's not a wild guess to assume so," Dimitri says. "Because they literally disappear, fall off the earth. No sign of them anywhere."

"Have you told Sergei?"

Dimitri's dark expression tells me he has, and it didn't go well. "He knows, but he doesn't believe me."

"Then why should we believe you?" Michael asks in an accusing tone.

Dimitri snaps his piercing blue gaze on my older brother. "Because I believe they're being kidnapped to be trafficked into the same ring responsible for Rose and Lily."

28

LILY

As I slowly drift toward consciousness, the warmth of a hand against my bare skin pulls me gently from the depths of slumber. At first, it's a distant feeling, barely registering amid the soft haze of sleep and the lull of dreams. The tender caress of a hand traces patterns down my side and thigh, reaching my knee before moving back up.

I shift toward the touch, seeking more of the feeling, upset when it fades.

A deep laugh echoes through the air, vibrating in my chest. A moment later, a mouth falls on my neck, soft yet firm lips kissing their way up to my ear. One suck, followed by a small nip, drags me further to the surface.

"Do you want to feel good, Lily pad?" Raphael asks, the warmth of his voice sending chills down my spine.

Moaning my consent, he laughs again. "Guess that means yes."

His hand returns, skirting up my thigh. I automatically part my legs, inviting his touch to reach the area where I desperately need him. He slips it beneath my panties, and one finger slides into my aching pussy before a second joins.

"Raphael," I beg him, needing more.

I can feel him readjust himself on the bed and open my eyes to the sight of burnt gold shrouded in the shadows his hair makes, staring down at me. He leans closer, putting all his weight on the hand he rests beside my head and steals a quick kiss.

My back arches, and my breath catches when he adds a third finger. Against my thigh, his anxious cock twitches, jealous of his hand. Sliding his thumb forward, Raphael plays with my clit while he finger fucks me. I can feel myself tighten around his fingers, the need to come as desperate as the air I breathe.

Raphael must, too, because he groans in my ear and whispers, "Not yet, sweetheart."

All at once, his hand leaves, taking my orgasm with it, but before I can protest, Raphael moves down my body and takes my panties with him. Our eyes lock for one moment before he tosses me a wicked smile and disappears between my legs. His mouth covers my sex, hot and wet, and I moan, unashamed at how loud I am. He runs his tongue along my throbbing pussy before clamping on my clit, and I come violently, my entire body seizing up as the waves of my orgasm crash over me.

Raphael props his chin on my pubic bone and peers up at me. His mouth glistens with the residue of my orgasm, and I lick my lips at the sensual sight.

"Thanks for breakfast."

I reach down and try to shove his head away, laughing when he playfully growls and nips the inside of my thigh. He slides up my body, purposely dragging his hard cock along my core, and I moan at the contact.

Since we returned to the penthouse a few days ago, we can't keep our hands off each other. As soon as Mei goes to bed, I find my way to Raphael's. Every touch wipes away another memory of pain. Every kiss heals a scar left behind. Raphael is there to chase any lingering nightmares away every time they threaten. With him, I'm remembering how it feels to be a woman worthy of affection and not a plaything to be abused.

Raphael captures my mouth and kisses me deeply and thoroughly. The kind of kiss that leaves me breathless and wanting more.

"God, I want to bury myself in this tight pussy and fuck you senseless. Fuck you until it's only me you remember."

I raise my hands and set them on his torso. Dragging them down, I enjoy every rippling muscle that dances beneath my touch. Almost like he's shivering. The rush of power it gives me is intoxicating.

"Don't tease a girl."

He chuckles but makes no move to stop me. "It'll have to be quick. I need to meet Michael."

Right.

At Dominic's funeral, the Russian Captain Dimitri shared some concerns about his workers and patrons disappearing. Evie and Enzo tracked one victim to a warehouse on the docks that was listed as abandoned. They already suspect Xiao is behind the human auctions in Miami but hope to identify who is behind the entire thing because someone is above him. Someone else is pulling the strings because this is bigger than Miami.

Tugging Raphael's face close, I tell him. "Then be quick."

With a deep groan, Raphael reaches down, lines the head of his cock with my core, and wastes no time burying himself to the hilt. He swallows my moan with a kiss as he groans. It always feels like coming home. Like a piece of a puzzle missing that has finally been found again.

He leans forward, bringing his arms to cup my head before cradling me to his chest. "Hold on."

I barely have any time to do as he asks before Raphael

pounds into me over and over, quick and brutal in the most delicious way. This close, he brushes against my clit with every thrust, causing my orgasm to rapidly climb.

"Fuck," he growls into my ear, his breath coming in harsh bursts that mirror his movements. "Fucking hell, Lily, your pussy is choking my cock."

If I had any breath left in me to spare, I'd laugh. Instead, I raise my hands higher, until I'm literally hanging on to his shoulders for dear life. He might have some red marks from it, but I doubt he'll mind.

"Come for me," he orders in a desperate voice. "I need you to come for me now."

Raphael reaches between us. With one pinch to my clit, I explode for the second time this morning. A second later, Raphael swells inside me, and then a rush of warm liquid fills me.

He rests his face on my neck but keeps his body weight off me. Every exhale of his against my sweaty skin sends shivers down my spine. Finally, Raphael kisses the side of my neck gingerly, then slips out.

"You are incredible," he tells me with a genuine smile that reaches his eyes. I believe him because he's never lied to me. "So perfect. Every inch of you. It's like you were made for me."

I smile and lean up to peck his lips. I'm still not used to his endearing comments and often am left speechless and unsure of what to say back. Raphael sees it and understands my reluctance because he knows it's not that I don't feel the same. It's just that sharing those feelings is a wall that has yet to come down.

Raphael's phone rings on the nightstand, and with a disgruntled groan, he reaches for it. "It's Michael. I have to shower and get dressed."

"Okay. Have a nice shower," I say with a lazy stretch, knowing exactly what I'm doing. When his eyes go dark, I know it works.

"And you're coming with me," Raphael says before he bends down to collect me in his arms.

THE ELEVATOR BEEPS, and I turn away from making lunch for Mei and me. Expecting to find Raphael, I'm surprised when it's Emilia.

"What are you doing here?" I glance behind her but don't see anyone else. "How did you get the code to come upstairs?"

Raphael put my mind at ease before he left, assuring me we were safe. He promised that only the family knew the code, and with Rose busy with her sister Grace and Evie, and Gabriella working at the hospital, there was no chance of anyone stopping by unexpectedly.

"The guard downstairs was easily persuaded," she admits with an innocent shrug and a sly smile playing at the edges of her lips.

The small hairs on the back of my neck rise. Something's not right.

"Raphael's not here. You should go."

Emilia holds up a cup holder. There are three foam cups set inside. "I brought a little peace offering. I've had time to think about my behavior at the DiAngelo estate, and I wanted to apologize."

I hesitate, but the sooner she gets done with whatever her goal here is, the better.

"Please? One drink, and then I'll go. I promise."

With a heavy sigh, I motion for her to follow me and then

gesture to the kitchen island. Emilia sets the container on the marble top.

Mei notices our new company and comes running over, the sounds of her cartoon show playing in the background. "Hi!"

Emilia turns and smiles at my daughter. "Hi, Mei. I brought you some hot cocoa." She glances over her shoulder at me. "If that's okay with your mother, of course."

I nod and watch as Emilia grabs the smaller of the three cups and hands it to Mei. Carefully holding the cup between her hands, Mei politely says thanks and then slowly walks back to the living room to enjoy her treat in front of her show.

Emilia hands me another insulated cup. "I wasn't sure what you liked, but I assumed everyone likes hot cocoa."

"It's fine." I'm not about to tell her how hot cocoa is my favorite winter drink. "Thank you."

I blow through the drink hole and then take a careful sip, testing the temperature. It's warm but not too hot, which is perfect. So I take another sip, savoring the taste of chocolate exploding on my tongue.

Emilia takes her cup and holds it between her hands. "You're welcome."

"So you wanted to apologize?"

She nods. "I realize that the things I said were cruel and unnecessary."

I wait for her to actually say sorry, but she doesn't. "I appreciate you saying that."

Emilia runs a manicured finger around the rim of her cup, studying the drink but never taking a sip. "Of course, I also realized that I acted out of jealousy, but there's no reason to be concerned."

"What do you mean?" The edges of my fingers tingle, and my legs go numb.

"Well, when I found out who you are and who you belong to, all of my fears disappeared."

Why is she smiling like that? Why is she fuzzy around the edges, too?

"What...did you...do?" My equilibrium falters, and I stumble into the island, barely catching myself in time. This feels eerily familiar. Like the time Dr. Rodriguez drugged me all those years ago. "Did you...drug me?"

"It didn't take long to get in touch with Xiao. I mean, the man is downright desperate to find you and his daughter. He's eager to have you home." Emilia reaches out and takes the cup from my hand seconds before it slips from my grip. "So I struck a deal. Return you and Mei, and he lets Raphael live for taking you two."

"What?" Black edges close in on my vision. I fight to look toward Mei and find her stretched out in front of the television, her cup knocked over. The bitch drugged my daughter, too.

"With you gone, Raphael will have no choice but to turn to me for comfort." She leans forward, and a wicked grin spreads across her face. "With you gone, we'll be married, just like we were supposed to before you came along."

Rage surges through my veins as Emilia's smile twists into a venomous sneer, taunting me. It's the last thing I see before the drug-induced darkness takes hold.

29

RAPHAEL

Michael and I have a nickname among our allies.

The Twin Grim Reapers

And over time, it became a name our enemies feared.

When we worked together, we moved as one. We know what the other is thinking with just a single look. We were the last thing our enemies saw before we brought death on their heads. And today is no different.

Muted daylight streams in through the warehouse's dirty windows. The scattered beams highlight the hazy atmosphere of dust and dirt among the maze of towering boxes and pallets, leaving us to move in the shadows like predators hunting our prey, silent and deadly.

Up ahead, a voice drifts, breaking the quiet, and we pause.

"When are they coming to pick up the shipment again?"

I slowly peer around a pile of boxes and count a pair of guards with their backs to us.

Idiots. You should never leave your back defenseless.

"Last time I heard, it was sometime tonight."

The guard on the right smacks the other's shoulder. "Hey, that gives us time to sample the product, yeah?"

"I like how you think, man. But I've got dibs on that young blonde kid. You know how I've got a thing for little girls."

Fury fills me with their conversation and I don't need to see

Michael's eyes to know he feels the same. These men are done breathing air now.

Silently, I approach the one on the right from behind, wrap a hand over his mouth, and bury my knife in the side of his neck, killing him instantly. Beside me, Michael is about to do the same to the other guard when he catches sight of me from the corner of his eye.

He turns on me, and I barely dive out of the way in time to miss the bullet he fires in my direction. Michael uses the moment to throw a knife at the man, his aim deadly and true, the blade burying itself in the guard's neck.

"They're Triads," Michael reveals after shoving one of the dead guards over to see his face.

Sure as shit. When I push the other guard over with my shoe and stare down at his face, his Oriental features stand out. "So Xiao's really behind this, then?"

Before he can say anything back, bullets start flying all around us. Seems the gunshot blew our cover.

Michael joins me behind a tower of crates with a sadistic smile. "Just like that time in Capri, huh?"

"You and I remember that summer in Italy very different-ly," I remind him while I reach for my gun and cock it back.

"You have to admit it was fun."

"We set fire and destroyed half an island."

"Allegedly," Michael corrects me. "We allegedly set a fire and destroyed half the island."

"Because of a dare."

"It was that or admit to Enzo that I fucked his cousin."

"But you did fuck his cousin."

Michael chuckles under his breath. "Exactly. But I wasn't going to admit that. Even at sixteen, Enzo scared the shit out of me."

Rolling my eyes, I count as the bullets start again. When they're forced to reload, we make our move. Leaving the safety of the wood tower, we each take a side and lay waste to the rat infestation.

"You know, you fucked his cousin too," Michael says when the last Triad member falls.

"Why do you think I joined you on that dare?"

We kick in a door at the very back of the warehouse and come face-to-face with a group of scared young girls and the pair of Triad members pointing guns at them.

One of them swings toward us, and Michael buries a bullet in his forehead before he can squeeze the trigger. His partner turns, and I shoot his knee out before he can do anything. He falls to the ground in a crying heap of blood and tears.

"Wrong move," Michael tells him as he steps forward and grabs the gun the guard dropped.

"We need this one alive," I remind my brother. "For information."

Michael concedes with a groan, like the idea of leaving the bastard alive for a second longer is highly inconvenient.

While Michael ties up the Triad guard, I tend to the frightened girls including the little blonde girl the guard talked about. A few of the younger ones just arrived from China with the promise of a better life, only to be met with the opposite. Two of the older girls work at one of the Russian's less exclusive sex clubs, which made them easy targets. And it's not a coincidence either because they weren't alone when they were brought here. So it seems Evie and Enzo's research was right, too.

Maybe a few would have ended up as prostitutes working the streets and others as slaves working until their fingers bleed from hard work, but all would have been treated like

Lily. Thankfully, nothing more terrible will happen to this group.

I call Enzo in, and together, we load the girls into a van. He offers to take them to the closest hospital, where the authorities will meet them. As they drive away, it finally feels like we've gotten a step ahead of Xiao, and I intend to have his head before the week's over.

"Well, well, well," I drawl when I rejoin Michael and our guest. "Who do we have here?"

"You fucking Italian bastard!" the man spits.

"Well, that's rude." Humming low, I take my knife out and spin the blade in my hand. "Do you know who we are?"

"You're the DiAngelo brothers," he hisses through clenched teeth.

"That's right. Then you also know—"

"That you're a pair of idiots who think you've won when you've never lost so hard." The man interrupts through a wet laugh as blood spurts from his mouth.

I glance at Michael, who stands watching the exchange with a blank expression. "That's funny. Because from where I'm sitting, you're the one who's lost."

"Don't you think it was too easy that you found this place?"

"What do you mean?"

"Xiao wanted you to find this place. He needed you out of that tower of yours to get back what's rightfully his."

Realization dawns on me, cold and freezing as if a bucket of ice water has been tossed over me. My breath catches in my lungs as my heart seizes.

"Lily."

30

LILY

Waking up is a struggle as each of my senses slowly returns.

The room is bright when I open my eyes, and I blink several times to adjust to the light. My head feels heavy, and my mouth dry. I'm lying on something solid but soft, a bed probably, and every joint in my body aches in protest when I try to sit up.

When I do, all at once, the memories of what happened with Emilia at Raphael's penthouse come flooding back.

"That bitch," I moan.

She drugged me.

Emilia was out of her fucking mind, claiming I was in the way of her and Raphael's nonexistent romance. And the only way to get rid of me was...Xiao.

Fuck.

An image of Mei lying down in front of the television flashes across my mind. That fucking bitch drugged my daughter, too.

"I'll kill her." If something has happened or does happen to Mei, I will go against every moral fiber of my being and kill that bitch.

"Mei?" I call out, twisting to look around for her, but the room is empty. Glancing at the window, I frown. It's small and circular. Not at all like the floor-to-ceiling windows at Raphael's penthouse.

I stand on shaky feet before losing my balance and stumbling into the wall. Is it me swaying or the ground beneath me? Peering outside, I see only water and nothing else in sight. What the hell am I doing on a boat?

Moving toward the only door in the room, I shout again with urgency, "Mei!"

I'm not sure what lies on the other side, but if it leads to Mei, I will face anything.

My hand reaches for the knob, but it opens before I can, and the lead actor in all of my nightmares fills the doorway.

"Baby, I've missed you." Xiao practically purrs, a sinister smile pulling at his lips.

The door closes behind him, and he stands in front of me, blocking my only way of escape.I back up right away to try and put some distance between us. It's useless, though. He simply eats up the space with every step he takes toward me.

He's dressed in a white button-down shirt with a matching black vest and slacks. He undoes the links at his wrists and then slowly rolls up his sleeves.

I watch each movement unfold with a wary eye as if waiting for the strike of a coiled snake.

"Did you miss me?"

My immediate response is no, but I swallow it down and stay silent. Mistake number one. I should have just lied.

His hand collides with my cheek faster than I realize, and the momentum pushes me back onto the bed.

"Or are you that Italian's whore now?"

Xiao stalks toward me, and I scramble backward onto the bed desperately hoping to put distance between us. But his hand wraps around my ankle, and pulls hard. I attempt to kick at him with my other foot, but Xiao simply grabs that one too, and now he has control over both my legs.

"Did you fuck him?" Xiao demands, spreading my legs wide so he can settle between them. "Huh? Have you given yourself to that bastard? Has he had what is mine?"

"Stop! Let me go. Please." I struggle, but he's too strong.

"Answer me!"

"No!" I cry.

Xiao slaps me again and the metallic taste of copper floods my mouth as an explosion of stars fills my vision.

"Don't fucking lie to me."

"Did you think of me when you let him fuck you?" Xiao goads. "Did you enjoy it? How many times did you fuck him, you fucking whore?"

His hands move from my legs to the waistband of my leggings. I push at his hands and try to keep my leggings up, but then he sends a punch directly into my gut that leaves me gasping and unable to stop him.

Cold air rushes over my naked bottom, and hot tears spring to my eyes as the realization dawns on me that Xiao is going to rape me.

It's nothing new. He's done it more times than I can count. But it's like the time I spent with Raphael wiped all those memories away. And now, every good moment between us will be washed away.

"Did you enjoy his touch?" Xiao asks before he shoves two fingers inside me, and I cry out at the painful intrusion. "Did he touch you like this?" He leans forward, buries his face in my neck, and bites me there hard. "Did he leave marks on you like me?"

I thrash around, arch my back, shift my hips...I try anything I can to get away but nothing works.

"I own your pleasure. Me! No one else!"

Xiao's wrong.

Raphael's face flashes across my mind. In such a short amount of time, he's shown me not only how to live again but also how to own my pleasure.

Because it's mine. Not anyone else's.

And if Raphael were here, he'd tell me to fight back and not give up.

So I do.

I reach for Xiao's hair and tug hard, taking the bastard by surprise. He hisses through clenched teeth, releasing me as his hand slips free from between my legs.

"You stupid bitch!" he hollers.

I kick at him, not caring where or what I hit, only that I hit something hard enough that he's forced to let me go. I don't even bother grabbing for my pants when I scramble away because modesty be damned when you're fighting for your life.

A hand wraps around my hair and yanks me backward. Xiao effortlessly flips me onto my stomach and uses his weight to pin my legs down.

"No!" I scream, desperate for someone, anyone, to hear me. "Please. Don't do this. I'm begging you."

Xiao's voice is heavy with sarcasm. "I do like it when you beg."

A crazy idea comes to mind. If I can't overpower him physically, maybe I can do so mentally.

"You're right," I start, drawing on every reserve I have left in me to put a poker face on and lie. "I'm sorry. I did sleep with Raphael, but it was terrible. He's nothing like you, baby. Nothing. You are so much better. I missed you."

Xiao eases his hold off my upper back, enough that I can

twist my head around to look up at him. He's peering at me suspiciously. Like he doesn't believe me. I need to try harder.

"He could never make me orgasm the way you do."

Xiao's lips jerk up. "That's right, baby. Only me."

He then thrusts forward, and I send up a silent thank you to whatever higher power is listening that he's still wearing his pants.

When Xiao rubs his bulge, his much tinier bulge, against me, it takes everything in me not to cringe. So, instead, to keep up appearances, I let out the most exaggerated moan, hoping he believes it.

As he does it again and again, I rack my brain for the right words to say that will stop this from going any further when there's a knock on the door.

Xiao freezes and peers over his shoulder.

"What?"

"Sir, we're ready to push off, and the captain would like to speak with you," a timid voice answers.

"Tell him I'll find him when I'm done here."

The voice clears his throat before saying, "I'm sorry, sir, but he says it's important. Something about international waters and permits."

When Xiao growls out his frustration under his breath and then all at once, he sits back and climbs off the bed. I fight the urge to crawl away, to hide myself from his seedy eyes, but I have to continue to play my part so I force myself to stay still.

Xiao straightens his clothes before reaching out to grip my chin. I force a smile on my lips when I peer up at him. "We'll finish this later. Welcome home, baby."

When he kisses me, a wave of nausea slams into me, and bile creeps up my throat. But it's only when he leaves me alone in the room that I double over and vomit with tears streaming down my face.

31

RAPHAEL

I hoped the Triad member had been lying about the kidnapping, but the silence in the penthouse when I return confirms he was telling the truth. Still, I rush into my home eagerly and shout out their names as if I expect them to be there.

"Lily! Mei!"

Turning the corner, I freeze when I come face-to-face with the last person I would ever expect to see standing in my kitchen as if she owns the place.

"Emilia?"

She looks at me with a huge smile. "Oh good, you're home. I was just about to make a pot of coffee. Unless you prefer tea? I'm not sure which is your favorite, but I'll learn."

"Emilia?" Michael repeats when he joins us in the kitchen. "What the hell are you doing here?"

"Well, I was hoping for it to be a surprise, but I wanted to have dinner with Raphael."

"What? Why?" I ask.

"So we could get to know one another better before we marry of course."

I hear Michael softly curse behind me. I don't blame him. Hearing her say the same thing repeatedly is becoming annoying, and I'm growing tired of it. No. I *am* tired of it.

"Listen to me closely, Emilia, because this is the last time I will say it." My voice is low and even and clear so she doesn't mistake a word I say. "We are not engaged, nor will we ever be engaged. Do you understand me?"

A look of disappointment washes over Emilia's face, swiftly replaced by a flash of anger in her eyes. "Why not? There's no one holding you back now."

No one?

A foreboding sensation crawls up my spine, spreading a chilling feeling across my body. I left Lily and Mei here alone and safe. But now they're gone, and Emilia is here. Something that shouldn't have been possible. Because I made sure the penthouse was locked down before leaving.

"How did you get in here, Emilia?"

"The guard downstairs was nice enough to let me up." Emilia shrugs a shoulder like it's no big deal. Only it is a big deal. The guards are under strict orders not to let anyone upstairs. Not even the Pope himself in all his grand holiness is allowed.

My eyes snap to my brother. He nods and pulls his phone out to message Enzo to pick up the guard and find out what exactly happened.

"What are you really doing here?" I ask, my tone grave.

"Like I said, I'm making—"

"The truth, Emilia. Now," Michael orders, and the girl shivers at the authority in my brother's tone.

"I am telling the truth."

Alright. I'm done with this.

Lunging forward, I wrap a hand around Emilia's throat and shove her back into the fridge. She hits the stainless steel door hard enough that she cries out. I said I would never lay a hand on a girl, but I can't bring myself to care. At this moment, she's not a girl; she's just someone who knows what happened to Lily and Mei.

"Where are Lily and Mei?" I shout. "What did you do? Tell me!"

Emilia scratches at my hand, desperately trying to get me to release her as her face grows more red from lack of oxygen.

Michael comes up beside me and rests his hand on my arm. "Brother, release her. We need her alive."

An unfortunate necessity, but he's right. If she dies, so does what she knows.

With a last squeeze, I release Emilia and take a step back, watching as she crumples to the floor in a fit of coughing. When it subsides, she struggles to stand, but neither of us attempts to help her.

"Start talking, or I'll send you back to Italy in a box," I threaten, my words hard as steel so she understands how serious I am. I don't care if it starts a war with her father and half of Italy. She is somehow responsible for Lily's and Mei's kidnapping. I know it.

Emilia visibly swallows hard. "She was in our way, Raphael."

"What the hell are you talking about? What did you do?"

"When I found out who she was, who she belonged to, I—"

I lunge at her once again, and she shrieks, cowering away, trying to find safety behind the island. Finally, she's afraid of me.

Michael stops me before I can make contact, and with a growl, I shake him off and step back. "It was you? You gave her up to Xiao?"

"I didn't give her up. I gave her back to him," Emilia answers. "You can't keep his family hostage here."

"Are you fucking delusional?" Frustration overwhelms me because I shouldn't have to explain this to her. "I rescued them *from* Xiao. I rescued them from an abusive asshole, who you've now given them back to. You stupid girl!"

"I didn't know," Emilia says in a meek voice. "I just wanted her gone so we could be together."

"Un-fucking-believable!" I shout at the ceiling.

Enzo returns, bursting into the space like a tattooed blond hurricane. "That fucking guard must have been bribed because the bastard dipped out the second he let Emilia up. I have our men searching for him. They'll bring him in."

"Talk, Emilia," Michael orders. "What exactly happened?"

Tossing a wary look at me, Emilia sits on a barstool at the island and explains, "After they passed out, I called the number Xiao's men gave me, and then I met a group of them downstairs in the elevator with Lily and Mei. They took them, and that was it. I swear. I promise that was it."

I grab a vase of flowers from a nearby table and throw it across the room. It shatters into a million pieces, mirroring how my soul and heart feel at this moment.

Lily trusted me. She trusted me to keep them safe, and the first time I leave them really alone, she's taken back to that abusive, sick bastard.

If I can't keep them safe...do I even deserve them? Do I deserve to be happy?

Michael rests his hand on my shoulder, pulling me from my dark thoughts. "I know what you're thinking, brother, and you can stop that right now."

Enzo approaches on my other side. "I have Evie already searching through cameras, tracking the car they left in. We'll find out where they went."

"Uh, excuse me. If it's all the same to you, I'll just be going now," Emilia says as she starts toward the elevator.

Enzo intercepts and grabs her wrist. "I don't think so. You have quite a lot to answer for."

Emilia tries to pull her arm free but with no success. "Let me go, you brute! This is no way to treat a lady."

Enzo barks out a laugh. "That's funny. I don't see a lady here."

"Take her back to the house and update our dad. We'll be there soon." Michael directs our friend.

Enzo leaves with a screeching Emilia, and the silence that follows is deafening and too large for the space. Funny how the mere presence of Lily and Mei in my home has drastically changed it to where I can't remember what it was even like before.

"We'll find her, Raphael," Michael says with a level of confidence I wish I felt right now.

"We have to, Michael. They're my family, and I won't lose them. I can't."

32

LILY

The second I'm alone, I'm off the bed, straightening my clothes and looking for a way out. I try the door, hoping like a fool that he left it unlocked, but of course he didn't. Wouldn't want his prized possession to escape.

I spin around, examining every surface of the room for anything I can use as a weapon, but the room is as empty as a cell. Besides a bed, there's a nightstand and a built-in desk in the corner and the tiny-ass windows that I'd be lucky to get a leg through, even if they could open.

I'm crawling under the bed in search of something I can use from the frame when there's a knock on the door. I freeze, my head snapping in the direction, and wait. I wait for it to open and for Xiao to storm in, intent on finishing what he started, but it remains closed.

Maybe if I stay quiet, they'll go away.

But then a second knock echoes.

"Miss?" It's a woman's voice. "May I come in?"

"Please go away," I say loud enough for her to hear. "I'd like to be left alone."

"I-I know, but…" she stammers, fear evident in her tone, which tells me exactly what I already know. She's as much of a prisoner as I am. "I need to get you ready."

"Ready for what?"

"Dinner."

I consider my options for a long moment. I could just refuse, but Xiao would no doubt send a guard, or worse...he would come get me himself. Backed into a corner, I wiggle my way out from under the bed and open the door.

A young Chinese girl stands on the other side, holding a garment bag in one hand and a metal case in the other. Behind her is a guard who looks at me with a stern expression, reminding me again that escape is impossible. So I step aside to let the girl in before slamming the door in the guard's smug fucking face, enjoying it immensely when I hear him curse behind the closed door.

The girl sets her items down on the bed and looks back at me. With a tentative smile, she says, "My name is Sasha."

"Lily."

"I know," she answers in a mousey tone.

"Do you know where my daughter is?"

Sasha shakes her head. "I haven't seen her."

"But she's on board?"

"I believe so. But I'm really not sure. They don't tell me anything except what to do."

Knowing Xiao, he'll use Mei as a bargaining chip against me, a way to control me like he's done before. If I play along and do what he says, then I'll get to see my daughter.

Sasha leads me across the hall to a bathroom, where she stands and waits for me to shower. Being under the water reminds me too much of Raphael, and the memories are painfully sweet.

Will he come after us? Does he even know where we are? What if Emilia concocts some bullshit story about me? Something like, I ran away to return willingly to Xiao. And what if Raphael believes her? Silly thought, I know, because he would never believe a single word out of her mouth...but the doubt still lingers. Mostly because if he believes her, then that means he won't be coming for me and Mei.

After a quick shower, Sasha helps me into a skintight little red number that barely covers my ass and chest. Just how Xiao likes it. If he wasn't so insanely jealous, I'd be naked all the time.

Sasha applies a stupid amount of makeup, another favorite of Xiao, avoiding my split lip as best she can and covering the blooming bruises on my cheek. After she blows out my hair and leaves it to hang in blond waves down my back, she steps back to admire my reflection in the mirror.

"You look beautiful."

I don't even bother looking and instead stand to slip on the heels she brought. "Thank you for your help."

Outside, a guard waits to take me to wherever Xiao waits. As I slip by Sasha, she squeezes my hand as if to give me strength. Or maybe she does it for herself. Either way, I squeeze back.

The guard leads me to the upper deck. The sun is just beginning to set over the open water as Miami fades further from view. It's a beautiful sight, and in any other situation, one might call this the start of a romantic and wonderful night. But to me, it feels like every mile we sail away is another knot on the noose around my neck.

"Mommy!"

My head whips around fast enough to cause whiplash. Mei sits at a cloth-covered table with a big smile on her face. She jumps down and rushes over to me. The white dress she wears flutters around her ankles, giving glimpses of her shiny black slippers. There's a matching white headband holding her hair back.

When she collides with my legs, I bend down to physically put hands on her to make sure she's really here.

"Hi, princess."

"Doesn't Mommy look pretty, Mei?"

I look up and see Xiao walking toward us. He's wearing a dress shirt that matches my red dress with a black suit jacket over it. It's like the sick bastard is trying to make this into some kind of romantic family date night.

"Yes!" Mei agrees.

Xiao reaches out and grabs my arm, giving me a silent command to stay still as he leans in to kiss me. He doesn't care that my lip is busted and bruised. He kisses me hard anyhow. Unlike Raphael, who kisses me like he's treasuring every brush of our lips.

"Come and sit down, baby," Xiao suggests in a tone that warns me not to ignore him.

His hand slips from my arm to my hand as he pulls me toward the table. Xiao gestures to the seat next to him, and I sit tensely, keeping my back ramrod straight and every muscle rigid and ready to move.

"Our daughter was just about to tell me about your time with Raphael DiAngelo after he took you two from me."

I swallow hard, my eyes dropping to the table. It's been decorated for a five-course meal, and I eye the knife set to the right of the plate, wondering if I can somehow take it without Xiao noticing. But then that leaves the next problem of where the hell do I hide it?

Under the table, Xiao sets his hand heavy on my thigh and grips me hard enough to leave a bruise. He knows what I'm thinking, and this is his way of saying I can just forget it.

"Go on, baby girl," Xiao says to Mei with a fake smile I can see through.

It doesn't matter what she says, Xiao will somehow find something to latch on to and twist it into something terrible. Like, for example, Raphael made us breakfast, which is innocent and nothing to dissect, but to Xiao, he'll assume it means that we enjoy his cooking more than Xiao's personal chef. Which is true, but nothing to get mad about.

"Did he buy you toys?"

Mei nods. "And books for Mommy to read."

Xiao's hand tightens on my thigh, his nails biting into my flesh. "That's nice. Did Raphael read to you too?"

Mei nods again.

"Did you have fun?"

Mei glances at me before lowering her eyes to her hands. No child should have to go through this kind of interrogation. No child should have to lie intentionally to avoid angering her parent. Especially a man who is supposed to be her father. A father is someone who protects their child. Not torment.

"Well, did you?"

Mei shakes her head. "Not really."

I know she's lying. So does Xiao.

"He didn't take you to his parents for Christmas? You didn't make cookies with him or go to the beach and make sandcastles?"

My head snaps to Xiao. How does he know about any of that? His questions are too precise to be mere guesses. Cookies maybe, but the afternoon we spent at the beach after Dominic's death? That's too specific.

The weather that day was unusually warm. Almost like Mother Nature was urging us to leave the chilly, depressive house to indulge in the sun and remember we're alive. With Dominic's funeral the next day, it felt like the right thing to do.

"Look, Mommy!" Mei cries out, pulling my attention from the ocean waves. "I made a castle like a princess."

In no way does her "castle" resemble one, but to her, it does, and I will never smother my daughter's imagination. I walk over to kneel beside her in the sand and smile widely at her master-piece. "It's beautiful, sweetheart! I love it."

"Maybe Raphael can make it real?" Mei asks. At hearing his name, Raphael glances over. "Like how the fairy made the pumpkin real for Cinderella?"

I smother a laugh because in her own way, she's just compared Raphael to Cinderella's fairy godmother. Raphael catches me and narrows his eyes at me playfully.

"Why don't you ask him, sweetie?"

Mei practically jumps to her feet and rushes over to Raphael. He catches her at the last minute when she stumbles and gently sets her down on the sand beside him. "Can you, Raphael?"

Raphael meets my eyes over my daughter's head, and I smile gently at him. I always wanted a true and loving father figure for Mei, and in such a short amount of time, Raphael was on the verge of becoming that. Something her real father could never accomplish in the four years of her life.

"Show me what you've built first, and we'll go from there. How does that sound?"

Mei smiles big. "Okay!"

For a few short hours, we enjoyed the break from reality, where we imagined a beautiful castle with a moat, flying horses, and talking candlesticks.

. . .

"DID YOU EVEN MISS YOUR BÀBA?" Xiao asks like the narcissist asshole he is.

Mei's on the verge of crying. She doesn't want to lie to her father because he'll know she is and get furious. But if she tells him the truth, he'll also get mad. It's a double-edged sword either way.

"Of course she did," I answer for her, trying to redirect Xiao's building anger to me. "We both did."

Xiao swings his black eyes on me. With a sneer, he hisses, "Don't fucking lie to me, woman. The only reason you're still breathing is because that Italian bastard seems to be entranced with your worthless and used-up body. If it wasn't for that, you would already be six feet under."

Mei squeaks at the violence in her father's tone and starts to cry. I try to move to comfort her, but Xiao grabs my arm in a viselike grip, stopping me.

"Please, Xiao, she's crying," I beg.

"Mei is no longer your concern. She is my daughter. You will never see her again. And in time, you will become nothing but a distant memory to her."

"Xiao, you can't, please—"

"From the moment you went with DiAngelo, you signed your death warrant."

Ice shoots down my spine.

"When the bastard comes for you, and he will, I will smile at him while I put a bullet between your eyes before doing the same to him."

"Bàba, no!" Mei shouts before she jumps off her chair and hurries to my side.

A guard approaches and tries to tear her off me, but I latch on because I know if he takes her, I'll never see her again.

"Let go, Mei," Xiao orders. "This instant. Let go of her."

"No!" Mei cries, gripping harder. "Mommy, please don't go."

Another guard grabs my hand wrapped around Mei and forces my fingers back, nearly breaking them before I'm forced to let go. Mei slips from my hold. The guard holds her against his chest to avoid her frantic kicks and flailing arms.

"Please, Xiao! Don't do this!"

"Mommy! Mommy!" Mei screams as Xiao orders the guard to take her away.

Time slows.

With Xiao's attention on the guard, my eyes fall to the knife on the table. Through tears, the silver glistens like a sword from one of Mei's books. I hoped a hero would save us. But maybe there is a hero. Maybe I've been the hero all along. And sometimes the heroes don't live. Sometimes they take the villain down with them.

Without a second thought, I grab the knife and lunge for Xiao. My first stab makes contact with his upper back. He cries out, reaching back in instinct to grab for the knife. But in my frenzy, I'm faster. I pull the knife out and stab him again in the same general area. Hot blood gushes from the wounds, covering us both, but I don't care. I'm about to stab a third time when arms wrap around my middle and pull me off Xiao.

"No!" I scream, kicking and trying to stab the person holding me. A guard wrenches the knife free from my hand and tosses it to the side. "I need to kill him! Let me go!"

Xiao turns toward me, his face bloody and furious. "You bitch! I was going to wait to kill you, but you're more trouble than that's worth. I'll just dump your severed head on Raphael's front porch."

He holds his hand out, and a guard places a pistol in his

palm. Adrenaline pumps through my body, but everything freezes when I see the gun.

The instinct to flight takes over, and I thrash in the guard's arms.

My fear of leaving Mei alone with Xiao threatens. I failed her as a mother. I failed to protect her.

I was so close to a happy ever after. But at least for a moment...I got to feel what it's like to be loved. To be treasured and cherished.

Xiao cocks his gun back.

And then the air is pierced by the deafening sound of a bullet being fired.

33

RAPHAEL

My entire body is restless and eager to spill blood. Every second I'm made to wait is another second Lily and Mei spend with Xiao being forced in to whatever hell he has planned.

For every wound on them, I will deliver three times over on Xiao and his men. They have no idea the devil that comes for them, but they will before the night's over.

My fingers tap against the knife strapped to my leg, my eyes on the yacht in the distance. We have to wait until night falls to approach. Otherwise, we'll be seen by Xiao's lookouts. Even then, to avoid radar, Michael and I will need to dive and board the boat from the back.

Michael hands me a mask and a respirator designed to pull air from the water while I swim. Genius piece of tech, really. Just like how our guns are specially designed to work after being submerged in the water.

Enzo, who's been keeping an eye on the boat through a pair of binoculars, curses. "Shit."

I freeze. "What?"

"We need to go now."

"It's not dark enough yet," Michael says.

"We don't have time to wait. Look." He hands me the binoculars and then starts the boat.

Mei is trying hard to keep hold of Lily while a guard tries to pull her away. Another guard wrenches Lily's hand back until Mei's hold gives out. I can't hear her cries over the ocean waves from this distance, but I can feel them in my gut.

"Hurry, Enzo," I order my friend, knowing he already has the speed boat going as fast as it can.

Lily struggles against a guard while Mei is taken away. And then in the blink of an eye, Lily is on Xiao's back, and blood flies.

"Fuck! She just stabbed Xiao."

"What?" Michael grabs a rifle and looks through the scope. "Holy shit! Does she have some kind of death wish?"

Lily doesn't know I'm coming for her. And while I hope she trusts I am, she can't be certain. So in her mind, she can only count on herself right now. As dangerous as that is.

A guard pulls a feral Lily off Xiao's back, and my chest swells with pride at the pure viciousness on her face. Blood covers her hands, her face, and hair, but she's never looked more beautiful to me.

Xiao spins around, and a second later, a guard hands him a gun.

"Enzo, we need to get there now. He's going to shoot her."

We're not going to make it. We're still too far away.

I'm going to lose her.

I'm going to lose her before we even have a chance to be together.

"Raphael, do you trust me?" Michael asks, his voice calm and steady over the rushing sound of the water.

"Yes," I answer without hesitation.

"Good."

And then he fires the rifle.

I don't even have a second to get angry because, through the binoculars, I watch the guard holding Lily drop to the ground. I can't see where she goes after, but I watch Xiao's eyes snap up and narrow in our direction. Michael ejects the casing and loads another bullet. But before he can fire the bullet, Xiao takes cover, and the bullet buries itself right where the bastard stood only a second before.

My eyes scan the deck and catch sight of a blond dressed in red. It's Lily. Relief floods my chest when I see she's been able to get away. My arms would be better, but I'll take the bottom deck for now.

"Hold on to something," Enzo warns. "This is gonna be quick."

At the very last second, Enzo decelerates and turns the wheel to steer clear of the yacht, allowing Michael and me to safely jump onto the swim platform. Originally, Enzo was going to stay close by and be ready when we called for extraction, but that's no longer the case. Even though he can't leave the boat with his bum arm, he can at least provide cover fire for us.

Xiao's men descend on us the moment we jump over the stern wall separating it from the swim platform. Moving as one, we send each one to the pits of hell without a second thought. They were dead the moment they signed up to work for the bastard.

"Lily!" I rush over to where I last saw her, but she's not there. "Michael!" I yell at my brother. "She's not here."

Michael joins me behind the bar table. "She probably went to find Mei. Don't worry, Xiao's men won't hurt them."

"But Xiao will."

Michael slams a clip in his gun before smacking me on my armor-covered chest. "Come on, let's go find them before he does."

Coming around a corner, I come face-to-face with a guard

who swings at me with a knife. I lift my arm to block his attack and hiss when I feel the hot slice of his knife cut down my arm. A gunshot cracks through the night air and sends the man flying away from me. A quick look to my side and I catch Enzo lowering the sniper rifle from the side of the boat he used as a prop before he revs the boat engine and moves to locate his next target.

Michael thumps my shoulder. "Let me see. How bad is it?"

It stings, but since I can wiggle my fingers and move my wrist, it's most likely just superficial. "I'm still alive."

Michael reaches for my arm. Once he confirms it's nothing too serious, he wraps a bandanna around my cut and cinches it hard. I bite back a groan and the urge to hit my brother in favor of concentrating on the goal at hand.

Find my family and kill Xiao.

"Let's go."

A woman's scream cuts through the chaos, followed by a ringing gunshot. Michael meets my eyes. It didn't sound like Lily, but I can't be certain. My heart pounds in my chest, blood rushing in my ears when we hurry toward the sound. The hall is empty except for a young Asian girl. Her eyes are open, staring lifelessly at nothing thanks to the bullet wound bleeding between her brow. I reach out and close her eyes. She didn't deserve to die like this. An innocent caught in the middle of a war.

We move on and come out on the bow of the ship.

"Lily!"

She spins around, her eyes frantic. She's terrified, and I see why. Xiao stands at the edge of the bow, holding Mei over the dark water below. She has her tiny hands latched on his wrists as she cries and pleads to her dad to stop and let her up.

My gun is locked on him, but if I fire, he'll drop Mei. And she can't swim.

"Oh look, the guest of honor has finally arrived," Xiao boasts.

"Xiao, please don't do this. She's your daughter," Lily begs, tears streaming down her face.

"Is she?" he taunts. "Because it seems like she'd prefer Raphael as her dad. Just like you do."

"That's not true," Lily urges, and I try to ignore the small stab of pain her words cause. I know she's lying to him, but it still hurts.

"Stop lying!" he shouts, pushing Mei out a little bit more over the water. She cries, and my fist tightens on my gun. "You stabbed me, remember?"

"You were trying to take Mei from me, and she was scared," Lily tries to bargain. "I was scared, and I was mad." She takes a small step forward. "Just like how you were mad after what I did and almost shot me." One more step. "Please, baby. You know I love you. Just let Mei go, and we'll go with you. We can fix this. Together."

Xiao sways on his feet, his face pale from blood loss. We don't have long before his strength gives out, and he drops Mei either way.

"Bàba," Mei cries.

For a moment, I think he believes Lily and will listen to her. But then a look of anger flashes across his face, and he opens his hand, dropping Mei to the water below.

34

LILY

Mei's scream as she disappears over the side of the yacht will haunt me for the rest of my life. Without a second thought, I jump in after her. Faintly, I catch Raphael's shout before the rush of air swallows it, and I hit the water.

Kicking to the surface, I shout, "Mei!" as soon as I break through.

"Mommy!"

Her tiny voice reaches my ears, but she sounds so far away.

"Mei, where are you?" I tread water, searching desperately for my daughter. The sun has set, and I can't see her anywhere. She can't swim. So if she goes under, that's it.

By some luck of fate or whatever, a light from the boat shines on a white dress standing out against the dark water.

"Hold on, sweetheart." I pray she can hear me before I swim as fast as I can to her.

"Mommy," she cries. Her voice is growing weaker. I can barely hear her now.

Another flash of light and I catch sight of her terrified face before she goes under with the next wave. Taking a deep breath, I dive, kick hard, reach out, and connect with her small arm seconds before she disappears into the dark abyss below. With another hard kick, we break the surface.

Supporting her tiny body against me, I push her wet hair

out of her face. "Mei? Mei? Open your eyes, please." I pat her cheek. "Mei, wake up. Please."

She coughs and spits up water before opening her beautiful blue eyes. "Mommy?"

"Oh, thank God." I hold her close, ensuring her head stays above the waterline.

"I'm scared, Mommy." She shivers in my arms.

My heart squeezes painfully at the fear in her voice.

"Lily!"

I spin around and watch Enzo pull up beside us in a speedboat. He throws it in neutral and leans over the side. I hand him Mei first, and he helps her into the boat without a second thought. Then, gripping me around the elbow, he hoists me up like I weigh nothing with only one arm. He carefully sets me down, and I collapse in front of my daughter. She's shaking from the frigid water and the adrenaline wearing off from her father throwing her overboard, but she's alive, and that's all that matters.

"Here." Enzo shakes out of his jacket and wraps it around us. Warmth and his signature woodsy scent envelop us instantly.

"Are you okay?" he asks, bending down in front of us.

"No," I admit honestly as I wrap my arms around Mei. "But we will be. Where's Raphael? What's happening?"

Enzo glances at the yacht with a tight jaw. His hand reaches for the throttle before he drops it and then reaches again. It's like he's torn about something. And then he makes whatever decision he was torn on. Throwing the throttle forward, he speeds the boat up...away from the yacht.

"What are you doing?" I shout.

"Raphael wants you and Mei safe," he bites out.

"And I need *him* safe." I stand with Mei in my arms and

stumble to the large man. "Enzo, turn the boat around. We have to go back."

He glances at me for a moment before shaking his head. "I can't. I'll get you two to safety, and then I'll go back for Michael and Raphael."

I grab his hand covering the throttle and squeeze. "Please, Enzo. If it was Evie would you leave her? Please…please. I-I love him."

Enzo pulls back on the throttle with a deep sigh, and the boat slows. Bowing his head, he closes his eyes and groans. "Fuck. He's gonna kill me for this."

Turning the wheel, he points the boat back toward the yacht and presses down on the throttle.

Mei grips me tighter as we get closer to the yacht. "It's okay, sweetheart. He can't hurt you ever again."

I can only imagine the shock she must be feeling over her father throwing her into the ocean. As terrible of a father as he is, he's still her father and the only one she's ever known. The betrayal of a relationship like that can be harmful, and I only hope she's too young to remember any of it. That she can move on from this entire ordeal and be happy.

"I want Raphael," she whispers into my neck.

I close my eyes and hug her closer. "Me too."

"I need you to stay on the boat, Lily," Enzo says as we get closer. "I'm already going against his orders to get you two far away from here. If you step foot on that yacht, he'll definitely kill me."

Fair. But unlikely.

But I won't tell Enzo that. He's likely to put the damn boat on cruise control or something, hop off, and send my ass back to shore just for suggesting it.

Enzo pulls the boat up alongside the yacht's swim deck in

the back. The opposite side of where we last saw Raphael, Michael, and Xiao.

"Stay put, both of you." Enzo points a finger at us both with a stern look.

"Okay."

"Promise me, Lily."

"I will not leave the boat. I swear." He should have specified which boat.

Enzo eyes me with skepticism before he finally nods and hops off the boat. I wait until he disappears from sight before I start counting to ten. When I do, I set Mei down on the captain's chair and wrap her in Enzo's coat, tucking her in until she looks like a little puffy penguin.

"Mei, I need you to stay here."

"But Enzo said—"

"I know what he said, but I need to go help them. Help Raphael. Okay?"

"Can I help?"

"Absolutely. You can help by staying here and guarding the boat. Can you do that?"

"Please don't go, Mommy."

I grab her head and kiss her forehead. "I don't want to, princess, but I have to. And I'll be back before you know it. I promise."

I should listen to Enzo and stay, but I can't. Something in me pulls me to the front of the yacht, pulling me to where I last saw Raphael. If I don't listen, if I don't go, I have this sinking feeling that something terrible is going to happen.

So many dead bodies litter the yacht. A gruesome sight for some, but all I see is proof of how hard Raphael and his brother fought to rescue Mei and me. And if they could do that, then I can ignore a bunch of dead Triad bastards.

I freeze just before coming around the corner when I hear voices.

"We found the warehouse, Xiao," Raphael says. "It's over."

"You think I care?" Xiao asks before he snorts. "I have a dozen more."

"So, you're the one behind the human auctions in Miami?" I can hear the anger in Michael's voice rise. "The one who sold Lily and Rose?"

"Maybe. There's been so many over the years," Xiao snorts. "They blend after a while, to be honest."

"I'm going to fucking kill you," Michael growls, his voice dripping with venom. "For Rose for Lily...for Dominic."

Xiao laughs. "Oh yeah, sorry about your cousin, DiAngelo. But he was getting a little too close, and it was bad for business. You know how these things go. The boss wanted him dead, and I wanted to send you a message."

"You're fucking dead," Michael threatens.

"You keep saying that, but do you really think this ends with me? This is a lot bigger than you realize, you fool. Cut my head off, and another two will grow in its place."

"But at least you'll be dead and will never hurt Lily or Mei again," Raphael says. His words are as cold as ice that a shiver runs down even my spine.

"Ah, speaking of my daughter. I saw your man pull her and that whore of a mother from the water. Once I get rid of you, I'm going to sell that slut to the first offer. Hell, maybe I'll sell the girl too. She's had her head filled with silly ideas for too long by that woman. I should have killed her years ago. She's been more trouble than she's worth."

I ball my hands into fists, my body wound up and ready to explode around the corner. Hearing him talk about selling my daughter has me seeing red.

"Tell me, Raphael," Xiao continues. "Did you enjoy that old cunt of hers?"

"Best breakfast I've ever had."

Xiao's angry growl is loud enough to let me know that Raphael's response struck a nerve.

Glancing around the corner, I catch the flash of a knife blade as Xiao lunges for Raphael.

"No!" I scream, leaping from my hiding spot and exposing myself to the group.

My outburst distracts Raphael.

"Watch out!"

Raphael's eyes snap from me to Xiao and the knife in his hand. He moves, but not quick enough. The blade buries into Raphael's shoulder when it would have hit his heart instead had he not moved.

But, if I had just stayed quiet, he probably would have been able to avoid the attack altogether. The momentum drives Raphael and Xiao backward against the railing. Xiao's feet get wrapped up in rope coiled by the railing, and he trips. Raphael meets my eyes a moment before they disappear over the side of the boat.

"No!" I dash forward, crashing into the steel railing where they fell overboard. "Where are they? I can't see them."

Michael and Enzo appear beside me, one on my left and the other on my right.

"You were supposed to stay in the damn boat," Enzo growls.

I don't bother arguing because what I should and shouldn't have done is irrelevant right now. I can't find Raphael or Xiao, and that's more important. Raphael's been stabbed, and he's bleeding in open water.

"Do you see them?" I ask frantically.

"No," Michael answers in a grave voice.

"Michael," Enzo says, the single word heavy and full of hidden meaning.

A single heartbeat later, Michael removes his vests and weapons, stripping down to only his pants and shirt. "Stay here and wait." He then sticks a knife blade between his teeth, steps over the railing, and dives into the dark ocean below.

35

RAPHAEL

Plunging into the ocean feels similar to when you first submerge in an ice bath. The shock that follows sends a brief wave of numbness through the body and soothes the burning coming from my shoulder.

Breaking the surface, I shake the hair from my eyes and take a couple of needed breaths before a hand latches on to my ankle below and pulls me under.

The salt in the water stings my eyes when I open them to look down at Xiao. He's practically trying to climb me like a tree to get to the surface, his eyes wide in panic, which is when I see what's wrapped around his ankle.

He somehow got tangled up in a rope. The weight is pulling him under, and the bastard is trying to take me with him.

Xiao's knife is still buried in my shoulder and is likely the only reason I'm not bleeding more profusely. But it's also preventing me from using my arm very much, which means I'm going to have to fight this bastard with one hand.

Reaching into my belt, I pull out another knife and swing at Xiao, catching his arm. Blood pours from the cut, instantly clouding the water.

I'm not afraid of sharks, but I know we don't have long before the blood in the water attracts them, and then I'll have another enemy to deal with.

Xiao uses his other hand to seize my wrist. As we sink deeper into the ocean, we wrestle for control of the knife in my hand. Xiao's desperate, causing his movements to be erratic, and I watch in dismay as the knife slips from my hand, vanishing into the unknown below.

That was my last weapon.

Except for.

No.

If I pull that knife out, I risk bleeding out. But I don't have a choice. I need to get free from Xiao.

A quick glance above makes my stomach drop. We're sinking farther and farther from the surface.

When Xiao grabs for me again, he reaches for the knife buried in my shoulder. I can't let him get it, so I lift my elbow and sock him in the jaw before wrapping my hands around the knife and yank it free.

Searing-hot pain explodes from my wound, causing black dots to dance in my vision, but I force myself to focus. Swinging my arm forward, I bury the knife in Xiao's neck. His eyes go wide, and his mouth falls open as all the air escapes his lungs. I watch the life leave his body, and the light disappear from his eyes.

Kicking his dead body away, I watch him sink farther down into the dark abyss, a cloud of blood surrounding him as he disappears into the black.

Xiao's gone.

He's dead.

He'll never be able to hurt Lily or Mei or anyone else ever again. The memories will fade in time, and Lily can rest easy, knowing he can never make new ones.

I turn my attention to the surface, illuminated only by the yacht's lights. It's so far away.

I'm not going to make it.

My lungs already burn from a lack of oxygen.

My strength is waning.

The sound of my rushing blood fills my ears.

I float in the water, weightless and numb, unable to keep going.

Black blurs my vision as I stare at the world above.

Lily's up there.

She's safe. They both are.

My family will make sure they stay that way. Even though I can't be with them, knowing they'll be okay, knowing that Xiao can never hurt her again...is enough for me.

I've always wondered what death will feel like. I always imagined that it would come from the end of a gun.

But this...death by drowning? It's almost peaceful. It's not the worst way to go, I suppose.

Death comes for me. Approaching from above, like a pale figure, here to take my dark soul back to hell where it belongs.

As I close my eyes, my last thought is a wish. A wish that I had gotten to tell Lily that I loved her.

36

LILY

Leaning desperately over the railing, my hands trembling and my breath shallow, I stare at the water, waiting for Michael to reappear with Raphael. Every second that passes is another second Raphael spends in the water without air. And as a doctor, I know the facts. A human being can hold their breath anywhere from thirty seconds to a minute and a half but very rarely any more than that.

"How long has it been?" I ask Enzo without moving my eyes from the water.

"Not long," he answers vaguely on purpose. Because we both know Raphael's been under for longer than a minute, at least.

Hot tears spring to my eyes, blurring my vision. Every heartbeat hurts, every breath burns. It feels like half of my body and soul is dying.

Bowing my head, I close my eyes, feeling the weight of the lingering truth press down on me.

"Lily, look," Enzo says, stepping forward just as Michael breaks through the surface with Raphael cradled safely in his arms.

"Help!" Michael coughs as he struggles to tread water while holding his brother. "I don't think he's breathing."

Enzo tears his arm sling off and reaches down to grab Raphael under the arms, heaving him up and over the railing.

Raphael isn't light in any regard, and Enzo's arm is still recovering from a dislocated shoulder, but Enzo just picks him up as if he weighs as much as a feather.

As a doctor, I'm annoyed at my patient, but as a woman in love, I've never been so thankful to the Viking for his incredible strength than at this exact moment.

"Set him down. Set him down," I repeat several times, gesturing to the yacht floor.

I'm trying hard not to concentrate on how pale and lifeless Raphael appears right now, flapping around like a limp doll in Enzo's arms.

Enzo carefully lays Raphael down, then kneels next to me. "What do you need?"

His question is the same one Raphael asked the day Dominic died. But I can't focus on that. Because today will be different. Raphael will not die today.

I lean over and put my ear to his chest, listening for a heartbeat...and hear nothing.

"I can't find a heartbeat. I need to start CPR."

Positioning myself over Raphael, I place the heel of my hand over his sternum, interlock my fingers, and begin compressions. Each push I make is deliberate and forceful, with my arms straight. Maintaining a steady rhythm, I count to twenty before blowing air twice into Raphael's mouth. Giving CPR is second nature to me, but I've never had to give it to someone I love.

My focus narrows in on the task and not how Enzo and Michael hover nearby.

After a minute of resuscitation efforts, I pause and place two fingers against his neck, searching for a pulse.

"Fuck!" I cry when I can't locate one.

Michael paces and occasionally coughs while Enzo stays close.

Starting a second round of CPR, I put my entire body weight behind each push.

"Come ON!" I growl through my clenched teeth. "You do not get to die on me, Raphael."

Michael chants something in Italian. Probably some kind of prayer or hymn. It's needed.

The tension in the air is thick.

Tears stream down my face when I listen again and hear nothing.

"If you die," I cry, my voice trembling with raw emotion, "I will hate you forever."

I'm exhausted, and my breathing has become choppy and irregular, but I push on.

"Do you understand me? You can't just make me fall in love with you and then die."

I feel Enzo place his hand on my shoulder. "I'm sorry."

With a violent shrug, I push him away. "No! He's not dead. He can't be dead."

"Lily," Enzo whispers, his voice cracking from emotion.

"Stop!" I slam my fists on his chest in time with my words. "He's." *Slam.* "Not." *Slam.* "Dead." Over and over. "Wake up! I can't lose anyone else. I won't!"

All of my strength leaves me, and I collapse on Raphael's hard, unresponsive chest.

"Please..." I sob. "Please, Raphael. We need you. We love you." I turn my face and bury it in his neck. He's so cold. Taking a deep inhale, I savor the lingering scent of his unique aroma mixed with seawater. "I love you. Come back to me... please."

Enzo once again grabs my shoulder, this time to pull me away, and I latch on to Raphael.

"No!" How will I explain this to Mei? I can't imagine it. I don't want to imagine it.

"Lily, please."

And then, suddenly, Raphael's chest expands as he takes a deep breath and coughs violently.

I pull away with a startled gasp. "You're alive!"

Raphael groans. His voice is scratchy when he says, "When was I not?"

"Holy shit, man." Enzo collapses beside us. "You gave us a scare."

"More than a scare," Michael adds, coming to kneel by Enzo. "You were dead, brother."

Raphael looks at us strangely and then tries to sit up. Enzo helps support him with a hand to his upper back. "I was?"

"Yeah." Enzo nods in my direction. "Your girl saved your life."

Raphael looks at me. His eyes are red from the salt water, and his face is still pale, but his smile is the same. "You saved me?"

"They helped."

His brother grasps Raphael's hand and squeezes. "Don't you ever do something like that again. I can't lose my brother. You hear me?"

"Deal."

Raphael reaches for me, and I burrow into him. He's shaking, and when I go to wrap my arms around him, he winces. That's when I remember the stab wound courtesy of Xiao.

"Yeah." Raphael reads my mind. "Let's go to the hospital."

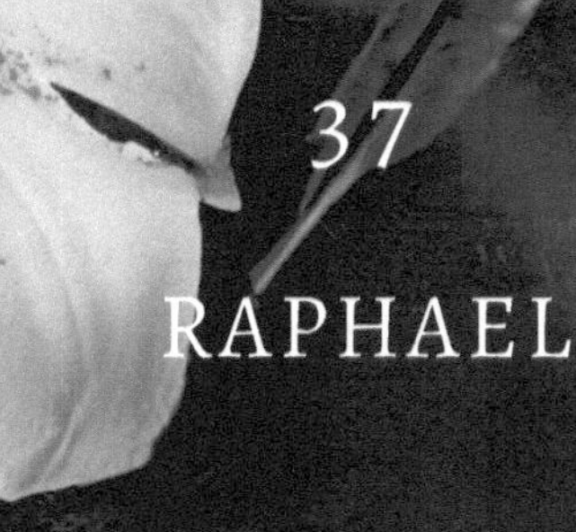

37

RAPHAEL

Turns out that being stabbed in the shoulder and then drowning takes a toll on the body.

By the time we make it back to shore, I'm on the verge of passing out from the blood loss. Once I'm resting on Lily's lap in the back of the car, my adrenaline crashes, and I surrender to the black.

The next time I open my eyes, I find Lily fast asleep in a chair pulled up to my hospital bed, her head resting next to my hand. My other hand is tightly bound to my chest, and I assume that's to ensure my injured shoulder remains immobile. I'll have to wait for the doctor's report to confirm, but if my arm is still present, it means Xiao's knife hit nothing critical. But I would happily sacrifice my arm if it meant Lily and Mei stay safe.

The harsh LED light highlights the bruises on her cheek and catches on the cut to her lip. They'll heal, and it will be the last time she ever suffers the same abuse because if I ever raise a hand to her, it'll be for pleasure and nothing more.

Lily stirs, raises her head, and yawns wide, covering her mouth with her hand. She hasn't noticed I'm awake yet. Watching her now feels like I'm getting a rare glimpse into the habits of an elusive, magical creature.

When she finally looks at me, her eyes go wide as she shrieks in surprise. "You scared me!"

"And you saved me." I smile softly at her, just happy to take her beauty in.

She appears somehow lighter...freer. As if the weight holding her down has finally been cut free. Which, in a symbolic way, it has been. By now, that weight is decaying at the bottom of the ocean floor.

She drops her eyes to my hand. I flip it over, and she slides her hand into mine. "I almost didn't. You were medically dead there for a moment longer than I liked."

Every day, I dance on the edge of death, and the thought of surrendering to eternal slumber has never fazed me...until now. Until Lily and Mei entered my world and gave me something more to fight for.

"I'm sorry. That was not my intention."

"I know." She looks up, and tears slip free from her beautiful blue eyes. "It's not fair of me to ask this because I know what you do is dangerous, but if you can try not to die again? My sanity would appreciate it."

"Just your sanity?" I tease.

Lily chuckles through her tears and uses her free hand to wipe them away before rewarding me with her brilliant smile. "Fine. Mei's too."

Before I can tug her to my chest and convince her sanity to appreciate other more...devious things, a knock on the door breaks the mood.

Mom and Dad enter, followed by my brother and Rose, and then Enzo with Evie, who holds Mei in her arms. The sight of them all gathered here serves as a harsh reminder of Dominic's absence. The sadness lingers, but his death has been avenged at last.

Evie puts Mei down, who then rushes over to her mother.

Lily picks her up and sets her down next to me on my hospital bed.

"Thank you for saving us," Mei says to me softly.

I reach out my hand, and when she doesn't shy away, I push her hair back so I can see her face. She looks at me through her bangs, her blue eyes so much like her mother's. A vivid image of a baby boy with the same eyes flashes through my mind, but it vanishes as quickly as it appears.

"Always, Mei."

Children wear their emotions on their sleeves. So it's easy to watch the nerves melt off her shoulders as confidence fills her again. Mei scoots forward and gives me a big hug, which, for her small arms, barely circles my chest. I hug her back before planting a quick kiss on the top of her head.

Rose approaches. "Come on, little one. The men want to talk, and I think ice cream sounds better. Don't you?"

"Yay! Ice cream!" Mei jumps into her arms.

Lily squeezes my hand before she follows Rose and Evie out of the room.

Once gone, the atmosphere grows tense the moment the door clicks shut.

"What is it about my sons and their incessant need to nearly die?" Dad asks with a raised brow.

Michael bows his head to hide his smile because he was in the same position as me not long ago after saving his family.

"Michael started it," I point out, knowing I'm playing with fire.

"And you will be the end of it," Dad snaps with a frown. "No more. It's upsetting your mother."

Dad knows we can't make any promise of the sort because death is a thin line we walk every day...but... "We'll try our hardest."

I peer around, noting an absence. "Where's Uncle Leo?"

Dad's frown deepens as he crosses his arms over his chest and exhales harshly. "Drinking himself into an early grave."

I catch Michael's eyes, and we share a look of concern. Losing a loved one is never easy on anyone, and while his ways of coping are understandable, our uncle has a way of taking everything he does to the extreme.

"And Emilia?" The taste of her name on my tongue is bitter, as her actions replay in my mind.

"On her way back to her father with her tail between her legs," Michael answers with a grunt.

"He has apologized for his daughter's actions," Dad says.

"He's lucky we didn't just kill her for what she did," Michael cuts in.

Dad shoots my brother a sharp glare for interrupting him, but continues. "And is forever grateful for sparing her life. He has also given me his word that she won't set foot in Miami again."

Good. What she did is unforgivable, and I never want to lay eyes on her again.

"We have news about the auctions," Enzo shares, changing the subject.

"Before we sank the yacht, we found evidence confirming what Xiao told us," Michael explains. "He had books recording every auction with lists of victims."

"Did you find the list for Rose and Lily?"

"Yes. I can show you Lily's, but there's not much to go on."

"Evie's checking, though," Enzo adds. "In case we missed anything."

I nod my thanks to my friend.

Dad steps forward and rests his hands on the railing at the bottom of my bed. "We've also found money transactions going to the same account. It seems our late friend wasn't lying about this boogeyman character. Xiao was probably just a manager, and we're looking for the fucking CEO."

"Can we track the money?"

Enzo frowns. "We've hit a lot of dead ends, but we're not giving up."

"Good. We need to find him," I say with certainty. "Before the bastard hurts anyone else we love."

"I LIKE when you order around the medical team," I admit to Lily once we're alone. "It's kind of hot."

Lily blushes and tucks a strand of hair behind her ear. "I don't mean to. I just want to make sure you get the best care possible."

I won't tell her that my father already made sure of that by bringing in the best of the best to oversee our care.

An idea comes to mind when I kiss the tip of her nose. "You know, Doctor, I am in a bit of pain."

Lily sits up in alarm, her eyes frantically scanning my body and vitals. "What? Where? Is it your shoulder? I'll go call a nurse."

She tries to slip off my bed, but I wrap my good arm around her waist and keep her close. When she sees the playful smirk on my lips, she relaxes, realizing I'm not being serious.

"Oh, really? Where does it hurt?" she asks in a teasing manner. Leaning forward, she hovers her lips over my cheek as she whispers, "Here?" She gives me a peck before moving up to my ear. "Here?" This time, she nibbles on the skin there, causing me to hiss at the sharp but pleasurable pain. I squeeze her waist tighter as she comes back to meet me face-to-face, our lips nearly touching. "Or here?"

I press forward and capture her mouth, exploring every inch meticulously and thoroughly. She moans and melts into me, eagerly handing over the power to command her pleasure. It feels like a cherished gift every time she does it, and I can't help but love it.

I reach down and tap her hip, pushing her to climb on top of my lap.

She breaks away and looks at me with a furrowed brow. "Are you sure?"

"It hurts there too, Doctor," I tease, falling into the role-play. "And aren't you supposed to help me feel better?"

Lily tugs her bottom lip between her teeth, her eyes scanning my face before her lip pops free, and she swings her leg up and over, settling on my lap. She rocks immediately against my hard cock with a deep moan that I mirror.

"Here?" she whispers before kissing me.

I hate only having one hand to guide her, but it doesn't seem to bother her. I thrust my hips up at the same time she rocks down. If we were naked, I'd have slipped inside easily. A problem I can easily solve.

"Yes," I groan into her mouth. "And there's only one cure."

"What's that?"

"Being buried in that glorious pussy of yours."

Lily raises up on her knees and bunches up my hospital gown, revealing my throbbing cock. Never thought hospital gowns could be so useful. Lily raises her skirt, flashing me her bare pussy.

"You naughty girl. Did you come here with expectations?"

Lily chuckles and tosses me a sinful grin. "Maybe. A doctor is always prepared."

I capture her lips, swallowing our moans when I slide home, filling her completely. Lily finds her rhythm, riding my cock and chasing her pleasure. I wrap my arm around her hips and hold her to me. Since I'm down an arm, I have to improvise. At this angle, she's able to rub her clit against my pubic bone.

"Oh fuck. Oh...fuck." Her body tightens up, her breaths shorter and faster. "I'm close."

"I can feel it," I grind out, my heartbeat racing.

Lily's body freezes, thrusting her chest forward and her head backward. Her pussy tightens harder than ever before, pulling my orgasm free along with hers.

"Holy shit, Doctor," I murmur into her sweat-lined neck. "Best medicine ever."

Lily giggles, and the sound makes my heart flutter. I want to hear that every day for the rest of my life.

Suddenly, the door bangs open, and a team of nurses and doctors rushes in. They freeze when they see the sight before them. Lily squeaks and tries to move away, but my arm prevents her. I'm still buried in her and have no desire to move. In fact, I'm almost ready for round two.

However, I don't care much for their eyes on Lily while she's on my lap. Even if she's clothed. So I reach for the blanket and toss it over us.

"Can I help you?" I ask nonchalantly, as if striking up a normal conversation with a girl impaled on my cock is an everyday thing.

One nurse steps forward, her face beet red. "We got an alert that your heart rate was high."

"Oh my God," I hear Lily groan into my chest. "I forgot about the pulse monitor."

With a soft chuckle, I set my hand on her hair and say to the waiting medical team, "For good reason. But as you can see, all is fine. In fact, why don't you ignore that alert for the rest of the night? I plan to do some cardio."

38

LILY

The sun is setting, casting a golden glow over the beach as it dips below the distant horizon. It's the last sunset of the year and it feels almost symbolic and therapeutic in a way. It feels like I'm closing the door on a past life and starting a fresh chapter. The pain of the past six years will linger, but I'm confident they will eventually fade to a dull ache. So when the sun comes up tomorrow, it will rise on a whole new year and a completely different life for both Mei and me.

The squeal of a child's laughter rings out, and I turn my gaze to watch my daughter run along the water's edge with Raphael. Pretending she's so much faster than him, he chases her with a mischievous grin. It's a picture of such happiness and joy that I wish I could freeze time.

The resilience of children is truly incredible. Less than a week ago, she was drugged, abducted, and thrown into the ocean by her own father, despite knowing she can't swim. She should be terrified of the water, yet here she is, running through it without a care in the world.

I'm thankful that she's young and that with time, the memories will fade, but I'm not as lucky. The memory of almost losing her still haunts me, and last night I found myself sneaking into her room and waking up next to her this morning.

According to Raphael, Emilia is officially back home in Italy. I'm glad because if I ever see her again, I can't guarantee how I will react. There is no way I can ever forgive someone for drugging a fellow woman and knowingly delivering her back into the hands of her abuser. The smell of hot chocolate still sends my heart racing, reminding me of that powerless feeling caused by the drug. I never want to feel like that again.

Raphael says healing will take time and I know it will.

One day at a time. One happy memory at a time.

I'll get there.

Mei stops, bends down, and collects a shell from the sand. She shows it to Raphael, who takes it and examines it in the fading sunlight. From where I sit on the sand with a towel under me, I can't hear their conversation, but whatever it is has my kid smiling from ear to ear, and that's all I care about.

Farther down the beach, Michael and Rose stand with Liam at the shoreline. He's far too young to stand on his own, so Rose supports him by holding his arms up. He's kicking at the sand and squeals when the cold water splashes his ankles.

I won't lie. Seeing a baby is making my ovaries ache. And it doesn't help when Raphael tosses me his insanely ridiculous sexy grin or when I watch his muscles move while doing the most basic things. Like breakfast yesterday. He was just flipping an omelet, and I about jumped his bones.

Having my IUD removed may have something to do with my desire for a baby and crazy sex drive. My hormones have been in overdrive ever since, and it's only been a few days. I also haven't told Raphael. I want it to be a surprise. But he'll find out tonight. I have something special in mind.

Raphael's shoulder is healing wonderfully. He no longer

needs to wear the sling at night when sleeping, but I still make him wear it during the day. Even though he's not fond of it, a few orgasms have a way of making his annoyance over the handicap disappear.

"May I sit with you, Lily?"

I look up to see Alice smiling down at me. "Of course."

Scooting over to give her some room, she sits beside me and stretches out her legs with a sigh of contentment. For a few seconds, we're quiet and simply enjoying the other's presence.

"I'm not sure if you know or not, but I am not the boys' biological mother." Alice reveals that truth bomb so conversationally, it's like she's commenting on the weather. "She passed shortly after they were born from delivery complications. I was brought in to help take care of them because Dante was overwhelmed with twin infants."

"I didn't know. The way you act around each other. I wouldn't have guessed it."

Alice smiles, her eyes on Michael and Raphael. "To me, they are my boys, and I am their mother. Family isn't always blood-related."

I peer out at Raphael and Mei. They're playing a game with the waves. Running out when the tide rescinds and then rushing back to the shore before the water can touch them. I can see their future together in an instant. Her first day of school, her first dance, her first boyfriend and the inevitable heartbreak that will follow, to her prom, and finally walking her down the aisle.

Xiao's DNA can make up half of who she is genetically, but again, I consider the idea of nature versus nurture. The idea that a person's behavior is shaped by either nature, like their physical makeup, or nurture, referring to the influence of the world around them on their behavior. As a doctor, I believe it's a mix of both. I believe that every person is capable of good and bad. And the way they're raised, the world they live in, will dictate which side prevails.

"You're right," I say, agreeing with Alice.

"He'll be a good father," she says as if reading my mind.

I chuckle softly. "He already is."

"I've never seen him so happy," Alice admits. "I'm glad he found you. Both of you."

I draw my knees up and rest my chin on them, keeping an eye on the pair. "I am too."

"Are you happy?" Alice asks after a long, quiet pause.

Twisting my head, I look back at her and say automatically, "Of course I am."

Her warm, dark eyes see past my lie. "You can be honest with me."

I huff out a small breath. She's not saying it out of malice but support, so I reward her with the truth. "Most of the time, I am."

"And the rest?"

"I'm getting there." Nodding in the direction of the beach, I add, "Days like this help."

Alice smiles, and the only sign of her age is the tiny laugh lines that appear. "Good. Because you deserve it. Every bit."

<hr>

HOLDING the box does little to quell my shaking hands and frayed nerves. It's a silly thing to be worried about. I know he's going to love the gift. Unconventional sure, but to be fair, he gave me the severed, flaccid dick of my first abuser in a box.

So what is conventional or normal, really, in the grand scheme of things? A gift is meant to be unique and thoughtful, special even. And when I thought about what Raphael wants, only one thing came to mind. I'm just worried he'll find it gross or something.

"Hey, what do you have there?" Raphael asks, coming up beside me and carrying two flutes of champagne.

"A gift for you," I mumble.

"For me?"

I shrug. "Yeah, it's no big deal." Deflection 101, folks. If you pretend to make something not a big deal when it is, in fact, a big deal, then you won't be disappointed when it turns out not to be a big deal.

"You don't have a dick in there, do you?" He eyes the box as if measuring the sides to see if one would fit.

"Ha, ha. Maybe there is."

Raphael sets the flutes down, and when he turns back to me, his eyes are dark with pleasure. He wraps his arm around my waist and pulls me snug to his chest. Dipping his mouth to my ear, he says, "The only dick you'll ever see again is mine," and then he nips playfully at my neck.

I giggle and attempt to squirm away from his grasp, but he effortlessly pulls me closer and kisses me in a way that makes me wonder if I'm the air he needs to breathe.

"Fair enough," I sigh out when we break apart.

"When do I get my gift?" Raphael asks, his eyes dropping to the white box.

"Midnight."

He glances at the clock on the wall. We have less than a minute until the ball drops. Raphael hugs me close while the time counts down.

"Five...four..."

Turning into me, Raphael cups my face in both his hands. I was feeling nice and let him ditch the sling for tonight.

"Three...two..."

"I love you, Lily."

My eyes go wide at his admission just as the clock strikes midnight. The air around us explodes with sounds of celebration from the television and the family as they yell out, "Happy New Year!"

Raphael leans down and softly kisses me. He doesn't push for more, but somehow, the kiss feels more intimate. Like an unspoken promise, we've sealed with a kiss. He pulls away just far enough that our noses barely touch.

His deep amber eyes bore into mine, scorching my soul and pulling the words free. "I love you too. Happy New Year."

His smile is dazzling and contagious. "Happy New Year, Lily pad."

We celebrate with his family for a few minutes before I pull him away to the outdoor lanai. It's now or never.

I hand him the box and step back, waiting as he opens it carefully. He lifts the top and goes still.

Watching his expression, I wait for a look of disgust or anger. Instead, when he raises his head, I swear his eyes are misty, but that must be a trick of the low light.

"Is this what I think it is?" He sounds almost hopeful.

"What do you think it is?"

"Your IUD." It looks like a smile is tugging at his lips.

I nod slowly. "You said you wanted a big family, and Mei's been asking for a little brother or sister. So I thought—"

Whatever words were about to spew from my mouth were cut off when Raphael grabs me and slams his mouth against mine. He devours my mouth like a man gone crazy, and I'm breathless when he retreats.

Grinning like a madman, he says, "Then we need to go practice."

39

RAPHAEL

When your girl gives you her birth control device as a gift and then talks about having a big family, you don't question it.

You get her fucking pregnant.

Or at the very least, you begin working hard at it. Because practice makes perfect, right?

Grabbing Lily's hand, I lead her upstairs to my old childhood room, choosing the back way to avoid the living room and where the family is still celebrating. As I shut the door and flip the lock, she turns toward me with a seductive gaze.

It's been beautiful watching her come out of her shell and bloom just like the flower she's named after. The nightmares still continue to haunt her, day and night, but instead of giving in, she fights. Hard. Every day. She fights for her future. A future entirely hers and Mei's. And I'm happy to just be along for the ride.

"So what now?" She asks, taking small steps backward as she does.

"Now, you're going to strip naked, climb up on that bed, spread your legs, and let me put a baby in you," I tell her while I undo a button with every stride toward her.

Lily flushes but does as she's told. Something else we've been working on. Having a man give direction with the freedom to say no.

Like I'm watching my own personal strip show, Lily slips out of her dress, revealing my second gift of the night. And this one I get to unwrap, too.

She's wearing an all-white lacy lingerie set that barely covers a single inch of her skin, and there's a garter holding her matching white stockings up. She turns and gives me a seductive glance, her perky round ass on full display in that revealing ensemble.

Climbing up on the bed, I physically groan and nearly go to my knees when I notice her panties are crotchless.

"Do you want me to get you pregnant?" I ask when she finally centers herself on the bed and turns to face me, propped up on her elbows. "Or do you want to kill me, Lily?"

"Depends on how many orgasms you give me," she sasses back.

Approaching, I drag my belt off and hold it up with a raised brow. When she raises her arms and holds her wrists together for me, I smile wide, pleased with how she continues to take steps forward. Still, even as I wrap the belt around her wrists, I keep it loose enough that if she wants or needs to, she can break free with little resistance.

Lily lies back on the bed, her arms above her head. She smiles up at me as she spreads her legs, giving me a clear view of nirvana.

Taking care not to strain my arm, I carefully crawl over her body until I can lean in and press my lips to hers. My stupid shoulder is still healing, but the ache I feel will not stop me from fucking Lily senseless. I do have some limitations, though.

"You wanna ride my face?"

"I thought you'd never ask."

Flipping over, I help support her as she straddles my face.

Gripping the headboard with her bound hands, she peers down at me. "You sure?"

"Sweetheart, if you don't sit on my face right now, I may just die."

With a light snort, she gradually lowers herself until she is fully seated. I hold her close to my face, wrapping my arms under her legs. After getting past her fear of me suffocating, it quickly became a new favorite position for both of us.

"You're already soaked, Lily pad," I share, my voice slightly muffled.

Whatever she's about to say back dissolves into a low moan when I run my tongue along the length of her pussy before blowing softly along her slit.

"Oh, fuck," she whimpers.

My cock is so hard, it's practically throbbing, but Lily's pleasure comes first. Always.

I groan as I suck on her clit. The vibration of my mouth makes her cry out and jerk before she rocks forward and back, seeking more. And I'm happy to oblige.

"Wait-wait," she moans. "I-I...need you inside me."

Releasing her, she moves down to hover over my thighs before making quick work of my pants and briefs. She bites her lip as she draws my cock free. It's like this every time. As if it's a sight to behold and wonder at.

Stroking me from base to tip, she squeezes with just the right amount of pressure, causing me to hiss and buck into her hand.

She continues to surprise me every day. Growing more bold, more confidant, as she continues to learn how to trust a man in bed again.

So when she leans down and takes my cock in her mouth, sucking down until I swear I feel her throat do that little flutter before her gag reflex kicks in, I swear my soul leaves my body.

With a guttural groan, I arch my back, chasing the feeling of her warm, wet mouth.

Lily hums her response against my shaft, swirling her tongue around the tip before she hollows her cheeks and swallows down my cock.

"Fuck, Lily." I'm so close, but I refuse to blow my load into her mouth. Not when we're supposed to be practicing for a baby. Can't do that if my seed rests in her stomach. "I'm close."

"Thank fuck," she says, popping off my cock with an audible *POP*. She rubs at her jaw like it's sore, and my heart sinks. Did we go too far? But then she winks and smiles. "Another thing to practice at."

This woman. This *fucking* woman.

I haul her up in a hurry and flip us over. Keeping pressure off my bad shoulder, I press forward, sliding home with one thrust.

I lean my forehead against hers and say, "I'm going to marry you."

Lily softly laughs before pressing a chaste kiss to my lips. "Is that a proposal?"

"Do I need one?" I raise a brow.

She purses her lips and admits in a meek voice. "It would be kind of nice."

"Okay, then. Lily—"

"But you have to ask Mei for permission first." She interrupts.

I smile. "Something tells me she'll give it."

"She loves you. You know that, right?"

"I love her too. And her mom."

Lily cups my face. "Her mom loves you, too."

I kiss her deep, my tongue diving in to tangle with hers as I start to move, slow and steady.

Even with foreplay, Lily's still tight. At least there's one good thing my bum arm can do. Lowering my hand, I caress her sensitive nub with my thumb, matching the rhythm of my intensifying thrusts.

Lily's heels dig into my ass cheeks, and her nails bite into my back hard enough to leave marks.

I kiss down her jaw, nibbling as I go, until I reach the junction of her neck and bite down harder. Her scream dissolves into soft mews and whimpers when I soothe the bite with my tongue.

"I'm going to come, Raphael. I need to come," she cries. "Please."

"Give it to me, Lily pad." I urge her, moving my hand so I can grind into her. "Let me fill you up."

Lily presses her mouth to mine and locks up. Her body seizes from an orgasm so intense, it literally draws out the cum from my balls.

Our kiss continues as we come down from the high, my cock still buried in her like a plug, ensuring that my cum stays inside. And we stay like that...just kissing. Neither of us fight for control or tries to move away. The kiss is peaceful, perfect... pure, fucking heaven.

I pull away to place several tender, sweet pecks on her lips. When she opens her eyes, I stare into the eyes that did me in all those weeks ago. If I had known then what I know now. If I had known that rescuing her and Mei from Xiao would result in death, and pain, and grief...I'd still do it. Because while sometimes good intentions can lead to unintended consequences... this is one I would make over and over no matter the consequence.

EPILOGUE

DIMITRI

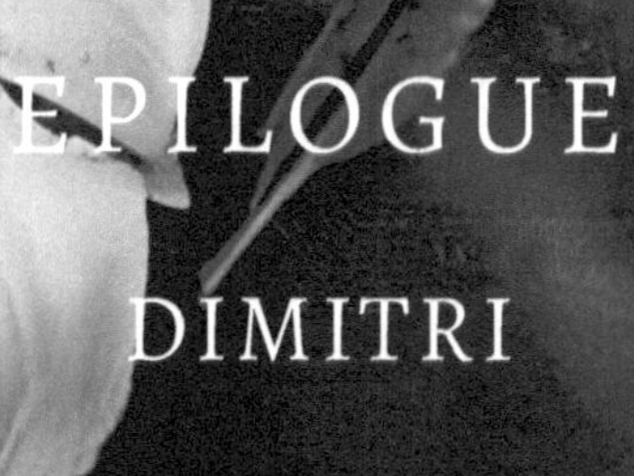

AN UNKNOWN NUMBER OF YEARS AGO

WASHINGTON, DC

"Hey, man. You want the usual?"

I tear my eyes away from my phone, and the email I'm certain will ruin not just my morning but also my entire week—a skill my boss has mastered—and smile at the man standing at the counter.

"Morning, Carlos," I greet him as I slip my phone into my suit pocket, effectively ignoring the problem hovering on the horizon in favor of a delicious cup of coffee. "The usual, yes. And if you can add an extra shot of espresso, please."

"Is it that kind of morning already?" he asks while he accepts the cash from my hand.

When he tries to hand back the change, I motion to the tip jar, and Carlos smiles gratefully before he stuffs the change in the jar. It's the same routine every time. He never just assumes or expects it, which makes for good customer service, in my opinion.

Still, it's not easy running a coffee stand in metro Washington, DC, when it seems there's a chain store on every corner.

So when he turns around to brew my coffee, I slip a twenty in the jar too.

"Just have a lot on my mind, is all."

Carlos bends down to look at me through the small window of his cart. "You're too young to have so much weight on your shoulders, you know."

I snort. If only he knew the half of it. As far as Carlos knows, I'm a simple lawyer who enjoys a coffee in the morning on the way to work.

But I'm the farthest thing from a lawyer.

"Listen, man, have I told you about my niece?" Carlos asks with a sly smile when he hands me my steaming cup.

"Yes," I answer. "You tell me about her almost every time I see you."

"And one of these times, you'll actually listen to me," he teases. "You need a lady in your life, young man. You're much too handsome to keep it all to yourself."

"Thank you, Carlos." I raise my cup in a farewell gesture. "Next time."

He shakes his head in exasperation. "And you say that every time."

While I appreciate his thoughtfulness and concern, my job doesn't leave much time for a relationship. Nothing serious at least. It's not that I'm against the idea of dating. My job is already stressful enough, and I don't need a relationship to add any more on top of it. So a date here or there that ends between the sheets for a little stress relief is all I can afford.

Look, I'm sure Carlos's niece is nice and all, but I wouldn't want to lose my favorite coffee joint because of her broken heart. She deserves to be with someone who wants *more*, who can give her that and doesn't have to hide who he is from her every day.

The weather is shifting in our country's capital, bringing a noticeable chill in the morning air. I turn the collar of my coat up around my neck to combat the cold bite. I'm much more of a warm-weather kind of guy, but this is where headquarters is, so I have no choice but to be here. When I eventually retire, I may find a tranquil private island with a charming little bungalow, where I can blissfully spend the rest of my life enjoying the sun and water. Until then, I'll drink my warm coffee and suffer through the snow and cold for a few months every year.

Crossing the street, I gaze up at the building, its name proudly displayed in large, imposing letters.

J. Edgar Hoover FBI Building

Most days, I enjoy what I do. I sometimes feel like I'm making a difference in the world. Other days, it feels like all I do is sit in my cubicle and analyze report after report, identifying suspicious transactions to investigate that end up being nothing half the time.

The elevator doors open to my floor, and I step out, nodding politely to Susan, a secretary who has been here longer than I've been alive. She's practically a grandma to the agents on the floor, and we love her just the same.

"Good morning, Agent Clark," she says before she holds out a wrapped caramel candy.

See? Grandma.

I pocket the candy with a smile. "Good morning, Susan. How's Dan?"

"Grumpy that the Cowboys lost last night."

Her husband, Dan, is a die-hard football fan. They met years ago when they were both widows. Susan claims her first husband sent Dan to her and vice versa.

It's a sweet story. But not one I ever expect to achieve.

Jacob waits for me at my cubicle with an eager grin on his

dark-skinned face. Digging out the candy from my pocket, I toss it his way. He catches it easily and makes a happy little sound before he unwraps it and pops it in his mouth.

"Those things will give you diabetes, you know," I comment casually while I shrug my wool coat off and stow my bag. "You should just tell Susan I give mine to you."

Jacob chuckles. "Where's the fun in that? If I did, you wouldn't get to see my handsome face every morning."

"Now there's an idea," I tease as I slip the chain holding my badge over my neck. "Did you get the email from Ford this morning?"

"Reason number two why I'm here. Come on, he's waiting in the conference room."

Special Agent Ford leads the Washington branch of the FBI's criminal investigative division. Young and new to the role, Ford is a boss with a need to prove something because he's a "legacy" or whatever the fuck you call someone whose entire family works for the agency. He's not my first boss, and he won't be my last. Something I have to tell myself over and over every time he sends an annoyingly vague email at the ass crack of dawn on a Monday morning ordering a meeting first thing.

"Nice of you to join us, gentlemen," Ford comments when Jacob and I walk into the conference room.

A glance around the large oval table tells me we're not even the last to arrive, but if I tell him that, I'm likely to get the short stick of whatever this meeting is about.

Once the last bit of the team arrives, Ford clicks on the screen hanging on the wall and a remote.

The image of a large older man in a suit with dark hair and dark eyes appears.

"This is Sergei Mikailhov," Ford announces. "He runs the Russian Bratva in Miami, and we have reason to believe Mr.

Mikailhov is also part of an organization called the High Table."

"The High Table?" Jacob repeats.

"Yes, we had a man on the inside, and that was all he could get us before he…" He looks uncomfortable, and it doesn't take a genius to know this inside man is no longer with us. "Anyway, the director has tasked me with sending in someone new undercover who can continue to gather evidence on the Russians and the identities of the High Table members."

I close my eyes and bow my head, already knowing where this is going. Jacob knows it too from the way he curses under his breath.

"Dimitri." The way Ford says my name with just a little too much glee in his voice makes my teeth grind. "You're Russian, right?"

I meet his eyes. "*Da.*"

He smiles like he's won some kind of prize. Probably has. Because this is the kind of job that could make his career. Mine too. "Excellent. You leave in a week."

So why does it feel like I've just signed my soul away to the devil?

EXTENDED EPILOGUE

LILY

For a place that is supposed to be the most magical place on Earth, I'm really struggling to feel it.

I need a distraction. But that's kind of hard to find when I'm literally surrounded by dozens of the very things bothering me.

A large, familiar hand pulls me into a warm embrace. I lean into Raphael's warm chest and savor the comforting beat of his heart against my back. He always seems to know exactly when I need him.

"You okay?" Raphael asks, his deep voice sending vibrations down my spine. "I know this can't be easy."

"No, it's not." There's no use in lying to him when he can see the truth on my face. "But we promised Mei, and it is her birthday."

Finding my daughter is easy in the crowd. The bright pink dress and the silver tiara on her dark hair stand out in the Florida sun. Focusing on her and concentrating on Raphael helps. And maybe if I try hard enough, I can forget about my absolute failure as a wife and mother.

"You're thinking about it again." Raphael leans down and lightly nips at my neck. I inhale sharply before softly exhaling a moan. "Stop."

"I'm trying. I swear I am."

Raphael hums low in his throat, like he doesn't believe me. Fair really, because I don't either. Raphael continues, "If you won't listen to me, then listen to your doctor." He reaches out and uses a single finger to lift my face to his until our eyes meet. Gazing into those amber eyes always brings me a sense of peace and security. But right now, they're just serving as a cruel reminder that I may never get the chance to hold a baby of our own with those unique eyes. "Stressing about it doesn't help."

He's right. I know he is, but it's easier said than done. It's simple for him to say this when it's not his body broken. When it's not his body preventing us from growing our family.

"Mommy!"

Raphael releases me, and I step towards her.

"What is it, princess?"

"Uncle Michael and Aunt Rose are here! Look!" She points in a general direction, and when I glance up, sure enough, Michael and Rose are walking toward us. Michael holds Liam, their energetic toddler, in his arms, while Rose pushes their newborn son in a stroller.

Rose meets me halfway and wraps me in a big hug. "Hey, you."

"Hey. I'm so glad you guys are here." I step back to peer down at the youngest DiAngelo. "How's Dean doing?"

Unlike Liam, Dean has the DiAngelo family's dark hair and amber eyes. My uterus hurts just looking at him, but I'm happy for Rose and Michael. Having only one ovary made getting pregnant more difficult for them, but not impossible. Unlike me and my hostile uterus.

"Us too. I can't tell you how much *I* needed this. Michael's been driving me crazy."

"If by crazy you mean doting on you every second of every

day," Michael comments after having overheard his wife. "Then sure, call me crazy for loving you too much."

Rose rolls her eyes. "Oh, for the love of—"

"Do I need to remind you what happens when you roll your eyes at me, *Rosa*?"

Rose points at the baby in the stroller. "Yes. Him."

The sarcastic grin on Michael's face says he doesn't regret a single thing. And when he leans over to kiss Rose fully on the mouth, the love-drunk smile on her face afterwards says the exact same thing.

"Hi, Aunt Rose," Mei says, wrapping her tiny arms around Rose's legs.

Rose sets a hand on her head, being careful of her tiara, and smiles. "Hey munchkin. Happy Birthday!"

"Thanks!" She steps back to look at Dean. "Hi Dean. Okay. Bye!" And then she's gone, skipping over to greet Michael and Liam in a similar fashion.

I watch her go, completely amazed at how much energy the child has.

"She's going to crash tonight," Rose comments.

"I sure hope so."

"Mommy, can we go on the ride now?" Mei asks when she literally comes bouncing up to us.

Raphael follows closely behind her, his hand finding the small of my back when he catches up. One thing I've come to discover about Raphael is that his love language is physical touch. Thanks to plenty of therapy, I've grown to accept it from others, like the hug from Rose.

It's getting better.

I'm getting better.

But trauma like mine doesn't just go away.

It lingers in ways I never imagined and comes when I least expect it.

Like at dinner, when the food triggers a memory and I have to fight to hold back the urge to vomit.

Or at night, when the silence feels so heavy that it's going to crush me.

Or how I still often pinch my arm to remind myself that this is real.

But for every hard moment, there are a dozen better ones.

Like how Mei hasn't woken up crying with the need to curl up in our bed in over three months now.

Or how I bought and picked up pizza all on my own a few months back. So what if Enzo followed to make sure I stayed safe?

And like how even now in this crowd, I'm not afraid to meet a stranger's eye and share a friendly nod. Again...so what if Raphael gave a sizable monetary donation to the parks foundation to block out the date for premium passholders only.

I want to believe that one day I won't need all the extra precautions and the weekly therapy visits. I hope I'll get there. I'll definitely fight for it. Just like I fought for the little girl being swung around by her Uncle Michael right now. Fought for the smile on her face. Fought for her laughter. Her happiness. Her safety. She's the reason I continue to fight every day.

I DON'T KNOW what sort of passes get us to the front of every line, but Raphael made sure we all got them. They earn us several nasty looks from parents who have been waiting in line for much longer. I do my best to ignore them, but it becomes more difficult when a few looks twist into something border-line seductive.

And because I'm feeling down already, seeing their outright audacity to look at Raphael and Michael with such frank open-ness sends a flash of jealousy surging through me. So hot in fact, that when I grab Raphael's hand, it's harder than I meant, which earns his attention.

He glances down at our hands, up at me, and then finally to the crowd. It takes him a second, but he finally catches on and then turns to face me.

Raphael raises his free hand to cup my chin, tugs it forward, and then up. I close my eyes just as his lips meet mine in a kiss that sends a different kind of hot flash racing through my system. A heat that settles in my lower stomach and makes me clench my thighs.

"Jealous, my love?" He murmurs against my mouth.

I pull far enough away to gaze up into his sun-kissed eyes, sparkling with mirth and desire. "Is that a bad thing?"

He smiles. "Never."

"What's going on? Why can't we get on the ride?" Michael's question is laced with a layer of anger we both pick up on and turn to look at him.

"I'm sor–sorry, sir," stammers the ride attendant. He's probably seventeen, if that, and is shaking like a leaf in front of Michael. "There's a man on the ride who is refusing to get off."

"And did you call security?"

"Ye–yes. Of course. But he..."

"He what?"

"He scared off the guards," the kid mumbles.

What?

Before anyone can say another word...we hear him.

"*It's a small world, after all.*" The voice grows louder as the boat comes around the corner. "*It's a SMALL world after all!*" No. It can't be. "*It's a small world after all!*" Sure enough, the boat comes into full view, and there he is. Enzo. His large, proud Viking form stretched out in the back row of the boat, clearly enjoying every moment. "*It's a small, small world!*"

"Please, sir," the attendant begs. "You have to get off the ride. There are children waiting."

Enzo's face goes stone cold. He gives the kid a one-over that makes the poor worker step back. Proud of his achievement, Enzo turns his attention to the group of us and smiles wide. "Hey! There you guys are. Took you long enough."

"How long have you been riding this thing?" Michael asks.

Enzo shrugs. "I don't know. I lost count after ten."

"You've been on this ride over ten times now?" Rose repeats.

"You guys told me to go hold the ride," Enzo defends his actions before he gestures to the frightened attendant. "And this idiot said he couldn't just stop the ride, so-" He motions to the cart. "Here I am."

"Unbelievable," Michael says. "I didn't mean literally, Enzo."

"Yeah, well. Are you guys gonna get on or not?"

"Yay!" Mei squeals when the attendant finally opens the gate. She takes off toward Enzo and climbs into the row ahead of him. He pokes at her tiara, which makes her giggle, before she pushes his big hand away.

Michael, Rose, and their children take the front row, leaving Raphael and me to sit with Mei. She's bouncing with so much excitement that I almost wish the ride had seat belts or a lap bar at the very least. I'm sure the water isn't higher than a foot, but I still eye it with concern.

Once the boat jolts forward, Raphael stretches his arm out

behind her and gently grasps her shoulder, helping keep Mei grounded and safe. I meet his eyes over her head and smile before mouthing *I love you*. He returns it with a wink.

There's so much to see on the ride that Mei begs to go through it a second time. It takes only one look from Enzo, and then we're off again to cruise through the dark waters and vibrant color animatronics. Yay.

"So did you get everything you wanted for your birthday, Mei?" Enzo asks when we finish our third ride through.

"Kind of," she answers in a somewhat subdued voice. I already know where this is going.

"What didn't you get?"

"Well, I really want a cat, but I'm not allowed."

"Why not?"

"Enzo," Raphael says his name like a warning.

I smile. This has been an ongoing argument in our house for a few months now. It's even gone as far as artwork explaining why she should get a cat, how she'll feed it all the time, clean up after it, and "love it lots". In Raphael's defense, I don't blame him for his hesitations. A pet is a big commitment, but what he doesn't know is the real reason why Mei wants a cat. She wants a sibling. She wants someone to play with. I want to give her that so desperately that getting a cat almost feels like giving up...and giving in to the very real possibility that it may never happen.

My smile deflates like a popped balloon.

"Oh," Enzo catches on. "I see. Well, maybe Santa will bring you one."

"Yeah! Mommy, will you help me write a letter and send it?"

I glance down at my daughter's face. Her beautiful,

hopeful face. I smooth my hand down the side of her head and try hard to smile again. "Of course, sweetie."

"Can we do it when we get home? I want him to have lots of time to get me the best kitty ever."

It's getting harder to keep a smile on my face. Especially when I know the look on my daughter's face. She's already given up on the idea of being a big sister.

"Of course." It's all I can choke out.

And unsurprisingly, Raphael notices. He always does.

"Hey, Mei, why don't you go with Uncle Enzo to get some ice cream?" Raphael suggests. "I need to talk to your mother."

We're coming up on the exit, and thankfully, the idea of ice cream is more enticing than another go-around.

"Okay!"

"You too, Michael," Raphael adds, his tone leaving no room for argument. Not that he'd get any from his brother. Dean's been growing increasingly fussy, and if the fresh smell in the air is any sign, he also needs a diaper change.

Raphael waits until we're through the first tunnel before he tugs me close. "What's going on, Lilypad?"

"It's nothing more than usual," I lie.

"Why don't I believe you?"

"Because you're stubborn?"

He snorts. "When it comes to you and your happiness, yes."

I'm quiet through another scene of the ride, taking the time to gather my thoughts before confessing, "It's bad enough knowing that I'm letting you down, but to see the acceptance on her face, to see that she wants a cat more than a sibling now...it kills me."

Raphael runs his eyes over my face, and whatever he sees is enough for him to growl out, "Fucking hell," and then stands.

The boat rocks slightly, but thanks to the track beneath, it stays steady beneath us. Raphael grabs my hand and tugs me up to my feet.

"Wha-what are you-Raphael, hey!"

He doesn't listen and sweeps me up in his arms instead. Before I can blink, we're off the boat and standing on a side maintenance deck. I trust Raphael not to drop me, but I still cling to his shoulders like a koala bear out of pure uncertainty of the unknown than anything else.

Raphael doesn't set me down until we're behind an extensive set of animatronics and puppets, hidden from view.

When he does, I spin around on him. "Raphael, we can't just jump off a ride in the middle of it. What is that poor kid—"

Raphael's mouth crashes down on mine, swallowing whatever more I was going to say with an intensity that sends a shockwave of pleasure crashing through my body.

"Listen to me, Lily DiAngelo," he says as he cups my face in his two big, warm hands and forces me to meet his eyes. "You are not failing anyone. Not me. Not you. And definitely not our daughter. Are we running into complications? Yes. Is it taking longer to get pregnant? Yes. But does that make you a failure? No. Does that mean I'm upset or disappointed in you? No. Never. Do you understand me?"

I nod mutely.

"I love you," Raphael continues, his amber eyes scorching the declaration into my very soul. "Just the way you are."

"Even if I can't give you a child?" I choke out the question that haunts me more than my past.

"You already gave me a child. Mei may not share my blood, but she is my daughter. Right?" He searches my face, and I nod again. "Do you want to stop the treatments?"

I inhale deeply and release a shaky breath. This isn't the first time he's asked me this. And the decision is always in my court. Because, unlike that piece of shit Xiao, who's thankfully rotting away at the bottom of the ocean, Raphael has never and will never force me to do anything I don't want to.

We're due to start another course next month. The eggs are ready for implantation. Three healthy embryos. This is the most we've gotten to this stage since we started. It's our best chance.

It could very well be our last chance.

But I'm not done fighting for our family.

"Not yet."

"Then we won't," Raphael says before he smiles and leans down to capture my lips in a way that pushes me forward, searching and needing more. He drops his hands and steps back, leaving me suddenly cold and hot at the same time. "Come on, we should go."

"No." The word slips out before I realize it.

Raphael glances back at me and chuckles. "What?"

"I just...I don't know. I mean...we're here. Alone...and Mei kind of interrupted us last night–"

"And this morning," he adds on.

"And this morning," I agree. "So I don't know..."

"Do you want to have a quickie?" Raphael asks.

I shrug, trying to look like my idea is no big deal, but fuck it kind of is. The man can turn me on with barely a kiss. That's all it takes. Sometimes even less than that. Sometimes it takes just a look.

Like that look. The one on his face right now. The one where he knows exactly what he's doing to me.

I reach for him and pull his face down to mine, giving him my answer.

Raphael responds by wrapping his arms around me and then spinning me so that my back is up against a wall. I wrap my legs around his waist, and his hands move to grip my thighs to keep me steady. He pushes forward, the heat of his cock burning me in the best way. Raphael smiles into our kiss and then rolls his hips, which turns my moan into a hiss at the sweet friction he causes.

I run my hands down his strong back, enjoying how his muscles flex beneath my touch. Watching him work out is still a favorite pastime of mine. Occasionally, I join him, but it always seems to end up with us doing a different type of workout that involves a little more cardio than weight lifting.

Raphael's hands move up my thighs and slip under my shorts...to find nothing.

Surprised, Raphael asks, "Lily, where is your underwear?"

I shrug innocently. "Oops, silly me. I must have forgotten them."

"You're going to be the death of me," he growls before he captures my lips in a kiss that feels more like he'll be the death of me. His fingers graze my core, and he moans, "You're soaked."

He slips one digit inside me...then two and curls them like a hook, seeking the spot he knows so well. I clench around him when he does, the spike of pleasure like a lightning bolt to my spine.

"Raphael, please," I beg.

"Please what?" He asks, moving to place open-mouthed kisses down my jaw and behind my ear. "Tell me what you want."

Another brush of his fingers.

A painfully sweet nibble to the sensitive place behind my ear.

Oh, for the love of—

"I need you inside me, Raphael." My hands move from clawing at his back to the waistband of his jeans. "Now. Please."

Raphael smirks like a cat who just got into a saucer of milk. He carefully sets me down, ensuring I'm steady on my two wobbly legs before he pops the buttons of his jeans and tugs them down far enough to reveal his boxer briefs and the massive bulge struggling to stay confined within the fabric.

I eagerly slide my hand beneath his waistband and grip him, stroking his dick from base to tip and then swirling the bead of pre-cum at the tip around the head with my thumb.

He hisses at my touch, and the rush of power the sound gives me is intoxicating. Knowing I'm the only woman allowed to bring this man this amount of pleasure feels like an honor and the best gift in the world.

Raphael firmly tugs my shorts down with his thumbs before lifting me up by my thighs once more. In one seamless movement, I wrap my legs around his waist, and he lines his cock up with my entrance and then impales me with one quick thrust.

We both freeze, needing a second to savor the connection because it always feels like coming home when we're together like this. I'll never be able to get enough of him...of this.

"We have to be quick about this, Lily," Raphael tells me.

A shame, really, but I understand. There's only so long we can be gone before Michael or Enzo comes looking for us. And I'd rather not be responsible for Raphael killing one of them for simply seeing me half naked.

"Then you better hurry up and fuck me," I tell him, squeezing my thighs to make my point.

"Hold on tight," he warns, giving me just a second to grip his shoulders before he slams into me, hard and fast.

In this position, I'm at his complete mercy, literally along for the ride. But unlike the one we abandoned, this is a ride I'll gladly go on over and over.

His thrusts bring me closer and closer to release, and he knows it, the familiar need filling him as well. He kisses me deeply before panting, "I love you, Lily."

"I love you more," I tell him.

He nuzzles his face in the crook of my shoulder, and I bring my hands up to bury in his hair, keeping him close. He's close. His hot breath on my bare skin grows ragged, his movements jerky and more uneven, as he swells inside me.

"Fuck!" I cry when he rolls his hips in a way that brushes against my clit. It only takes a few thrusts before my orgasm crashes down hard and fast over me.

Raphael follows with a deep roar a few seconds later, coming deep inside of me. We stay like this for a long minute; him buried in my pussy, throbbing the last of his release, and me clinging to him like a koala bear.

"I'm serious, Lily," he finally says after he regains his breath and pulls his face back to look deep into my eyes.

"About what?" I ask, bringing my hand up to swipe hair from his sweaty brow.

"You need to know that I am happy with our family the way it is. If you want to keep trying, you won't hear me complain because I love being buried in this tight pussy of yours," he smacks my ass to prove his point before continuing, "If you want to adopt, we'll adopt a dozen. And if Mei ends up being the only child we have, then she's the only child we have. And that's perfectly fine, too. Besides, my brother and sister are likely to breed like rabbits, so there'll be plenty of nieces and nephews to spoil."

I want to believe him. "You're sure? You won't feel regret… or disappointment?"

"Never." Raphael gently sets me down, his hands steady and careful as he helps straighten my clothes before adjusting his own. When he looks at me again, something in his expression softens. "Lily, you've given me more than you'll ever realize."

I open my mouth to speak, but the look in his eyes silences me. There's more he wants to say.

He reaches up, brushing a loose strand of hair behind my ear. His fingers linger warm against my cheek, and without thinking, I lean into his touch. "You showed me there's more to life than just existing," he murmurs. "Before you and Mei, I didn't even realize how numb I'd become. But you–" His voice falters for a moment. "You reminded me what it means to love and to be loved."

His words steal my breath, and my heart stutters, aching in the best possible way. "Raphael…"

His thumb traces a slow line along my jaw. "You and Mei… you're not just part of my life. You *are* my life."

He leans in, and I rise on my toes to meet him halfway.

When our lips meet, time slows because there's no rush in the kiss. Only the quiet, certain promise of tomorrow. Of every tomorrow we'll spend together as a family. And that whatever comes, I'm home.

RAPHAEL

An alert from my phone pings, and I glance at the notification.

Enzo: Left the munchkin a gift. Look outside.

I read the message twice with a furrowed brow before I leave my office toward the front door. It's nearing midnight now. We got home from our week vacation earlier this afternoon, and Mei went to bed several hours ago, so whatever present Enzo got her is going to have to wait until the morning.

Passing the master suite, I peer in the open door. Lily is curled up under the covers, peacefully asleep, just where I left her after fucking her brains out a few hours ago. There's no reason to wake her. She needs all the rest she can get.

So I leave her be and continue toward the front door, wondering if I'm going to open it to a giant fucking teddy bear. But if whatever it is wakes up Lily or Mei, I'll likely beat the shit out of that Viking bastard.

I swing the door open...

...to empty air.

"What?"

Meow.

My eyes fall to the floor, to the basket where a small white fluffy kitten waits with a pink bow on top of its head.

That motherfucker.

ACKNOWLEDGMENTS

The list of people I am thankful for has grown which is not good considering how terrible I am at this. So, if you feel left out, my apologies and belated thanks.

Mandy, you're more than my PA...you're a dear friend and I'm so thankful everyday for you. Especially on the days where I send you dozens of voice messages freaking out about something or another and being ready to talk me down when I start a message with '*now hear me out*'.

Sam and Holly, my two lovely Alpha readers and friends. The love you two have for my characters makes my little dark heart so happy. Your comments along the way were the best part. I'm so happy to have been introduced to you two!

To my ARC team, those new and old, thank you so much for taking the time to read, review, and share my books with the world. Thank you for your support!

To every friend that has believed and supported me, even with my endless droning on about my books and then still bought them. I'm proud to be introduced as the *"smut author"*.

Thank you to my family for continuing to be my biggest fans and supporters. To Dad for sharing my books at the clubhouse, and Janice for your ear and great ideas. To my big sister, thank you for answering every medical question I had, especially the one asking if a guy can die from having his dick chopped off. (Did you know they can't? Cutting off only the dick will not cause enough blood loss to warrant death.)

And finally...a big thank you to my Mom for always looking after me. I'm lucky to have you as my Guardian Angel.

ABOUT THE AUTHOR

Connect with me
I love interacting with my readers!

instagram.com/author_k.boozer
facebook.com/author.k.boozer
tiktok.com/@authorkboozer

ALSO BY K. BOOZER

DARK ANGELS SERIES

Dark Choices

Michael and Rose

Dark Consequences

Raphael and Lily

Dark Truths

Gabriella and Dimitri

DARK ANGELS SPINOFF

Dark Memories

Enzo and Evie